"Mom, yo   **your fami**   **your dues," Kate said.**

"Not really," Beth answered quietly, and both her daughters glanced at her sharply, on the point of arguing, but she spoke again.

"I'm married to Doug. I'm his *wife*. My 'dues,' as you call them, include helping my husband if he needs my help. And this time he does. And so does his precious three-year-old grandson. No. Don't say anything. Just pause a second and think about that. I talked to our pastor when he was in the hospital, and he reminded me of one important fact."

"But, Mom—"

"He said, 'When you do it for the least of these, you do it for Me.' Just think about that," Beth said, hoping she sounded decisive.

Books by Virginia Myers

Love Inspired

Helpmate #36
The Dad Next Door #71
September Love #230

VIRGINIA MYERS

has been writing stories since childhood. She has published ten novels, historical and contemporary, for the general book market. A few years ago she decided to write novels reflecting her growing religious faith. She has now written four faith-based novels.

Virginia has taught the art of novel writing in several Washington colleges, and a number of her students are now published novelists. She has lectured, participated in panel discussion and conducted workshops at several writers' conferences and is a faithful worker in her church.

Having lived most of her life so far in a series of big cities, Virginia has now settled happily in the small town of Longview, Washington. This is the only town that has built a special bridge for squirrels from tree to tree over the street so they won't get run over by cars.

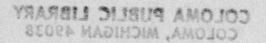

SEPTEMBER
LO...

VIRGIN...

Love Inspired.

Published by Steeple Hill Books

STEEPLE HILL BOOKS

Steeple
Hill®

ISBN 0-373-87237-2

SEPTEMBER LOVE

Copyright © 2003 by Virginia Myers

Printed in U.S.A.

When you do it for the least of these,
you do it for Me.

—*Matthew* 25:40

To those many people
who raise their children's children.
They go so much, much farther than the extra mile.

Chapter One

At first Beth thought the thin blond girl was going to ask her for spare change. She had the look of a street kid, with her long, unkempt hair and her odd assortment of clothes. She wore a long, very faded, green-and-white print dress, topped by a man's brown jacket, worn and much too big. On her bare feet were old floppy sandals. But street kids didn't come into residential neighborhoods. They stayed in Seattle's various business districts.

Beth sighed. If only she had come home from her errands a few minutes sooner or later, she might have avoided this. Then, as the girl came closer, she saw the small child, a little blond boy. He clung with grubby desperate hands to the flowing skirt, half hidden by it. She thought, *He shouldn't be barefoot. It's too cold a spring.*

She was immediately sorry for her rush of impatience. What right did she have to be impatient with this woman and her child? They were obviously destitute. She, in her classic gray spring suit, about to enter her beautiful old home, was blessed far beyond anything she deserved. She paused, beginning to open her handbag. True, the classic suit was in its second spring, and the lovely old home was now a bed-and-breakfast. And it had not been a good day. As her younger daughter, Jill, might have said, it had been a mega-stress day, full of problems and worry—and two new guests were due before five. For just an instant she longed intensely for Doug's good-humored acceptance of life as it happened. He would bring out his favorite calmdown comment: "Lighten up, Beth my true love. The sky will not fall today."

The blond girl, close up, wasn't a girl. She was a woman of about thirty. When she spoke there was a whine in her tone and she looked exhausted.

"You must be Beth. You've simply got to be Beth. I'm beat. And you look just like my aunt said—dark hair with no gray, dark eyes and dressed like a model. I must say this—you've sure kept your looks."

Who in the world *was* this woman? "Yes, I'm Beth," she said cautiously.

The woman gave a sigh of relief. Clean, with her hair styled, she would have been pretty. Now, in sudden exasperation, she turned on the little boy and smacked at his grubby clinging hands.

"Leggo my dress. I'm tired of you hanging on to me."

The child, scowling and silent, let go and backed away a step, watching her intently. Then, as if this burst of anger had taken the last of her strength, the woman persisted tiredly. "And you married Douglas Colby?"

Sudden alarm bells sounded in Beth's mind. She half knew and dreaded what was coming. Surely, this *couldn't* be Kayla, Doug's daughter. No. Definitely not. Doug had said that Kayla had a child, but that child was a girl who would be about eight. This child was a boy, not more than three or so. But her quick sense of relief was shattered.

"I'm Kayla, Doug's daughter," she said flatly, and Beth saw the little boy's hands creep toward the flowing skirt and grasp it again, as if it were some sort of lifeline. Now she noticed that both his knees were skinned. Sometime some place today he had fallen and scraped his knees, but no one had cleaned them and put on protective bandages.

Beth swallowed her disappointment. Well, they didn't call her "perfect hostess" for nothing. She must do her best for Doug's daughter.

"Kayla, how lovely to see you. Doug and I were so sorry you didn't get to our wedding." It sounded hollow, but Kayla didn't seem to notice.

"Yeah," she said. "Dad and I have our ups and downs. We're not what you might call close." She shivered, seeming to huddle inside the large jacket.

"Well, come in," Beth said quickly. "I'm just getting back from some errands. Your little boy must be freezing. This is such a cold spring. Usually by April it begins to warm up a bit." She fumbled for her key as they went up the steps to the big porch. She longed for the sense of security she always felt when entering the big front door with its heavy oak panels and oval of etched glass. This was the house she had fallen in love with thirty years ago.

Talk, Beth! Put Kayla at ease.

"One of the things that first brought your father and me together was the fact that we both had grown daughters, and both had been widowed." *September love,* her daughter Kate had called her midlife marriage to Doug Colby.

Inside the hallway, she remembered Doug's words after he had met both her daughters, Jill and Kate. "You and your husband did a wonderful job raising your girls. I'm afraid I failed there." And Doug's eyes, reflecting some inner sorrow, had seemed to be looking at something in another place and time. "I was away so much. On my job, you know. Whenever Kayla needed me...I wasn't there for her." Then quickly, defensively, he had added, "Kayla's a lovely person, but she's had...some problems. I blame myself, of course. I... Right now, I don't even know where she is.'' The admission had cost him a lot. They had just come from the big Thanksgiving dinner at Kate's. He had seen her daughters at their best. Kate, so steady, so competent, so stable. And Jill, so bright and resourceful. And both married to good husbands and raising their own families.

''Well, now that you're here, Kayla, you and your dad can catch up.'' She knew her voice was too bright, but Kayla didn't seem to notice. She was looking around the large entry hall.

''You've certainly got a big house,'' she said. The child was looking around, too, still frowning slightly, pressing himself against Kayla's leg.

''The house is old,'' Beth explained. ''Built back when architects didn't mind wasting space. But I never think of it as wasted. I like some space.'' She looked around the familiar hall. She had worked for years at the decorating, budgeting carefully to get the very best in antique-designed wallpaper for the large dining room, or the brass andirons for the several fireplaces, or the special paneling for her late-husband Ralph's study. He had so liked to read in there. In the house's heyday, before its bed-and-breakfast incarnation, it had been featured in several Gracious Homes of the Northwest tours for charity.

The grand old house had settled gracefully into its new life as a B and B when she had learned that the pension of a city librarian's widow wasn't going to be enough. And she had been determined not to be a burden on her daughters. For the first time in her life she had needed to earn money.

Not too many changes had been required, just a little remodeling to meet city codes. A small registration desk had been added to the front hallway, plus an attractive rack

to hold Seattle postcards, printed recipes of house special-
ties, along with some tourist leaflets for the guests to take.

Beth led Kayla and her child into the large living room.
"What's his name, your little boy?" Beth asked.

"Oh, him? His name's Adam."

At the sound of his name, he looked up expectantly at
Kayla and said the first word he had spoken so far. "Hungry." His voice was somewhat husky, and his frown deepened.

"What a lovely room. Lovely chairs," Kayla said, ignoring Adam, a sigh in her voice. "Mind if I just collapse
awhile?" She sat down in one of the deep chairs.

"Hungry," Adam persisted, standing close to her.

"Kids are always hungry." Kayla opened her large
satchel-like tote of limp gray vinyl. "You can have the rest
of the fries." She rummaged in the big bag and pulled out
a greasy paper bag. "I'll level with you, Beth. I've just
about hit bottom again. I guess Bottom is my hometown.
But I had enough after bus fare to get us something to eat
in a burger place. I tried to make it last awhile, but Adam
whined all the way from Phoenix. Kids are bottomless pits.
Here." She handed the greasy bag to Adam.

To Beth's dismay, the little boy took it eagerly and sat
down on the floor beside Kayla's feet. Carefully, with deep
concentration, he opened the bag, took out a limp string of
potato and ate it hungrily. Then he poked his dirty little
fingers into the bag again.

Beth bit back a dozen questions. What could she say to
Kayla? This was Doug's daughter. A daughter who had
some problems. She felt a kind of inward weeping. *I will
help you. I have food. I will feed your child. I will give you
a place. I will fix your lovely hair. I will find you something
to wear. I will… I will… I will…* Unable to speak for a
moment, she looked at Kayla.

"Yeah. I know I'm a mess," Kayla said dully. Then, as

if she had read Beth's mind, she added, "I don't suppose you have a place I could wash up. And I'd like to clean Adam up. You know my dad…doesn't even know he has a grandson—" Her voice broke.

Beth, unable not to, went to her side and put her arms around the thin shoulders.

"Of course you can wash up. Adam, too. And why don't I fix you a snack? It's a long time until dinner." She was thinking swiftly. Only three of the bedrooms were taken for tonight. There was that big room at the back, with an adjoining bath. She could put Kayla and Adam in there for the night. It was reserved for tomorrow. Then she would move them to what she called the "bed-sitter." It was the small, ground-floor room that had served as her sewing room when she had had time to sew. She had made it into a small, extra place for the peak season when everything in Seattle was full and someone called desperately from the airport. There was a sofa bed and no bath. But behind an ornamental screen there was a basin with hot and cold water.

"Where is your luggage, Kayla?" she asked. Kayla would certainly need a change of clothing, and the child… She glanced again at the little boy. He was digging fruitlessly into the now empty bag. All the limp fries were gone. Determinedly, he began to lick the remaining salt from his grubby fingers.

"I did have luggage when I started out," Kayla was saying. "Believe it or not, I did come prepared. But I fell asleep in one of the stopovers and somebody ripped it off. So we came in what we had on. This is it. What you see is what you get." There was an attempt at bravado that didn't quite come off. Kayla was embarrassed.

"I can help out there, I think," Beth said briskly. "My daughter, Kate, lives only a few blocks from here. She's collecting for the annual spring rummage sale at church. I happen to know that some very nice things have been donated. I'll give her a call while you're cleaning up. You look like you're Jill's size. Jill is my younger daughter. I think that she gave her blue challis. It's lovely." She noticed how blue Kayla's eyes were and was filled with sadness. *Kayla's such a lovely person,* Doug had said. Doug mustn't find her like this. And certainly his first sight of his grandson mustn't break his heart.

"Come upstairs. My big back bedroom isn't taken for tonight. You and Adam can have that. It had a large dressing room from when people used dressing rooms. I had it remodeled into the most gorgeous big bathroom you've ever seen. And while you're doing that, I'll make Adam a snack."

"Oh, Beth, that sounds wonderful." Kayla followed her to the stairs. Adam scrambled up.

"Mommy!" In a panic he rushed to grab her skirt.

Kayla turned. "It's okay. I'm just going to take a bath. Beth will give you something else to eat. It's okay to go with Beth." She turned. "Kids this age are a pain. He won't let me out of his sight."

One of the dozens of questions in Beth's mind popped out. "I thought Doug told me you had a little girl...."

Kayla's blue eyes suddenly clouded. "I have. I mean, I had. My Becky. She's with her father. I...I lost custody when my marriage went haywire." She sagged against the banister. "I don't know what Dad has told me about me, but..." She paused a moment and then, as if she were speaking to a group, she said, "My name is Kayla. I'm an alcoholic." She grimaced. "I'm sorry but that's the way it is. But I'm going to try again. I've got responsibilities. I've got Adam to look after. And now you know the worst. Where is that lovely bathroom?"

"It's right down this hall," Beth said in sympathy. "You have a view of the back garden—for today, anyway. Your father painted a picture of the back garden. My daughter, Kate, has it. It's hanging in her living room.''

Beth opened the door of the big room, furnished with the antique brass bed with the hand-pieced quilt covering. The marble-topped dresser was catching a thin sunbeam from the nearby window. The vase of old-fashioned roses looked lovely. She heard Kayla sigh softly.

''And the bath is in there. This is a double, so there are plenty of towels for both you and Adam. I noticed that Adam has skinned knees. I always keep those little colored bandages on hand for when my own grandchildren visit. I'll get you some of those.''

''Lovely,'' Kayla said, her eyes sweeping the huge bathroom with its deep tub and separate shower. She reached out to touch, almost lovingly, one of the downy aqua-colored towels. Then she turned her attention back to Adam, who was again clinging to her skirt. ''Adam's poor knees are my fault. I was out of money by then and couldn't even afford bus fare. A nice old guy who was leaving Seattle gave me this street map. I thought we'd never make it. Adam is so slow. I guess sometimes I walked too fast and he couldn't keep up and he fell a couple of times. Really did mess up his knees.''

Beth's throat ached at the thought of the frantic little boy trying to keep up. His lifeline, the green-and-white skirt, getting farther and farther away down the strange street.

Kayla bent over, talking directly into the small frowning face. ''Look, I'm going to take a bath, see? I'm not going anywhere. You go with Beth. She's got— What have you got to feed him, Beth?''

''Cookies,'' Beth said. ''I've got cookies, Adam. And milk.'' This child needed milk, and lots of it.

''Okay,'' he said after a moment. ''Okay. Cookies.'' And he held out one dirty little hand.

Beth took it in hers, clasping it warmly. *This is Doug's*

grandson. And again she felt a sense of inward weeping. It shouldn't be like this. Her beloved's grandson should be happy and healthy and secure. Living in a stable home, with loving parents. She went slowly down the stairs, matching her pace to his short little legs that couldn't keep up.

"Adam, do you like peanut butter?" she asked as they reached the bottom of the stairs. "I can make you a peanut butter sandwich, if you like."

He stopped, and she glanced down. He was looking up at her, angry and disappointed. "You said cookies!" he accused.

"Yes. Cookies, too." How many times had this small child been disappointed? It didn't bear thinking about.

In the kitchen she quickly found one of the wood booster seats her son-in-law, Greg, had made for short grandchildren. She put it on a kitchen chair. She lifted Adam up and sat him on the seat, wishing fervently that she could wait just long enough to wash him, but she knew with certainty that her promise of food must come first. And from somewhere in her mind rose the conviction: *I will never break a promise to this child.*

She didn't call Kate until Adam was devouring his small feast with total concentration—the peanut butter sandwich on her delicious home-baked bread, a house specialty, with a stack of three sugar cookies waiting. She even found in the back of the cupboard the two-handled mug she had used when her youngest grandchild, Meggie, had needed two hands to drink her milk. Then she rang Kate from the kitchen phone.

"Kate, darling, this is Mom. I need a favor." Some inner caution stemming from a need to save Doug's pride about his problem daughter made her less than candid. "You remember Doug talking about his daughter? Kayla?"

"Yes. She didn't come to your wedding. I remember."

"Well, she's here now, late but welcome. But she had

some bad luck. Her luggage is missing. She's kind of travel-stained, and I was wondering…didn't Jill donate her blue challis dress for the rummage sale?''

''Yes. She did. Do you want that for Kayla? It's clean.''

''Yes, I do. She wants to tidy up for her father. And wasn't there some stuff in there that Ben had outgrown? Kayla brought her little boy with her.''

''I thought Doug said Kayla had a daughter.''

''She has. But she also has a little boy. About three. His name is Adam.'' She glanced over to the kitchen table where Adam was pausing to lick some peanut butter off his hand. He heard his name and, just for an instant, the frown was gone and he gave her a timid smile that she knew she would cherish. Recklessly, she plunged ahead. Kate was such a practical, sensible person.

''Look, what I really need is a lot of things, well, several things. Kayla is about Jill's size, but thinner. Will you look through what you've got and pick some out? She has nothing but what she's wearing. See what you can do for Adam, too. Just until she can make other arrangements?''

Kate's unquestioning ''Okay, will do. What else?'' made her wonder again how she could have had two such wonderful daughters.

''You do most of the pricing at these sales, don't you?''

''Yes. You mean you want to *buy* this stuff?''

''Right. It's iffy if Kayla will get her luggage back. So she'd better have something to wear until she can start replacing things.''

''Okay, Mom. I'll do it now, and send one of the boys over with the stuff.''

''Thank you, Katie. This is really a help. I've got two guests coming in before five so I'm going to be busy.''

''Wait. Don't go yet,'' Kate said. ''Did you visit the hospital today?'' And as Kate said it, the afternoon's other worries came crowding back. Kayla's arrival had pushed them aside for the moment.

"No, but Bessie called me. It's not good, Kate." Even as she said it, her voice broke. "I don't think Cyrus is going to recover soon." She paused, a thousand and one images welling up in her mind. Their pastor, Cyrus Ledbetter, had always been there for all of them. He had married her to Ralph Bennett years ago. He had baptized both their daughters. He had supported them in joy and in grief. And he and Kate had a special relationship. They had worked so hard together to establish the church school, Gilmartin Academy. The very idea that he might not always be there was unbelievable.

As they ended their conversation and rang off, Beth recalled the other problem she had pushed aside. Kate was in the midst of her third pregnancy, and things were not going very well for her. Beth had the sick feeling in the pit of her stomach that always came when people she loved were at risk.

Still standing by the phone, she watched Adam. No longer wolfing down food, he had lain his head on the table and was finishing his cookies, half lying down. He must be exhausted. Did he have regular naps? Did he have regular anything? He was using one grimy hand to slowly break up his last cookie into small pieces, which he put tiredly into his mouth. His eyes were heavy. Any moment now he would simply fall asleep where he was.

Beth hurried to make a snack for Kayla. She had forgotten to ask what she might want, so she improvised. While she made a quick grilled cheese sandwich and sliced an orange, she watched Adam fall asleep. When she had these and a small pot of tea on a tray ready, she went to him and gently placed her hand on his tousled head. Instantly, he struggled out of sleep.

"Is it Adam's nap time?" she asked.

He sat up quickly. "Mommy?"

"Mommy's upstairs taking her bath. Do you want to go up?" she asked reassuringly.

"Mommy," he said again, and started to get down, almost falling. Beth caught him and held him close for a moment.

"Come on. We'll go up to see Mommy. Let me get this tray."

Holding the small tray in one hand, she reached out the other, and Adam confidently put his small hand in hers. It was the beginning of trust. *Well, Adam, you* can *trust me.* She was surprised at the fierceness of the thought as it crossed her mind. Then, just as fiercely came another thought. *Don't get too attached to this child.*

Upstairs again, Kayla was glowing. "Beth, you have no idea how good it feels to be clean again. Lucky I keep my hair dryer in my tote, isn't it?" She started eating hungrily of her snack. "This is so good!"

Beth brushed aside the idea that the lost luggage was a myth. There had never been any other luggage. The ugly tote was all there was. "I can cut those split ends off for you, if you like. I used to trim my daughters' hair all the time."

"I'd love it if you would, as soon as I finish this. I want to look nice for Dad."

"Fine. I'll put Adam down for a nap. He was falling asleep at the kitchen table."

"Okay, but make him go potty first," Kayla said, taking another bite of her sandwich.

"Go potty," Adam said sleepily.

Beth had almost finished styling Kayla's hair when the doorbell rang. Not the guests so soon, surely. But it was only Kate's boy, Tommy, with two shopping bags balanced on the carrier of his bike.

When Beth came back with the clothing, Kayla was looking at her reflection in fascination. ''Beth, I can't thank you enough. I look great.''

Beth had cut off quite a bit and had used her curling iron to cup the hair under Kayla's chin line. A middle part had let her draw back both sides and hold the fine, fair hair back with two antique ivory clips. Kayla reminded her of Alice in Wonderland. She looked young and innocent in her slim blond prettiness. Doug would be pleased, and that was what mattered.

Kayla was elated at the clothing donations.

''Just until you can start replacing things,'' Beth said tactfully as she emptied the shopping bags on the bed next to the sleeping child.

''Yeah, right. I love this shade of blue.'' Kayla picked up Jill's lovely blue challis dress. ''Perfect! I love it!'' She was like a happy child at Christmas. ''And look at these. Adam's never had a pair of jeans. He'll be ecstatic. He'll think he's like the big boys now. And look at this!'' She held up a small yellow T-shirt with ''Mariners'' printed across the front.

Kate had even sent some underwear, and Beth wondered if she had taken things from her own wardrobe. Kate was good at reading between the lines. Well, it was little enough to do for Doug's daughter.

''Will you be all right for a while now?'' Beth asked. ''I have some things I need to do.''

''Oh, I'll be fine. Thanks a million. And don't worry about Adam. I'll clean him up nice for Dad.''

Beth held back surging questions. Where is Adam's father? Where are your first husband and your little girl, Becky? Did you really bring any luggage, or did you just run away from someplace, or something, or someone, in a panic, with no clothing, no money? And why? And, as she was going down the wide stairway, there came the question she really didn't want to know the answer to: *What do you expect of Doug?*

With a sudden feeling of lassitude, Beth wandered back into the kitchen. She'd need to clear the table where Adam had scattered crumbs. She looked vacantly at the small mess he had made and she sat down.

She and Doug were so happy. By some miracle they had found each other in the autumn of their lives. Never had she loved anyone as she loved him. And she knew that he returned that love. It was as if they had both lived all their lives, carefully going through the motions, faithfully doing all they needed to do, or had committed to do, but marking time. Waiting. For this ultimate happiness. Was there such a thing as a perfect life? If so, she and Doug had found it.

They had married just after last Thanksgiving. She loved her small B and B business that she had created and he seemed quite willing for her to continue with it. And he, having worked all his life, was not content with just painting his beautiful landscapes. He had found other satisfying work to do. His work in the textbook field had made him a natural for a place on the board of trustees for the church school. He volunteered to teach Kate's Raymond and Tommy how to play golf, and they were getting quite good at it. And he constantly helped her with the B and B work. *Beth, don't lift that. I'm your heavy-lifting guy.*

She wished intensely that Doug would come home. Now. This minute. She wanted to see his big frame coming through the doorway, the ready smile on his rugged face. She remembered when he had first registered as a guest. She had thought of him as a man who might climb mountains, or wrestle heavy, wet sails on choppy water. She glanced at her watch: four-fifteen. The minutes were sliding by. She had so many things to do. Instead she went to the wall phone and dialed Doug's cell phone. He answered almost immediately.

"I'm heading home soon," he said. She loved the sound of his deep voice. He had been down at the church for a meeting. "I suppose you're anxious for news. Well, the Elders have appointed an interim pastor to keep things going until Pastor Ledbetter recovers."

"Oh? Yes, I had wondered." She should tell him about Kayla. He shouldn't come home and just find her here.

"He's a nice enough guy," Doug was saying. "I met him. He's a bit young for a pastor. I don't think he'd have been my choice, but I guess the Elders know what they're doing. Name's Philip Cooper. He'll take the service Sunday, so you'll meet him then. I meant to be home to carry suitcases, but things got busy here."

"The new guests haven't come yet. I don't expect them until about five. Listen, dear. I want to tell you something, and this is a nice surprise. Your daughter, Kayla, is here. She came in this afternoon. Such a lovely girl."

There was dead silence for a moment, then his astounded voice. "Kayla? Here?" The joy in his tone was clear.

After Beth hung up the receiver she lingered by the wall, feeling oddly indecisive, almost confused. Doug was happy. Her beloved was thrilled that Kayla had come. Why then did she have this strong feeling that something was very wrong? It just didn't make sense. *Get on with your work, Beth.*

Then Adam's piercing wail cut the air, chilling her.

"No! Mommy! No!"

Chapter Two

Beth rushed upstairs, her heart pounding with anxiety for Adam. What now? There was the distinct sound of an open palm smacking bare flesh. Adam and Kayla were in the big bathroom.

"Kayla! Stop!" Beth grasped Kayla's uplifted arm. Both Kayla and Adam were crying.

"But he's so dumb," Kayla wailed. "Why can't he be smart, like Becky is? He's just plain stupid. He won't get in. He kicked water on me!"

"Let me do it," Beth said, making her voice calm when she wanted to scream. "Kayla, you're tired. You're impatient because of it. Let me bathe him. Go back in the bedroom. Lie down awhile. I'll clean Adam up."

Kayla rubbed tears from her face. "Okay," she muttered. "You do it. He's too much for me." She turned, but before she left the bathroom she glared through angry tears at the naked, trembling little boy. "You dumb brat. How can you get clean if you won't get in the tub? Beth, can you comb my hair again? He messed it up."

"Yes," Beth said evenly. "Just go lie down awhile."

She turned to the little boy. He was backed up against the wall like a small animal at bay.

"Why don't you want to get into the tub, Adam?" she asked gently, hoping that he remembered that she was his friend, the one who had given him food. The tears had made streaks in the dirt on his face. What went through the mind of a three-year-old child when confronted with big, angry adults?

"Too hot," he said finally. Beth reached down to test the water. It was too hot, at least for skinned knees.

"Would you like some cold water in it?" she asked, and he nodded reluctantly. She turned on the cold tap, cooling the temperature to just barely warm. Cajoling, coaxing and explaining, she persuaded him into the tub and began bathing him. She was getting water all over her lavender silk blouse. At some point she had taken off her jacket. She couldn't recall where she had left it. The minutes were ticking by. She managed to get Adam washed, including his hair. It was too long and somewhat shaggy, but there wasn't any time to cut it. Doug would just have to see his grandson with shaggy hair. At least it would be clean.

When she took Adam, clean and dried, back into the bedroom, Kayla was lying flat on the bed, staring at the ceiling.

"You know, I'm scared. That's the whole problem. When Dad and I parted company last, he was pretty fed up with me, with my drinking problem. And it is a big problem. I don't know what he's going to think now."

Beth glanced at her watch. Almost five. And Kayla showed no inclination of getting up to dress Adam. Maybe it would go more smoothly if she did it herself. Mentally gritting her teeth, and hoping the new guests would be late, Beth hurriedly picked out some clothes intended for Adam.

"Here, Adam. Would you like to wear these jeans?" She held up the pants. He stared at them, his wide eyes questioning. Then he reached out to touch them. "Adam's new jeans," she assured him. Then he lunged past her and grabbed a small pair of red sneakers. He looked at her desperately.

"Adam's shoes?" he asked. "My shoes?" He gripped them to his narrow chest. "Mine!"

She had a sudden need to cry. "Yes, Adam. Your shoes." And she was rewarded by his sudden, radiant smile.

"Mine!" he said exultantly. "Mine!"

She managed to dress him, although he kept trying to hold the red shoes, which made it awkward. As soon as she had Adam dressed, she got Kayla back to the dressing table for another combing session. She tried not to keep looking at her watch. How long was this going to last? She had a business to run. She made herself speak kindly.

"Don't worry about your dad, Kayla. He was delighted when I told him you were here. He's coming home as soon as he can."

"He was? When did you talk to him?"

"Right after you came upstairs. I called to let him know you'd come. He was *very* pleased," she said firmly. Well, he *had* been pleased. Fair was fair.

Kayla was looking at her reflection with satisfaction. "That sounds hopeful. The right clip is pulling a bit."

Beth loosened the clip. "Is that better?"

"Fine. You see, Dad doesn't know that I got married again."

"But he knew you were divorced from Becky's father, didn't he?" Beth wanted to ask about Adam's father. Maybe Kayla would tell her without being asked.

Kayla continued to gaze at her reflection. "Yeah, he knew that. You sure do have a way with hairstyling. I look great. Thank you, Beth. You're an amazing woman."

All right. She would ask. "Why didn't Adam's father

come with you?'' That was blunt enough. She put down the comb and got a glimpse of herself in the glass. She was positively disheveled! Bathing small children was something she hadn't done in a long time.

"Mitch *died*," Kayla said almost accusingly. "He was... Well, he got into some trouble about a DWI. And he was sent into rehab. Being *sent* is a lot different than going in on your own. He wasn't ready, see. But he *had* to go. It was that or a jail sentence.'' She was staring angrily into the mirror. "He was fighting it, see? And I guess he drank the wrong stuff. It's hard to get anything decent to drink in rehab. They thought...afterward...that he'd drunk something like maybe rubbing alcohol. Anyhow he...died. And he left me with Adam to take care of. Just on my own. That's why I've really got to get squared away. And the last time Dad and I were together he said if I ever really meant to get dry he would help me. But I really had to mean it. Well, I mean it now. I got to. No ifs, ands or buts. This is it.''

Beth's heart sank. "Of course he will help you,'' she made herself say. This *was* Doug's daughter. She tried to sound sympathetic. Poor, desperate Kayla, fighting her demons and trying so ineptly to care for a small child at the same time. She was thankful her own daughters didn't have such difficulties.

Kayla's eyes suddenly filled with tears. "Thank you, Beth. You can't know how much I appreciate this.''

Then Beth felt guilty. She really had no right to judge Doug's daughter. Her own life had been so good.

Beth was about to say something comforting when the front door chimes rang out. The new guests! Without thinking, she hurried out into the hall and down the stairs as the chimes rang out again. Almost at the door she remembered that she hadn't combed her own hair, and she noticed that her gray skirt as well as her blouse was liberally splashed with water. Well, so be it. She pasted on her perfect hostess smile and opened the door.

"Mr. and Mrs. Driscoll," she said brightly. They were a stocky middle-aged couple. Mr. Driscoll smiled but Mrs. Driscoll didn't.

"Yep. We got here and only got lost once, finding the place." Mr. Driscoll dropped the big suitcase onto the porch.

"Come in," Beth said, smiling. "Everybody gets lost at least once finding this place. Didn't you get the little map I sent?"

"He lost it," Mrs. Driscoll snapped. She was looking at Beth's wet skirt intently as they went into the entry hall. Mr. Driscoll had picked up the big bag again and dropped it inside the hall. It sounded heavy.

"If you'll just register here…" Beth said, indicating the registration cards on the small neat desk. "And feel free while you're here to take postcards and things as you need them. We have some good views of Seattle." She was going automatically into her welcome-the-new guests routine. But she wished fervently that Doug would walk through the door. She had to at least offer to carry the big bag upstairs.

As Mr. Driscoll registered, Mrs. Driscoll finally said what was on her mind.

"Do you know there's water all over your clothes?"

"Yes, I know it," Beth said, laughing. "I was bathing our little grandson. I forgot how small children splash about. I'm going to change in a minute."

Mrs. Driscoll's face went dark and forbidding. "Are there *children* here? The bed-and-breakfast directory said there were no children here."

"Th-there aren't, actually," Beth stammered. "I mean, he doesn't live here. He's just visiting." As soon as she said it she thought, *But he does, at least for a while.* Was this going to be a problem?

Mrs. Driscoll was still worried. "Does he cry at night? I have a sleep disorder. I'm a very light sleeper. Anything—even the drop of a pin—wakes me up. Oh, dear, I really must get my rest. Is our room near his at all?"

"No, it isn't," Beth said quickly, instantly rearranging the room assignments in her head. She would put the Driscolls in the very front bedroom. And when Mr. Bryant arrived later, she would put him in the room next to Kayla and Adam. Justin Bryant was a regular who came up every spring from San Francisco to look for "collectibles" for his antique shop. He was a pleasant, good-natured man. He wouldn't care about not getting his regular room for once.

"Well, we'll just hope for the best," Mrs. Driscoll said wearily, as if the weight of the world rested on her thick shoulders.

Beth reached the top of the stairs, out of breath from carrying the Driscolls' suitcase. What did they have in it— lead weights? There were guests and then there were guests. She huffed her way to the very front bedroom, wondering what Mrs. Driscoll would find wrong with it. Mrs. Driscoll let her know immediately.

"Oh, dear, this bed has a canopy," she said with a worried glance around the lovely room. "Canopies are pretty but they are dust catchers. I have several allergies. Dust is just deadly for me."

"I don't think you'll find any dust in here," Beth said briskly. "My cleaning service vacuums everything, including all fabrics, draperies, upholstered furniture and canopies. I'm sure you'll be very comfortable here."

"Well, we'll just hope for the best," Mrs. Driscoll said with weary patience.

Mr. Driscoll tried to help. "Oh, come on, Myrtle. This

is a lovely old mansion. Be glad the lady opens it to the public.''

Whereupon Mrs. Driscoll turned to Beth and said with woman-to-woman frankness. ''Actually, Bert is the one who likes these bed-and-breakfast places. I'd much rather have the anonymity of a motel—so much more privacy.''

Beth's perfect hostess smile remained fixed while she wondered who in the world could possibly dream of invading this woman's privacy. She indicated the small desk.

''You'll find house stationery in there and postcards with a picture of the house on them. There's also a city map and a what-to-see leaflet. Mrs. Driscoll, are your allergies food related, too? Our breakfast menu offers a fairly wide variety. Both for low-cholesterol people and high-cholesterol people. We have eggs, any style, with sausage or bacon. Plus a wide selection of muffins or home-baked bread. The muffins are small, two-bite sized, so you can have different kinds. Then, for those who need to eat more carefully, we have muesli, nonfat milk and, of course, lots of fruit and juices.''

''You're very kind,'' Mrs. Driscoll said sadly. ''I'm sure I can find something.'' And Mr. Driscoll patted her shoulder in a comforting manner.

Beth escaped into the hallway with a suppressed sigh as she heard Doug enter the front door. As always, her heart lifted and all fatigue vanished. She ran down the stairs like a teenager.

''Doug!'' She flew into his arms and was held for a moment against his strong body, raising her face for a kiss.

''Where's Kayla?'' he asked anxiously, glancing around.

Beth drew back, letting her hands linger on his arms. ''Upstairs resting a bit. She was tired from her trip.'' Should she tell him about Adam? No. Let that come from Kayla. Presenting Doug with a grandson might be part of Kayla's fence-mending with her father.

"Did I get here in time to carry suitcases?" Belatedly he kissed her, but it landed on her temple as she was drawing away from him.

"No. I did it all, and I'll have you know it weighed a ton. Their name is Driscoll. Mrs. Driscoll requires pampering, so I put them in the front bedroom."

He frowned. "Isn't that Justin Bryant's regular room? Isn't he coming tonight?"

"I'll explain later, darling. Why don't you go up and see your daughter? They—she's in the back bedroom. You two have a lot to catch up on and I have to change."

"You're all wet," he said, suddenly noticing, and just then the doorbell chimed again.

"Go on up. I'll get that. It's probably Justin Bryant," Beth said, touching the side of his face briefly. She found herself listening intently to Doug's steps as he went up the stairs. She had an odd little sense of dread, which she quickly brushed aside as she hurried to open the front door. She knew Justin Bryant well and was ready to welcome him on his spring foraging among the collectibles of Seattle.

"Come in," she said eagerly. "And yes, I know my clothes are wet. I was just about to change. I'll show you up this time. I'm sorry, Justin, but I had to put you in a different room. I hope that's all right."

"Oh, I can't stand that," he said in mock despair. "You know how set in our ways we middle-aged guys get. Well, how many kinds of muffins will I get for breakfast? Maybe that will make it right."

"Four kinds," Beth assured him, and, as they mounted the stairs, she explained tactfully about Mrs. Driscoll's sleep disorder.

As she spoke she couldn't help but look toward the back bedroom, but the door was shut. Would Doug be shocked at finding a grandson he had never been told about?

Justin Bryant was still talking. "...and I intend to beat Doug at Scrabble this time. I have a new dictionary. Who else is here besides the fragile lady who took my bedroom?"

Beth found herself telling him about the sudden arrival of Doug's daughter and the other two guests who were arriving tomorrow.

"Oh, good. Full house," Justin said. "You can always find somebody interesting in a full house."

After she left Justin, she finally managed to change into an at-home outfit, one of Doug's favorites. A soft heather jersey with a swishy draped skirt. Doug was trying to paint a picture of her in it. He had made dozens of sketches but he wasn't satisfied.

"I guess what talent I've got is for landscapes," he had said. "Trees. Rocks. Hills. Sea. Those I can do. Why can't I capture your beautiful face?"

She went into the kitchen to start dinner and realized she was still listening intently for some sound from upstairs. Twice she couldn't resist going to the bottom of the stairway for a moment. When would they ever come down? Would Doug really be happy? Was he as pleased as he had sounded on the phone? From the kitchen she heard the Driscolls leaving, and the murmur of Mrs. Driscoll's voice, sounding plaintive. She hoped they wouldn't come back early, but they probably would. Then, a few minutes later, she heard Justin Bryant bounding down the stairs. He had friends in Seattle, so he would probably be back late.

Finally. Beth heard Doug and Kayla coming toward the kitchen. *Oh, please, God, let Doug be happy. Let this be right for Doug.* Then, belatedly, she prayed, *And let it be good for Kayla, too.* She breathed a sigh of relief at Doug's wide grin. He was carrying Adam. The little boy wasn't frowning, but his small face was dead serious.

"Ah, something smells wonderful. And I'm famished. Why didn't you tell me my grandson had arrived?" He leaned over to kiss Beth, and she felt herself flushing like a schoolgirl on her first date.

"I wanted Kayla to tell you," Beth said. She couldn't help but smile, too. Kayla looked radiant, so the reunion must have gone well. She *was* a pretty woman.

"Everything's almost ready," Beth said happily. "Just go in and sit down. I'll bring in the food." She had set the dining room table with her best china and silver in Kayla's honor. There was a low centerpiece of early white crocus. She had put the wooden booster seat on one of the chairs for Adam. As the three seated themselves, Beth began serving. The London broil marinade had tenderized the meat so it could be cut with a fork. The roasted red-skinned potato wedges were perfectly done. Beth sprinkled grated cheese over them, knowing it would melt by the time it reached the table. Then she quickly filled the chilled salad bowls with greens. She took everything in on the big silver tray because she didn't want to get up from the table again until dessert, and because she knew Doug would leap up to help her. *Let me take, Beth, it's too heavy for you.*

It was a lovely, comfortable meal, enriched with talk and laughter. Kayla's tension was gone. She was relaxed, pleasant and sometimes quite funny. Adam tucked into his food with sober concentration, as if he hadn't had a peanut butter sandwich and cookies in midafternoon. Kayla ate hungrily, too, with little approving comments. "Oh, Beth, this is so good."

Looking at Adam fondly, Doug said, "I had a bit of trouble getting acquainted with the little guy, but he loosened up after a while."

"Adam's kind of quirky," Kayla said. "He'll probably

end up like his daddy. Mitch was a loner. I don't think he ever had any real friends.''

Beth met Doug's eyes across the table in time to see the quick look of rejection. She could almost feel his thought: *No. Not Adam. Somehow, some way, life must be better for Adam.* And again, Beth felt the sense of uneasiness.

Kayla's energy didn't last long after dinner, and Adam had already fallen asleep, curled up on the floor beside Kayla's feet, soon after they had gone into the living room.

''Why don't you go to bed, sweetheart?'' Doug asked her. ''I know you're beat. Traveling does that.''

Kayla hid a yawn behind a slender hand. ''I think I will, Daddy—if that's all right with you, Beth. Tomorrow I'll be a new woman. And I intend to be some help. I'm a pretty good house cleaner when I get going. Daddy, will you carry Adam up for me?''

Beth went back into the dining room and cleared the table. She was putting the last things into the dishwasher when Doug came into the kitchen. He sat down at the kitchen table and she joined him. Both reached out and clasped hands as they often did. Doug was looking at her intently.

''Thank you for what you did, my love.''

''What? I don't—''

''For Kayla. For Adam.'' His voice was unsteady for a moment.

''What do you mean?''

''I know Kayla. I'm her father, remember? I know how grungy she can be when she reaches the point of going back on the wagon again. And I recognized Jill's blue dress.''

''Oh, that,'' Beth said in sudden embarrassment. ''I... She lost her luggage and she needed—''

''And if anybody *needs,* you fly to the rescue. I love you, Beth. I hope I deserve you.'' He tightened his hold on her hands. "And it salvaged Kayla's pride a bit, too, not having to face me looking like a ragamuffin. I know she must have been."

"How…how did things come out?"

He released her hands and got up. "Pretty well, I guess. With Kayla I'm never sure. But this time I think she really means it. Endicott's death got to her, I believe."

"Who's Endicott?"

"Adam's father. Mitch Endicott." He went over to the refrigerator. "I'll start the breakfast preparations while I tell you. No, don't get up. You've done enough today." He took the melons out of the fridge and put them on the long drain board.

Beth sat back as he took things out of cupboards and drawers and rolled up his sleeves. She loved to watch his big hands working. The big hands that could saw logs for the fireplaces or wield a tiny paintbrush to put sunlight on leaves or, as now, use the small scoop to create melon balls for breakfast.

"Kayla wants to go back into rehab. This time for the complete cure. She knows it won't be easy, mainly because she's tried before and failed. The rehab treatment takes about three months and will cost the earth. But I can afford it—though my emergency fund is taking a bit hit."

"But if she really means it and is successful, won't it be worth it?" Beth felt a surge of relief. She had a quick mental image of Kayla, not an alcoholic. Kayla not depending on Doug, but competent, successful. Kayla taking her little boy and going away.

"More than worth it. But she wants us to take care of Adam while she's away. She can't take a three-year-old with her into rehab." He turned from the sink, the melon baller held loosely in one hand. "What do you think about that?"

"Of course we can take care of Adam," she heard herself saying firmly. *What am I thinking of? I have a business to run!* And at the same time she had a recollection of Adam clutching the red sneakers to his chest. *Mine.* Well, Doug was worth it. If he wanted Adam to stay here for three months, so be it.

"I didn't doubt it, love. I know you too well for that. And when I saw Kayla in Jill's blue outfit, I figured it was practically a done deal. And, you know, I believe it will come out right this time. I feel sure it will. She'll stick with it. She means it. I don't know if you can understand this or not…how much this means to me. Your girls, Kate and Jill, don't seem to have any problems at all. They seem so *right* with life. I want that for Kayla, too." His voice was unsteady again.

"Kayla's life is screwed up because of me. Don't shake your head, Beth. I know what I know. You may have wondered why I've never talked about my first marriage, but it wasn't…very good. My fault, too, I guess. I did have a good, solid live-at-home job, lecturing on economics at our local college. But I didn't like academia. I didn't like…my marriage. I wanted *out.* At the time I was thinking of no one but myself. I couldn't walk out on the marriage commitment, but I got a job as a textbook representative because it demanded that I travel. It got me away. It set me free. When Kayla needed me—and she did—I was never there for her."

He worked silently for a time. Beth didn't know what to say. When he finished with the melons he put down the scoop and began gathering up the rinds for the disposal. The kitchen was filled with the drone of the grinding. Beth stared at the large platter of melon balls. The bright orange cantaloupe, the red watermelon, the pale green honeydew. It looked like a picture and would be tempting on the buffet in the morning. She watched as Doug carefully covered it with plastic and put it in the refrigerator. Then he took the two bun warmers out of the cupboard and put them near the electrical outlets so she could fill them with Kate's tiny, home-baked muffins in the morning. At last the grinding noise stopped.

Doug had never talked to her before about his first marriage. Nor had she talked to him about her long marriage to Ralph Bennett. Nor her guilt because she had never loved Ralph as he had loved her. Perhaps everyone felt guilty about some things—things done wrong, or things not done when they should have been done. She got up and went to him, taking his big hands and raising them briefly to her lips. Her heart ached for him. She knew what it was like to feel guilty.

"Beth, are you sure about this? I'll help out more than I have been doing, but running a busy B and B and looking after a three-year-old kid won't be a piece of cake."

Beth put her fingers over his lips. "Don't worry. We can do it. We *will* do it." But even as she said it, there was that sick feeling in the pit of her stomach. How ridiculous. Really ridiculous. Of course they could do it. It was only for three months. So why wouldn't the sickness go away?

Chapter Three

Mrs. Driscoll was happy with her muesli and nonfat milk breakfast because of the melon balls and the "little tastes" of this and that from Bert's overloaded breakfast choices. He had scrambled eggs, bacon, sausages and a large collection of muffins, heavily buttered.

"My doctor told me to cut way back on fat, but those little sausages looked so *good*. Bert, let me have a little taste of yours." Whereupon Bert would move three or four of his sausages from his plate to hers.

"Bert, those scrambled eggs look so fluffy..."

Breakfast at Beth's B and B was a time of pleasant confusion, much talk and laughter, and comings and goings. Beth enjoyed this fully. It was a nice feeling to give people a good breakfast and send them off in happy anticipation of their day's adventures in a new city—and one of the things she enjoyed most about her work.

Kayla, true to her word, was up early, having dressed Adam and brought him downstairs. Then she helped in the kitchen. Relaxed and at ease, she was a happy addition to the group, getting up quickly now and then to refill the coffee carafe or fetch more muffins from the kitchen. Beth could sense how pleased Doug was at Kayla's efforts. *Please, God, let this be right for Doug. And let it be right for Kayla, too. Soon.*

Justin Bryant was the last to leave. Beth hurried to the kitchen to get the two sack lunches she had prepared. She sometimes did this for guests who wanted to eat on the run. He and an associate were going out of town on business for the day. He had told them all with great gusto of his hopeful plans. They would go out to the country to see an attic full of "old things."

"Every antique dealer's dream come true," he said. "A granddaughter is getting rid of her late granny's stuff—and estate matter. We're hoping to see an attic full of priceless antiques that the granddaughter thinks are junk, that we can pick up for pennies. But it will probably be an attic full of junk granddaughter thinks are priceless antiques. Wish us luck."

Beth laughed and handed him the two sack lunches, for which he always paid generously. "Roast beef," she said. "The sack with the *B* on it is the one with barbecue sauce. I remember you said your friend can't eat anything spicy."

When the guests had gone for the day, she, Doug and Kayla settled down with comfortable sighs and Adam came back to the table. He had stolidly disposed of the large breakfast Kayla had placed before him. But he had a habit of sliding down from his place and wandering off for a while. Then he would come back, let Doug help him back up on the booster seat to resume his meal. Later, tactfully, Beth thought she'd better persuade him out of this habit. Since he ate much of his food with his fingers there was the matter of greasy fingermarks on walls and furniture. Now she watched his sober efforts. He was immaculately clean, neatly clothed, well-fed and safe. Doug must be happy about that.

As they were leisurely drinking second cups of coffee, the kitchen phone rang and Doug got up to answer it. She and Kayla could hear him talking and laughing, and when he came back he was still smiling.

"That was Jill," he said, sitting down. "They're both coming over for lunch. But they're bringing it." He turned to Kayla. "Jill and Kate are Beth's daughters. You'll like them. They're a lot of fun."

"I know I will," Kayla said, smiling warmly, but Beth happened to be looking at Kayla's expressive eyes. She sensed Kayla's instant withdrawal. How difficult would it be for Kayla to meet women of her own age who had solved their problems as they arose and hadn't made the mistakes she had? Was this going to be another difficulty? Both girls had accepted her marriage to Doug and liked him very much.

"Are they bringing their children?" Beth asked. "They have three each," she added for Kayla's benefit, "and Kate will have another in a few months."

"Three each," Kayla said. "I have trouble taking care of one." She made a move to leave the table. "You wanted to change our room," she reminded Beth.

"Right," Beth said quickly, sensing that Kayla suddenly wanted to escape. "We'd better get on with it."

"Mommy!" Adam said in panic as Kayla left. He slid down from his place. He followed closely behind them as they went upstairs to strip the bed and put on fresh linen for the guests tonight.

Beth could hear Doug whistling and the clatter of dishes as he cleared the table.

Kayla turned out to be an excellent helper, scouring the tub and shower, working quickly and efficiently. When Beth commented admiringly, Kayla answered, wringing out the cleaning cloth, "I had a job once as a maid in a motel. I learned a lot about cleaning fast."

She frowned slightly, and Beth wondered about Kayla's hectic and uncertain existence. What a way to live.

"Incidentally," Kayla added. "I've never mentioned to Dad some of the jobs I've had, so this is just between us, okay?"

"Fine," Beth agreed. "Past history is past history."

Beth's cleaning service came once a week for vacuuming, mopping, polishing—all the heavy work—but the daily bed making, bath cleaning and tidying up, Beth did, and today she found Kayla a real help. They finished in half the time and began to move Kayla's and Adam's things into the small downstairs bed-sitter.

Adam fell in love with the bed-sitter on sight, especially when she and Kayla opened the queen-size sofa bed to put on the sheets and blanket.

"Izziz our house now?" he asked, looking around the small room. There was the made-up sofa bed, a small chest of drawers, a pretty chair and the wide window seat that magically opened up to reveal the big empty space below the seat. He had already discovered the basin with running water behind the folding screen. He was standing in the center of the room, legs spread out, hands on hips, like a tiny lord of the manor. Beth had to admit he was kind of cute.

Kayla laughed at him. "This is our house for the time being. You know, I told you this morning that I had to go away for a while, but just a little while. Beth's going to take care of you. Remember what I told you. Don't play dumb now."

Because suddenly the little lord of the manor was scowling fiercely.

"It's just for a little while," Kayla repeated placatingly.

"I'll be back. You know when I leave I always come back."

Beth wondered how many times Kayla had left him "for a little while." With whom had she left him? How well had he been cared for? It took an effort to remain silent. Kayla wouldn't be gone for a *little* while. She'd be gone for three months in rehab. Three months would be forever to a small child. Well, somehow she would have to deal with it. Anything was possible…for Doug.

When they finished in the bed-sitter, Doug remembered the box of toys Beth kept for grandchildren's visits. He brought it into the room. Adam was fascinated. Had he never had toys of his own? Beth wondered. Doug sat down on the floor to show him how to connect the bits of yellow plastic with which Ben, Jill's little boy, built and dismantled wonderful structures when he was here.

They had almost finished in the bed-sitter when the doorbell chimed twice in quick succession. Eleven-thirty. That would be Jill, Beth thought. She always pushed the bell twice. Hard. *Please, God, let this work out.*

There was an interval of happy chaos as Beth and Doug introduced everyone. She watched carefully, hoping that Kayla would not be intimidated by her daughters. Jill, tall and beautiful, with her striking dark hair and eyes. And Kate, only five feet tall and to anyone but a mother probably rather plain, and very pregnant.

They came in carrying plastic and foil-wrapped containers, which Doug took charge of and carried to the kitchen for their lunch later.

"Everything in plastic goes in the fridge," Kate called after him. "The big box has tomorrow's muffins for the B and B folks." Then they all settled in the large living room. Adam, suddenly surrounded by strangers, stayed close to Kayla's legs, looking at everyone with a steady frown. A sudden thought popped into Beth's mind. What had made this little boy suspicious of the whole world?

"I should have brought Meggie," Jill said, smiling graciously at Kayla. "Then Adam would have someone to play with. She's four. But I left her with my support group. We all help each other out with baby-sitting now and then. We're all former career women who have put our work on hold until our kids are grown."

Kayla looked at her blankly, and Doug intervened to explain that Jill had been a successful restaurant owner early in her marriage.

Beth mentally sighed. It wasn't working. Lunch was going to be a disaster. Both her girls were trying too hard to be nice to Kayla, and Kayla was trying to respond, her little boy pressed against her legs looking like a small thundercloud. Neither Jill nor Kate could forget that Kayla hadn't shown up for the wedding and—clearly—her arrival now had been a complete surprise to Doug. Kayla was tense and on guard, obviously feeling inferior to all these people and their successful lives, and resenting it deeply. *I'd better talk to the girls about this,* Beth thought. *But what can I say to them?* Each daughter, in her own way, was doing her best in an awkward situation.

What would Cyrus say? Suddenly she was thinking of her pastor. *Dear God, help Cyrus get well soon.* Cyrus had always been there for them, all of them. If only she could call Cyrus's well-known number, knowing he would pick up the phone at the other end. *Ah, Beth, how can I help you, my dear?* Then she could pour out her worries to him, counting on his kindness, his loving knowledge of the predicaments human beings got themselves into, his willingness to advise, to guide, to help. By sheer willpower she shut out thoughts of Cyrus and made herself pay attention to the here and now.

They labored through lunch. She could sense Doug's discomfort. Jill, whose talent for working with people of all sorts in her business, was still being too cordial. And Kate, who couldn't hide her obvious growing irritation as Adam ate his own lunch in installments. He kept getting down, wandering away, then coming back to the table. Each time, Doug had to get up to lift him back onto the booster seat on his chair. Kate's children were better rule-obeyers than Jill's, or anyone else's, for that matter, and she managed to do it in such a way that her children didn't seem to resent the discipline.

Lunch ended on a rather contentious note. Doug had looked at his watch for perhaps the fifth time.

"We've got to cut out, love," he said to Beth. "Kayla and I have an appointment. We're going to have to leave the clearing up to you."

"That's all right," Beth said quickly, trying not to sound relieved. "We'll make out fine." She stopped herself from asking about the appointment, but Kayla spoke out, more loudly than necessary. There was defiance in her tone.

"My dad and I have an appointment at a rehab clinic." She turned to Jill and Kate, adding deliberately, "I have a drinking problem. I don't know if Dad has mentioned it to you or not." Then, as if this hadn't been enough to startle both Jill and Kate, she added coldly, "I'm a drunk."

"Oh, come now," Beth said weakly, as she saw the stunned expressions on her daughters' faces. Doug had never actually explained to them what Kayla's problems were.

Jill, always the quickest in the Bennett family, tried to rescue the situation. "Good," she said decisively. "If you think it's become a problem, then treatment is probably your best course. Good for you." She reached over and patted Kayla's hand.

"It's a preliminary interview," Doug said uncomfortably. "We'll be back later, but we need to make arrangements and so on."

Kate had recovered her poise. "How long will it take, Kayla?" she asked politely.

"The brochure said three months," Kayla answered, and then added with a hint of venom. "Beth's going to take care of Adam while I'm gone."

"We'd better get going," Doug said hurriedly, getting up.

But as Adam realized that Kayla and Doug were leaving without him, he began to cry. He had to be pulled away from Kayla.

After they had gone and Adam had quieted down—Jill was very good with small children—Beth prepared herself to answer questions. They came immediately.

"Did she call? Write? Give you any notice at all? Did she just show up? What kind of person just shows up?"

"Mom, those rehab places are expensive! Doug's not rich by any means."

"If Kayla's reduced to wearing rummage sale castoffs—and yes, we noticed the dress—*who* is going to pay for three months in a rehab facility?"

"*How* are you going to care for a three-year-old child and run a B and B? *Moth*-er!"

Beth recognized the exasperation in the "*Moth*-er" and spoke commandingly. "All right! Let's clear away this stuff. I'll explain everything." She did her best to downplay the inconvenience and explain how important it was to Doug to help Kayla, that Kayla was a widow now, that Adam's father had died. And that Kayla was serious and *intended* to recover. This was important. She omitted how and where Mitch had died for the moment.

"It's only three months, after all," she ended, but neither daughter was satisfied. They had always been a close family, and protective of one another. They were both worried about her now, and wondered how she would cope. They knew how happy she had been with her new marriage, how well she and Doug got along. They calmed down, but with an obvious effort.

Fortunately, Adam then became sleepy by his toy box. It was Jill who went looking for him and put him down on the sofa bed for a nap. While she tended to Adam, Beth and Kate were left alone in the kitchen.

"How have you been doing?" Beth asked. Kate hadn't been much help with the clearing up, which was unusual for her. She seemed tired and lethargic. Her baby wasn't due for another three months, and Kate had gotten easily through her previous pregnancies.

"Okay, I guess," Kate said. "I was lucky before. Maybe I'm really too old now, but Ian and I—" She shrugged, adding, "I wish—"

"Probably the same thing I do," Beth said, turning from the dishwasher. Now was a good chance to change the subject. "I'd give a pretty penny to talk to Cyrus today. Have you heard how he is?"

"Yes. I call the hospital every day. He's stable and as well as can be expected. He had a good night. You know how it is. Depends on who you talk to. They've sent—" She paused because her voice was suddenly unsteady. "They've sent for his son and daughter."

"Oh, no! Not really! Is it that serious?" Then immediately, she added, "Where will they stay?"

"I told Bess down at the church office that we have a spare bedroom. Several other people have volunteered, too. Or they could just stay at the rectory, I guess."

"I can't offer," Beth said. "The B and B is booked solid through the whole summer. People tend to come back. Probably because of your muffins, Katie."

That got a wan smile.

"I've met the substitute pastor. Flip Cooper." Kate's tone was decidedly sour.

"Flip? His name is Flip? Are you kidding me?"

"It's a contraction of Philip, which is a perfectly good name for a pastor. But I think he thinks 'Flip'' is clever. He seems awfully, uh…*young* for a pastor."

Beth had to laugh. "Kate, you sound absolutely testy." And Kate laughed with her.

"I guess the poor guy has a hard path to walk here, coming in to substitute for Cyrus. Everybody loves Cyrus. We all go back so far together."

"When did you meet this, uh, Flip?"

"I'm still going down Thursdays to help with the food bank stuff. He was there. You won't believe what he wears for casual clothes."

"Maybe you'd better not tell me. Not until I get used to calling my pastor 'Flip,'" Beth said.

Then Jill came back into the kitchen. "Adam's off in dreamland," she said. "How long does he sleep—about an hour?"

"About that, I think. Now, listen, girls. I want this to *work*. I know you both have reservations, but your mother can be very resourceful when the need arises. So bear with me. He is Doug's grandson, don't forget. That's important to me. Doug adores that little guy."

Jill said softly, "He'd be hard not to love. Poor little mite. If I…can help in any way, Mom, anytime."

"Me, too, Mom. You know that." Kate reached out to her and they suddenly clasped hands. Then Kate, who had always been "Daddy's girl" while Ralph was alive and had been so devastated when he died, surprised her, adding, "I know how much Doug means to you. And the more I know him, I get the oddest feeling that he and Dad would have been good friends. I mean, if Dad had known him."

Deeply touched, Beth turned away. She didn't want to

be reminded of Ralph—good, kind, faithful, loving, grateful Ralph. He was at peace now. Let him rest.

"Thank you, Kate. I agree. I think they would have talked books until the small hours of the morning."

"That's right," Kate said, smiling. "Doug spent his work life among books, too. I'd forgotten that. He looks like such an outdoors type."

Her daughters left soon after lunch. They had accomplished what they had come for. They had met Kayla. Beth sat down at the kitchen table, trying to quell her uneasiness. Neither daughter had liked Kayla, although they had tactfully tried to hide it. And both of them were worried now about how she would cope with the situation.

But she would. For Doug's sake.

The silence now in the large house had an eerie quality, and she felt a sense of foreboding. *Will I be able to handle it? I've already raised my children. I haven't had the care of a small child for years. Can I keep up with a lively three-year-old boy with all my other duties? And a problem child at that, a child already filled with deep anger at a world he has come into and found hostile, and far too young to understand why?*

Oh, dear God, let me be able to do this.

The front door chimes rang out. What now? She got up quickly, hoping whoever it was wouldn't ring again and wake Adam up. But of course the person did ring again, just as she reached the front hall. It couldn't be guests this early. She opened the door.

He was young, tall and rangy, with an unruly mop of reddish blond hair and clear, very light brown eyes. He was dressed in a once-white T-shirt that had seen better days and old, limp jeans that had been cut off at the knees. His bare muscular lower legs ended in the oldest, dirtiest running shoes she had ever seen. Propped against the porch railing was a battered bike, apparently his mode of transportation.

"Yes?" she inquired politely.

"Hi. Is Mr. Colby in? Doug? I wanted to catch him down at the church but I missed him. I'm Flip Cooper, uh, Pastor Cooper. I need to talk to Doug about new ninth grade science books. I'm told he knows all there is to know about textbooks." He ended on a questioning note, as if he wasn't quite sure of his welcome.

"Of course," Beth said, hoping her surprised expression hadn't intimidated him. *This is our new pastor? Unbelievable!* She opened the door wider. "Please come in. I'm afraid you missed Doug again. He and Kayla—that's his daughter—he and Kayla have gone out. But they'll be back soon. Would you like to wait?" She hoped that he wouldn't and that he hadn't heard it in her tone. *Put on your perfect hostess smile, Beth.* What a contrast he was to Cyrus. What had the Elders been thinking of? He was just a kid, not more than twenty-five surely. Well, he'd have to be older than that, to have gotten through college and seminary. He must be at least thirty. *Don't ask the pastor how old he is.* "Or, if you're busy," she continued, "you can just leave a message with me and he can call you."

"That might be a better idea," he agreed, strolling on through the hall into the large living room. "I've met your daughter, Kate. Lovely woman. Very generous with her time. And I've met Doug, of course. This is certainly a beautiful old house," he added, looking around appreciatively.

"Thank you. It's a bed-and-breakfast now. I started a small business after my first husband passed away. Won't you sit down?" *No, don't sit down. Just go away. How in the world can you hope to take Cyrus's place?*

"No, thanks. I know you're busy. I won't stay. Just tell Doug to give me a call. I'll be at the church—I guess you know the number." Suddenly he smiled and there was laughter in his eyes.

Beth felt herself flushing, wondering if he sensed her disapproval. If he had, he didn't seem to care much whether she approved of him or not. It made her feel defensive. He really shouldn't run around looking like a grubby teenager.

"I stopped at the hospital and saw Cyrus this afternoon," he said. "He's been with this congregation so long, I'm sure he's very important to you all."

Beth felt her flush deepen. It was as if he had been reading her mind. "Yes, he is," she said. "How was he today?"

He paused a moment before answering, "I'm sorry. I can't con you by telling you he's fine when he isn't. Cyrus is a very sick man. His son and daughter are coming in today. I sent for them at his doctor's request."

Beth said down suddenly and looked up at him. He seemed so tall. "Yes, my daughter told me that," she said faintly.

"I'm more sorry than I can say. Can I...get you something?"

"No, I'm okay. It's just that— Cyrus has always been here." How stupid she must sound, she thought.

"I'm not going to say he won't recover—somewhat. But I think we must face the fact that he won't be coming back as your pastor." There was an odd gentleness in his tone now.

Maybe he wasn't so young, after all.

"It's going to take some getting used to by all of you," he added.

"I know," Beth said bleakly. *Please go away now. You can't help me. You weren't there when I was afraid I would die before Jill was born. Cyrus was there. He made me not afraid to die. And Cyrus was there when Ralph died. And it wasn't you but Cyrus who helped Kate through the dif-*

ficult early part of her marriage to Ian. And it was Cyrus who guided us all when we worked together to create the church school.

Beth stood up, embarrassed by the long pause. What must he be thinking of her? He was looking confused and uneasy. She was rescued by the sound of the front door opening. Doug was back. *Thank you, God.*

"That must be Doug now."

"Oh, good." There was pure relief in his tone, and he grinned. "As you've probably already guessed, I'm better at coaching the kids' basketball game than some other of my pastoral work. I'll need to bone up. But take hope. I'm working on it— Hi, Doug," he said, as Doug and Kayla came into the room.

Kayla had been crying. She made an effort when Doug made the introductions, but it was an uncomfortable moment.

"Doug, can I tear you away from your family for a couple of minutes to talk new science books for the ninth graders?" Pastor Cooper asked, his gaze lingering on Kayla.

How odd. Kayla didn't look that bad.

"Sure," Doug answered. "Come on into the study." And he led Pastor Cooper out of the room.

As soon as he had gone, Beth went to Kayla. "What is it? What's the matter?" she asked. Had something gone wrong?

"Oh, it's just me, Beth. I did okay at rehab." She sat down on the couch, all hunched over, putting her face in her hands. "I'm so embarrassed. Poor Dad. After we made all the arrangements and we were back in the car I...I kind of fell apart. I was so stupid. I know I've got to go through with it. I've got Adam to take care of. I don't have a choice, but I'm so...so scared to go in again." She raised her face and her vivid blue eyes were full of tears. "I'm such a...loser."

"No. You're not a loser," Beth said firmly, and sat down beside her. "You are doing a sensible thing. And you *can* do it. When you've got this far you know you've turned the corner. It's going to be fine." This was Doug's daughter and, somehow, she had to be helped.

"I know," Kayla said wearily, her voice low and defeated. "But, Beth, you don't know how many times I've screwed up. Other people don't seem to—"

"But think ahead, Kayla. Think of three months from now. All this will be over. It will be behind you. You will have done it. Think about that." Kayla mustn't become discouraged. She mustn't give up.

Kayla straightened tiredly, as if she were an old, old woman. "Beth, you know, you're a sweetheart. I'm glad Dad found you. He deserves some happiness. Where did you stash my dumb little kid?"

"Adam isn't dumb," Beth said quickly, surprising herself because she sounded so defensive. "He's taking a nap. He's in the bed-sitter."

"The bed-sitter sounds pretty good to me, too," Kayla said. "I think I'll sack out awhile. Unless you need me to do something," she added.

"Not a thing. You just take it easy. You've had a rough afternoon. We've got guests coming, but not until later."

She watched Kayla leave. Kayla was young. She shouldn't walk like that, as if she was too tired to put one foot in front of the other. A phrase came to her that Doug sometimes used when he was tired from heavy work, like chopping the firewood: *Tired to the center of my bones.* Kayla shouldn't look that tired.

She heard the approaching murmur of men's voices and knew that Flip Cooper and Doug had finished.

After Flip left, Doug sat down beside her, reaching for her hand. How good it felt to be here alone with Doug, feeling the strength of his big hand. They didn't speak for a moment, savoring the privacy and peaceful silence.

"How did it go at the rehab place?" Beth finally asked.

Doug sighed. "Good, I think. It's a nice place. The staff—we met some of them—are competent, well qualified. Kind. Patient." He sighed again. "But it's a...*facility.* It's a rehab center, just short of a hospital, never mind the decor, the fact that the staff don't wear uniforms. It's a *rehab.* People go there who need help. I can't imagine being in such a place myself, of being so...controlled. So...confined. Being told what to do, hour by hour. Kayla..." His voice dwindled away.

"But Kayla needs that kind of help," Beth said. "She knows that, probably better than we do. It won't be easy for her. Nothing like that is. But people who need that kind of help are broken people, Doug. Somebody has to...put them back together again." Doug mustn't become discouraged about this.

"I know," he said sadly.

"Kayla told me she broke down in the car after the interview."

"Yes. She did. I pulled the car over to the side street, I never know what to do in a situation like that. It worried me. There was such a hopelessness about it. It was as if once she started crying she couldn't stop. And there was nothing I could do. I felt so desperate. Finally, she managed to get control. Or maybe she had just worn herself out. I kept thinking I should be able to...I don't know. As a father I'm just not..." There was such regret in his voice, it tore Beth's heart.

"You were probably better than you thought as a father," she said. "Raising children is a never-ending challenge. And we all think we should have done better."

"Well, I certainly could have done better. Kayla isn't the only one paying the price. Much as I hate to admit it, she's way out of her depth in parenting, too. Poor little Adam. He's being cheated, big time. I guess that's what it means when it says in the Bible about the sins of the fathers being visited on the second and third generations. On the rare occasions when I was home, I couldn't wait to get back on the road again. And leaving always meant I was leaving Kayla when she might have needed me. And now, after all this time, I can see the result of my running away. It has become the burden of a little three-year-old kid named Adam—one of the most insecure kids I've ever seen, who can't even begin to understand—''

"Doug. Don't do this to yourself. You couldn't have been that bad a father. Kayla must take some of the responsibility. She's an adult. Did you mention any of this to Pastor Cooper?''

"No. It simply didn't occur to me. He's a nice enough guy, but, really, I don't think it would ever dawn on me to take him any personal problems—not the way I would with Cyrus.''

"Yes,'' Beth said, suddenly distracted. "He said he doesn't think Cyrus can come back as pastor.''

"I'd heard that from some other people. I guess we're stuck with Pastor Cooper. Actually, he's okay, really. You just have to get used to him. And there was another thing,'' he added, looking at her keenly. "I got the distinct impression that he could become interested in Kayla. He's a single guy, isn't he?''

"Yes, he's single.'' Beth started to laugh. "And you think he might be looking for a wife? That's usually a woman's reaction when she sees a single man.''

Doug grinned sheepishly. "Well, he's single. And Kayla is a lovely young woman. He did ask me about her. Rather persistently, I would say. I think he noticed she'd been crying but was too tactful to mention that.''

"What did you say?''

"I told him she was a widow. I guess I just let him assume she had reason to cry now and then. I didn't go into any detail."

"That was probably best," Beth agreed. "At least until we know him better. Kayla is entitled to some privacy," she added.

They fell silent as they heard the front door open. It was the Driscolls, coming back from wherever they had been. They could hear Mrs. Driscoll's plaintive voice and the deep murmur of Mr. Driscoll reassuring her about something.

Doug raised his eyebrows. "When are they leaving?"

"Tomorrow," Beth whispered, as they heard the Driscolls going upstairs. When the sound faded, they settled into silence again.

Beth finally asked, "When will Kayla go into rehab?"

"Tomorrow. I take her over tomorrow morning. That was her decision. She was fine during the interview. She said the sooner she got started, the better."

"That was sensible. I think—" She paused as someone was coming down the stairs with a heavy tread, loud and purposeful. Both Beth and Doug turned to the hall door as Mrs. Driscoll came majestically in, very obviously upset. Doug stood up as she entered, and after a moment, Beth did, too. What now?

"Ah, I was hoping to find you both. I *don't* understand this!" She gingerly held out a limp, half-eaten piece of old toast. "You *said* you had a good cleaning service. If so, *why* in the world would I find *this* in our room? Really!"

Beth reached out, and Mrs. Driscoll placed the piece of toast on her palm. "I...I don't understand it either," Beth said uncertainly. "Where did you find this?"

"In our dresser drawer. The bottom one. Bert and I *always* use the bottom drawer because most people use the top one. I believe that the bottom one is cleaner. This piece of toast was in our bottom drawer.''

"I don't…understand," Beth repeated helplessly.

"Well, I think I do," Mrs. Driscoll said portentously. "I think it was that little boy. I saw him in the hall this morning. He had a piece of toast in his hand. I do *not* approve of children leaving the table carrying food. I'm sure he's running about in the guest rooms, leaving bits of food here and there."

"I'm sorry," Beth said. "I'm really sorry. I'll see that it doesn't happen again."

"I should hope not!" Mrs. Driscoll turned and angrily left the room.

As she left, Beth and Doug turned to each other in confusion. Then, they both saw it at the same time. On a lower shelf of a bookcase in a back corner. Half hidden behind the bookend—unmistakably—was a small cookie.

"Adam?" Beth said faintly. So that was why Adam wandered away from the table during meals. "Can Adam be hiding bits of food? Why would Adam hide bits of food?" But even as she asked it she knew the answer, and felt a little sick.

It took an effort but Doug replied. "Because he *expects* to be hungry, Beth." His voice was oddly grim, not sounding like Doug at all. He turned away and she couldn't see his face. "It would seem that my grandson—in his three-year-old wisdom—is trying to provide for his very uncertain future in the only way he knows how. He's learned a tough lesson. If you have a piece of food today, hang on to it. Because tomorrow you're going to need it.

"I did this to him, Beth."

Chapter Four

Morning was hectic. Neither one had gotten much sleep the night before. Doug had been miserable about Kayla and Adam, and Beth was miserable because he was miserable. They had talked until very late. Then Seattle's frequent night rains had found another hole in the roof over the Driscolls' bedroom, in, of course, the area over the bed canopy. Someday they might recall and laugh about Mrs. Driscoll's outrage, but not today. Then Doug had had to get Kayla to the rehab center before nine-thirty because she was to begin with a complete physical exam and the rehab doctor was only going to be there until eleven. Kayla and Doug had left before anyone had finished breakfast.

Kayla's leaving had resulted in Adam's near hysterical crying just as the Driscolls wanted to check out. The other guest, Justin Bryant, stepped in and showed remarkable child-consoling ability in calming Adam down while Beth dealt with the Driscolls.

"They'll probably never come back," Beth said resignedly to Justin when she returned to the dining room.

He glanced up from Adam and grinned. "And that would devastate you, of course?"

And she had had to laugh.

"No, I suppose not," she said, sitting down at the now disordered table. "Are you off antiquing today?"

"Yeah, as soon as I can leave my little friend, here."

Adam seemed content enough now. He sat at his place with his half-eaten breakfast before him. His small face was still flushed and tear-smudged, but he was methodically eating. She couldn't help but feel sorry for him, so little, so confused.

She thought, Where else has he hidden food? Should she find all his carefully saved little scraps and throw them all away? What if more guests find half-eaten fragments in their rooms? What if Adam feels hungry in midafternoon and discovers one of his cherished fragments gone? How is it possible to explain to a three-year-old child that he will not be hungry in this house? Should she gather up all his tidbits and put them in one place for him? Maybe she could secretly throw away any that got too stale. Maybe that would make him feel secure until he had learned he would not be hungry here. She was startled by Justin's voice.

"Earth to Beth. Are you out there somewhere?"

"Oh, Justin. I'm sorry. I was a thousand miles away."

"I know." He was laughing. "I've got to go now. We have big business afoot in the world of old stuff, and I've only got two more days. Can you take care of my little buddy now?"

"Yes, I'll take over." She got up to see him to the door. "Thanks more than I can say for stepping in. I'm sorry this morning was such a hassle."

"Glad to help, Beth. Hassles make life interesting. See you later."

She shut the front door behind him. There was one great thing about running a bed-and-breakfast. Wonderful people occasionally came and went in her life—many more than were not so wonderful.

Then her mind flew to Kayla. What were Kayla and Doug doing now? They would have reached the rehab center half an hour ago. Had Kayla made it through without breaking down again? She wished she had had more time with Kayla this morning. Perhaps she should have encouraged her more. But Kayla had seemed distracted, with a kind of vacancy that had puzzled Beth. She turned and went back into the dining room. The silence of the big, empty house pressed upon her. Adam was still at the table, observing his empty plate. He looked up anxiously, his blue eyes wide with worry. *A three-year-old child should not have to worry.*

"Mommy come back?" He had heard the door shut.

Beth forced herself to speak brightly when all she wanted to do was cry. "Not yet, Adam. It's too soon. Mommy's coming back but later. Not today." She mustn't get too attached to Adam, she warned herself.

He gave a small sigh and started to climb down from his booster seat. She hurried forward and caught him before he fell. He never waited to be helped. He wasn't expecting to be helped. But he should. Little children *should* expect help. And get it.

"Toy box," he said firmly, and Beth felt a surge of relief. He wanted to go to the toy box and perform his version of playing. This meant he would sit there soberly for a while, taking out the toys and looking at them, then putting them back. Now and then he would piece together some of the small yellow plastic pieces to make some oddly shaped creation. He played so differently, not like Jill's little boy, Ben. Ben was often lost in his own imaginary world, but it was a secure world. He emerged from it now and then to play with other children, and Ben's laugh was a delight to hear. Would they ever hear Adam laugh? Had Adam *ever* laughed? What had he to laugh *about?*

She cleared the table, tidied up the kitchen, and was making beds when Doug came back. She heard him go into the bed-sitter. Could Adam stay in the bed-sitter alone at night? One more question. One more thing to worry about. When would this end? Leaving a half-made bed, she hurried downstairs to talk to Doug.

"Did everything go all right?" she asked him after she had kissed him.

"I guess so. She's in there, anyhow." He sounded tired. He was watching the little boy intently.

"I wanted to talk with her this morning," Beth said. "But there was so much else to do, I couldn't."

"I know, love. I don't think it would have mattered. I think you'll probably find an empty vodka bottle in here when you clean up. She'd had a few for courage before we left. Didn't you notice?"

"No. Not really. You mean you think she'd been drinking? In the morning?"

"Beth," he said gently, "it's clear you've never lived with an alcoholic. Yes, she'd been drinking. One of the first things to learn when dealing with an alcoholic is that the alcoholic will have a stash of booze somewhere. Food? Only a maybe. But booze? Yes. Always. I suspect that ugly big gray tote bag she hangs on to as if it were full of gold bullion is the receptical of choice for our Kayla."

"I'm sorry," Beth said weakly. "Should I have done something?"

"What? She had already decided on rehab, on giving it another try, but until she actually went into rehab it would have been Kayla just doing her thing. God help her. Let's just pray that it works this time. That this time she makes it. She was serious about it, I'll give her that. It takes some guts to admit you've screwed up and even more guts to admit you can't handle it and need help. She's really trying and…it kind of breaks my heart because…''

''Because why?'' Beth asked softly.

''Because I'm scared that she'll fail, I guess.''

''Oh, Doug, she will succeed this time. I just know it. She's got to.'' She couldn't stand Doug feeling so defeated, and so guilty.

He spoke quickly, turning his gaze to the sober little boy. ''And if she doesn't?'' he asked.

''What do you mean?''

''We've got to talk some more about this, consider all the possibilities.'' He indicated Adam, without speaking his name. ''We must be sure about him. Nothing can change that. If Kayla makes it this time, fine, his place is with his mother. But otherwise…''

Yes, otherwise. What was Doug thinking? Beth made herself think about the possibilities. She suddenly knew to the bottom of her soul that they couldn't stand by, if Kayla failed, and watch her leave with Adam. She couldn't do that to Doug or Adam. She could not stand at the door and watch his little legs trying to keep up with the billowing green skirt going rapidly to—where? To somewhere that didn't have enough for him to eat? Never again did she want to think of his digging dirty fingers into a limp bag for leftover french fries— But what about the rights of grandparents? What *right* did Doug have to dictate to Kayla how Adam should be cared for?

No, they couldn't forget about *otherwise*. She had loved being a grandparent. There was so much joy in it. All the fun of welcoming her daughters' children trooping up the front steps for a visit. None of the commitments of keeping lists of booster shots, of dental appointments, of the sudden edge-of-death illnesses of small children that went away the next day after a sleepless night for the parents. Oh, *that* otherwise. If worse came to worse and Kayla didn't make it this time, could she really handle the *otherwise* again? For this little boy? All the unending problems of parenting?

Doug was looking at her with a question in his eyes. "That little bundle to take care of now, at this time in our lives, could be a real handful. Or, as they say today, a 'challenge.'" He was speaking tentatively, with uncertainty in his voice. She felt an inner chill. He went on. "Our life is good, Beth. You and me. Here. Now. Together. If anything should put it at risk, I don't think I'm above falling on my knees and howling like a banshee. That's what I mean when I say we should talk about this more, consider all the possibilities. Even the possibility—make that probability—that Kayla could blow it again."

And Adam was already a psychologically abused child, a child with many problems.

"I agree," Beth said. "We need to get serious, think about solutions, all the what-ifs, of raising a child." *What am I saying? No way could we take on a child to raise at this wonderful time in our lives.*

"Whatever way it goes with Kayla," she said carefully, "I think we should try to persuade her to stay in Seattle. So we can be aware of how he's doing. So we can at least have a, er, monitoring position. For whatever reasons, Kayla has shown herself to be…vulnerable. She's not as…strong as most people. Even if she recovers completely but some sort of pressure mounts, she might need help again. So I think she should be *here*. I mean in Seattle. Don't you think so?" Even as she spoke her reassuring words her mind was silently screaming, *I can't do this!*

"Besides the fact that I would probably agree with anything you say, yes, I think we should try to keep Kayla in Seattle. I'm going to stay vigilant about Adam."

Beth felt a little sick. Nothing must ever separate her from Doug. He had sounded uncertain, uneasy. There was one absolute in this wonderful part of her life, this marvelous second chance at love: she must never—*for any reason*—lose this closeness with Doug. Together, with the operative word being *together,* they would have to handle this. Somehow.

"When will we know how Kayla is doing?"

Doug sighed. "Not for six weeks. At first the patients aren't allowed to call out or receive incoming calls or visits. It's a period of orientation, sort of. Training, I guess. Redirecting the person's mind-set. Broadening the focus *off* getting that next drink to some sort of realization that there is more to life than getting that next drink. And that life entails responsibility, that other people are out there who need thinking about. They seem to know what they're doing. Their success rate is quite good, keeping in mind that once a person is an addict—to whatever—that person will always be more vulnerable than someone who has never had a dependency on something. The fact that a person becomes addicted in the first place indicates a cry for help, that the person has—needs help in some way." He paused. "And isn't getting it."

Beth went into his arms and he held her tightly for a long moment. *Oh, Doug, I love you so much.* They were both looking somberly at Adam by the toy box. Adam put two pieces of yellow plastic together, struggled with them before they clicked into place together. Then he paused and stared off into the distance.

"Mommy, come back," he muttered softly to himself.

"Yes," Beth said. "Not right away, Adam. Not today. But she will come back." And Adam nodded, turning his attention back to the bits of plastic in his small hands, as the phone ringing broke into the pensive mood.

With Doug following, Beth went to answer it in the hall by the desk. It was someone to make a reservation, and

Beth flipped through the booking schedule. The entries for summer were mounting.

"No, I'm sorry. There's nothing left in either July or August for your friend. No, not even the bed-sitter. That's booked solid." *The bed-sitter is Adam's place.* "I still have about eleven days in June. And more than that in May, and a few dates this month. Yes. I have that big room available on June fifteenth. And, yes, it's big enough for a roll-away for your third person." She wrote down the reservation and credit card number, and said goodbye. As she hung up the phone it rang again.

"Party of three from Denver," she told Doug as she picked up the phone again. "That couple from Denver coming in later today have certainly spread the word— Hello?" she said into the phone.

"Yes, of course I can, Mrs. Reese-Talbot. No, it's not too short notice. I understand you get these sudden assignments. No trouble at all." And she booked in another returning guest. As she hung up the phone she smiled at Doug. She really liked this part-time career she had built for herself. She was proud of it. It was her own achievement—her very own.

"It's that elderly professional photographer from New York. She's working on some assignment to photograph inner-city street people, and I guess Seattle's Pioneer Square qualifies."

Doug sighed. "She worries me. The woman doesn't know fear. I mean commonsense fear. Pioneer Square at 3:00 a.m. isn't for little old ladies with cameras, old pro or not."

"Well, cross your fingers because she's coming in on an 8:00 p.m. flight today. I promised to have a snack for her." But she said it absently, aware that she was thinking on two levels. What was wrong with refusing a few reservations? Better start leaving a few days vacant. She might need some spare time later. No need to book solid this year. It might cost them a little money, but she and Doug both had moderate pensions and Doug was selling more and more of his beautiful landscape paintings now. They could get by comfortably without a full house. It was certainly something to consider.

Sunday morning brought another small problem. Checkout time was 11:00 a.m. On those rare Sundays when people were still here by eleven, when church began, Doug waited to see them off and slid into the pew a little late. But now, what about Adam?

"Adam's not secure enough yet for us to drop him off tomorrow at Sunday school, is he?" Doug asked.

They were in the bed-sitter, with Adam, sound asleep, looking very small in the middle of the big sofa bed. One or both of them were coming down during the night to check on him. It was another little task, a little worry. Tomorrow afternoon Jill's husband, Greg, the family fix-it expert, was coming over to install an electronic child-monitor intercom between the bed-sitter and their bedroom. That would help.

"No, not yet," Beth answered. "He's such a little loner, he might not fit in with a group of children yet anyhow."

"I'll baby-sit," Doug offered immediately. "The sky won't fall if I miss a few Sundays at church. You've got your Coffee Hour duties."

"Yes," Beth said, frowning slightly. She was on the rotation two Sundays a month to serve coffee, tea and cookies at one of the big tables in the church rec room after Sunday service. Should she think about giving that up? *No. No way.*

Doug continued. "And Coffee Hour will be a sellout this Sunday because everybody will come to church just to hear how Flip Cooper preaches a sermon. Cyrus is a hard act to follow in the sermon-preaching department."

Beth's frown deepened. "You don't suppose, Flip Cooper will wear those awful cutoff jeans, do you?"

Doug started to laugh but stopped as Adam stirred in his sleep. Beth gently adjusted the boy's covers although they didn't need adjusting.

On Sunday morning Beth arrived at church a little breathless and almost late. She met Kate and Kate's husband, Ian, coming out. Kate looked awful, her face pasty and her brown eyes deeply circled.

"Kate, Ian," Beth whispered, hugging them both. "Aren't you going the wrong way?" The congregation was already into the opening hymn. The beautiful words and melody of "Amazing Grace" flowed around them.

"We're not staying. I told Kate we shouldn't come today. She's not feeling too great." Ian's sandy hair had fallen down over his forehead the way it usually did, and his tall, lean frame was tense with worry.

"I'm okay, really. I shouldn't have gotten out of bed, so I'll just go home and get back into it again." She tried for a smile, which wasn't quite convincing. "Go on in, Mom. They've already started. And you may feel a little better about flippy Philip."

"You mean he's not wearing denim cutoffs?" Beth tried for the same light tone. She was thankful Kate's marriage was good and she knew that Ian would care for Kate better than anyone else could. It was a second marriage for both. Kate had been a widow with two small children, and Ian divorced with custody of his son. The first year of their marriage had been rocky. Proud Kate hadn't known that she knew about the troubles, but Beth and Jill had worried privately, never letting her know.

"Actually, you'll be pleasantly surprised," Ian was saying. "He's stashed the cutoffs, at least for today. He looks pretty good. Not exactly suit-and-tie but he's wearing brown slacks and a sort of tan jacket over a rust-colored turtleneck. Sorry I couldn't see his shoes."

"Not as dignified as Cyrus always looked," Kate said, "but not really undignified, either. Ian, we'd better get going."

"Yes, sure. Bye, Beth. Love ya."

Beth looked after them fondly for a moment and then entered the nave, slid into a back pew and reached for a hymn book to join in the last bars of "Amazing Grace." A feeling of comfort gently touched her soul. *Trust and believe.* Somehow everything would be all right.

She was thinking of Cyrus again as Pastor Cooper ended his sermon, and she felt a lot better. Philip Cooper wasn't Cyrus, but his sermon had been quite good. She was able to file out with the others, pause to shake his hand and honestly thank him, as the congregation slowly dispersed. Then she hurried down to the rec room, to take her place at the tea end of one of the long tables.

Coffee Hour lasted longer than usual. It seemed that everyone was relieved to see that Philip Cooper could, and did, act like a pastor when necessary and that, somehow, even with the worry about Cyrus, things might still turn out fine.

"How'd it go?" Doug asked as he met her at the door when she got home. "Greg called a minute ago. He's coming over to install that gizmo. Jill begged off. Laurie is coming down with something and she wanted to keep the kids home."

"Oh, dear, I hope it's nothing serious. At church things went quite well." And she told him about Pastor Cooper's well-written sermon. "Where's Adam?" she asked.

"I left him in his bed-sitter. He's a sad little guy, love. He asked about Kayla at least once every hour. And he's apparently missing you, too. What'd you tell him to call you?''

"Gramma Beth. We started that for Jill's children, since they have two grandmas. Greg's mother, Laura, and me. She's Gramma Laura and I'm Gramma Beth.''

He grinned. "Well, he gets it fairly close. It comes out more like 'Gamma Beff.' I told him you were at church. That drew a big blank. I'm afraid church hasn't been part of his life experience so far.''

When Greg Rhys, Jill's tall, blond husband, came over, as always Beth's heart warmed to him. He was so good, so steady. Always there when needed. In addition to being a successful CPA, it seemed there was nothing he couldn't fix, mend, put together or build from scratch. During college he had spent every spare moment building a beautiful wooden sailboat he had name *Far Horizon.* It didn't seem to bother him that he had never sailed it to any far horizon. He and Jill had found their happiness here at home.

But he had told them a number of times, "It wasn't wasted effort. If any of us needs a sailboat in the future, well, I can do that.''

He and Doug kept up a steady flow of easy conversation while he installed the child-monitor intercom. Adam stood close to Beth's side, glowering at this strange blond man who had invaded his bed-sitter domain.

When Doug tried to pay Greg for the cost of the monitor, Greg brushed it aside. "Jill got it on sale at some discount place. Not worth worrying about.''

Doug accepted this pleasantly, but when Greg had gone he said, "I wish they wouldn't do that. They're always trying to do something for us. Makes me feel over the hill. I wanted to at least pay for the thing.''

Beth held back a smile, looking at his rugged face and strong frame. "Trust me, Doug. You're not over the hill.'' And they looked into each other's eyes.

"I love you, lady."

"I love you, too."

It was the last tranquil moment they would have for some time, as the ringing of the phone ripped into their serenity.

"Don't forget," Doug said quickly, as Beth answered it, "we decided we didn't need to book solid."

"Right. Hello?"

"Hi. I mean, hello. This is Estelle Yager." And there was the sound of something like a gulp.

"Were you calling about a room?"

"No. I mean, I guess you remember me as Estelle Led-better. Does that ring a bell?"

"Oh, Estelle. Yes, of course." She covered the mouthpiece, turning to Doug. "It's Cyrus's daughter, Estelle. She went to school with Kate." She spoke into the phone again. "I'm so glad to hear from you. I'd heard that you and your brother were coming home again. Have you seen your father?"

"Yes, we have, and—" There was another little gulp. "And he's, uh, not feeling too badly. I'm here at the hospital now, Mrs. Bennett. I mean, you're Mrs. Colby now, aren't you? Well, Mrs. Colby, could you come down to the hospital for a little while? Dad is...Dad said he wanted to visit with you for a few minutes. And they, uh, they said it would be okay."

"She's crying," Beth said almost soundlessly to Doug, sudden anxiety seizing her. *Oh, dear God, not Cyrus. Not yet. Not my dear, dear friend.* "Of course I can come down for a while," she answered, surprised that her voice was so steady.

She turned to Doug almost as soon as she hung up, going into his arms.

He said, "Think a minute, sweetheart. What do you want me to do? I'll come with you if you need me and cope with Adam, or...whatever."

She drew away from him. "I guess it might be best if you just stay here. I got the feeling that...I won't be there long."

"Shall I call a cab or do you want to drive?"

"I'll drive." She looked up at him, loving every line of him. "I'll be all right. You just hold the fort here until I get back."

"Will do."

There wasn't too much traffic downtown on a Sunday afternoon, so Beth made good time. And after parking in the big gray garage across the street, she walked swiftly to the great gray mass that was Swedish Hospital. She paused a moment just inside the large entrance. This place held so many memories. She felt a kind of inward shaking. Kate, darling Kate, had been born here, her first child. Beth nodded and smiled politely to a receptionist behind a counter. It was here she had sweated and twisted during Jill's birth, with Cyrus waiting in the father's lounge with Ralph.

Now a teenage volunteer smiled and came forward. "Do you know which room you're going to, ma'am? If you don't, I can take you."

Beth smiled back. "Thank you, yes. I know."

It was here, years later, that Ralph died. She had felt so helpless, but her family, and Cyrus, had been here for her, supporting her. She walked steadily to the first bank of elevators and pushed the up button, listening to the strange sounds that come from behind closed elevator doors.

When she reached Cyrus's room she paused. It said No Visitors. Then she recognized Estelle, sitting in a chair against the wall. Estelle got up quickly.

"Oh, Mrs. Bennett— I mean, Mrs. Colby. Thank you so much for coming. We can go right in." And she pushed the door open.

"Here's Mrs. Colby, Daddy," she said as they entered. "Do you want anything else? Or shall I wait outside?"

"Take a break, Stell. Get yourself a cup of something. Beth, my dear. Thank you for coming." Cyrus's voice was rasping, with small pauses for breath that hadn't been in his speech before. Beth hurried to his side. There was that monitor thing with the little lines and blips; a drip stood beside the high bed, with its needle in Cyrus's gnarled old hand, more bony now with the knuckles rising sharply. There was the faint *hiss* of oxygen from the small plastic tubes and, over and under and through everything, the constant hospital noises.

"How are you feeling today?" she asked, sitting down and taking his free hand in both of hers. *Oh, dear friend, please hang on. For my sake. For all our sakes.*

"Not too badly, Beth. I've never had so much attention in my life, which is nice. I seem to have attained star status just because my body is conking out. Congestive heart failure, they call it."

"What do they say, the doctors?"

"What do doctors ever actually *say?* I think one of the first things they learn in med school is how to never actually say anything. Luckily, I'm good at reading between the lines. It's been part of my job description. But let's not talk about me, Beth. I've got no complaints. I've had a good run. What I really want to do today is ask you a couple of questions. You've got one of the levelest heads I know of when it comes to level heads."

"Ask away." She pressed his hand. It felt so frail.

"We don't have a whole lot of time, you see. Privacy is something I don't get much of. Everybody is standing by. Good people. One of the Elders is always here. Sentry duty, I guess. Anyhow, thing number one is this. That young Pastor Cooper wasn't my choice at first, and I insisted on talking with him myself when I was told that the Elders thought he was the best applicant for the job—mainly because of his school experience, I think.''

"To tell the truth, Cyrus, yesterday I wasn't too impressed—he seemed too young, I guess. But today, after his sermon, I felt differently. And if he has had school experience…'' She let it rest there. This wasn't the time to distress Cyrus with any lingering doubts about Flip Cooper.

He sighed. "He's sound, Beth. I talked with him a long time. I should be elated, I suppose, and I feel guilty because I'm sure that some of my doubts about him were probably just my ego—reluctance to hand over my baton to anybody. And ego shouldn't have any place in my line of work.''

"Don't worry about your ego,'' Beth said firmly. "And Pastor Cooper really looked good this morning. Very pastorlike. And his sermon held considerable insight. It was good, thoughtful.''

From Cyrus there was something like a chuckle, which ended in a gasp. She felt his hand shake.

"Don't reach for the bell,'' he said. "I have these little tremors now and again.''

"And then,'' Beth continued, "he was talking to Doug about new ninth grade science texts.''

"Good sign,'' Cyrus agreed. "Science changes faster than, say, grammar, so he's got his priorities right.''

His eyes closed and he lay silent for a time, visibly gathering strength. She wondered if she should leave.

"Now, about thing number two,'' he said, opening his eyes. "Having people constantly hovering tires me out, but the flip side is it keeps me plugged into the church grapevine.''

Beth couldn't help but smile. Same old Cyrus. Always the underlying droll humor. "What's the latest on the grapevine?''

"You. And your new little grandson. How's that going?'' *Cyrus never missed any need. He was always there to help.*

"Okay," she said, and told him as briefly as she could about Kayla and Adam. She knew she wasn't quite hiding her own dismay at the situation, but she had always been honest with Cyrus.

He was quiet for a time when she finished. Then he spoke slowly. "I believe that God may have blessed you with a special assignment, did you know that? You must have a very reliable record. It won't be easy, you know. Two of His most vulnerable children are in your and Doug's care. Especially the little boy."

Beth knew her voice quavered but she couldn't help it. "Both Doug and I know that. He's so— I mean, he can't understand the *why* of anything."

"I know." She felt him press her hand. "Fortunately, there are also some instructions for this task, so you'll know, sort of. At least a reason to succeed, to give it your best shot."

"What is the reason?" she asked. What possible reason could there be for Kayla's intrusion into her perfect life now?

"Quote. 'When you do it for the least of these, you do it for Me.' Unquote. And that's a capital *M* on the *Me*, so you know who said it."

She was silent for a time, dread lapping at the edges of her mind. Had God sent Kayla and her angry, confused little boy into her life? Why now? At this late date? She was fifty years old—and her life was so good.

"Thank you, Cyrus," she said hollowly. "I think. You do sum things up very well."

"Comes of writing sermons for fifty years. Did you know that both my kids are here? That's a real treat. And since I'm sick I don't get any argument when I tell them to do something, which is a first. And Beth, don't be discouraged. I think I hear discouragement in your voice. We go back a long way, girl. But you may have the life of that little person in your hands.''

Beth left shortly afterward with Cyrus's words in her mind. *''Remember, Beth, your best shot, your very best.''* She made it clear across the street into the parking garage and was seated behind the steering wheel before she started to cry. Was she crying for Cyrus? Or for the burden he had just handed her? The garage, somewhat dim and with few cars in it today, offered a sort of privacy, so she let herself sob, balling up one tissue after another to put into the litter bag. Finally she was able to stop.

Maybe, if she dumped the litter bag and took her time driving home, by the time she got there Doug wouldn't know she had cried. She reached for her handbag and flipped on the overhead light to repair her makeup. *''When you do it for the least of these, you do it for Me''* echoed dimly in her mind, like a chant.

Doug knew the moment he saw her that she had been crying and held out his arms. He held her for a long time, finally asking, ''Would a cup of tea help?''

''Yes, it would. And,'' she added in surprise, ''I think I'm hungry. How odd. Quite hungry.''

They were in the bed-sitter, and Adam, who was sitting on the window seat, was staring at them soberly.

''How about a muffin, too? Would that help?''

''Perfect.''

''You stay here with Adam. I'll go fix it,'' Doug said.

Beth sat down on the sofa bed. Adam was looking at her steadily with his usual serious expression. *''When you do it for the least of these, you do it for Me.''* She felt an odd sort of yearning and couldn't help holding out her hand to the sober little boy. He started clambering down from the window seat. At first she thought he was coming to her, but instead he ducked in behind the sofa bed. He came out almost immediately. What an odd little child he was. He came to her now, one small hand extended.

"You c'n have dis," he said. "You're hungry." He was holding a broken piece of sugar cookie. One of his hidden scraps, so carefully hoarded against tomorrow's hunger. Looking into his wide, worried blue eyes she felt her resistance melting away. Somehow, some way, she must help this child.

"Thank you," she said steadily, taking the piece of cookie. Carefully, she brushed from it a piece of lint or dust. *Nothing on God's green earth can keep me from eating this broken bit of stale cookie.* "Thank you, Adam. This is exactly what I needed."

Chapter Five

The 5:00 a.m. alarm blasted both Beth and Doug out of sleep. The child-monitor intercom had disturbed them several times during the night. Both testy from lack of sleep, they nearly had an argument about it.

"Greg set the sound too loud," Beth complained.

"No. We set it together. We just have to get used to it," Doug objected. They glared at each other.

It made a bad start to the morning, as both were tired from the repeated wakings. They had heard every time Adam sighed, coughed, murmured or rustled his covers. Together or separately they had made five trips downstairs to check on him. They both apologized immediately, both speaking at once. Then they had to laugh at themselves—and suddenly the world was right again. Showering and dressing as quickly as they could, they hurried downstairs to start the guests' breakfast. This daily rush took their minds off domestic problems for the moment.

Beth was watching the scrambled eggs and lifting sizzling sausages out of the cooker, and Doug was setting the table and noticing the salt shakers hadn't been filled, when

Adam wandered into the kitchen. He was wearing only his pajama top and was barefoot.

Doug came in after him. "Where're your pants, Adam?" There was laughter in his tone.

"Wet," Adam answered, and went over to Beth. Not expecting any help, he must have tried to go to the potty by himself. The results hadn't been good. He'd probably left his wet pants in the downstairs bath.

"I'll get 'em," Doug said quickly, picking Adam up.

Mentally Beth added a child's potty-chair to her list of things-to-buy-for-Adam, as she heard Doug head for the bathroom. At least no guest who used it later would find Adam's wet pants. An unpredictable little child didn't fit too well in a B and B.

At breakfast, Beth found she didn't have time to sit with the guests and enjoy breakfast. When they started coming down, she was still piecing together the table settings and saying things like, "I'm so sorry, I'll get you a napkin." Or, "Let me get you a full salt shaker." Doug had simply disappeared to get Adam bathed and dressed.

When he finally came back, he said with a sigh, "I guess we're going to have to rearrange a little. How did you manage before I came into your life?"

"Come to think of it," Beth said distractedly, "I used to set the table at night. I guess we'd better go back to that."

"Looks that way," he said as he put Adam at the table.

Beth set down a slice of cold bacon she had picked up. "Everything's cold," she said, "I'll fix something for us." And she went into the kitchen. "You didn't hear that Mrs. Reese-Talbot say she thought Adam was too thin, did you?"

"No, I didn't," he said, coming to the kitchen door.

"But now that you mention it, he is kind of skinny. You think we should get him checked out?"

After they had finished breakfast, Beth called Kate for the name of her pediatrician. Then she made an appointment for Wednesday afternoon for Adam's physical exam. She wanted to do what she could until Kayla took him and left, and they certainly must maintain some sort of watch on his well-being. She wondered how Doug would persuade Kayla to remain in Seattle. Well, Doug could handle that.

The morning had gotten off to a slow start and she seemed to take forever making the beds. She was only in the second bedroom when Adam peeked in the door. He had followed her upstairs and he was carrying a large, flat book from his toy box. She felt a quick rush of warmth. Maybe he was beginning to bond with them. Was that a good thing or a bad thing? What would he think when he and Kayla had to leave his bed-sitter?

Then, somehow or other, it was after eleven and she was sitting in a big easy chair beside a half-made bed with Adam cuddled beside her, listening to her raptly as she read of the adventures of Doctor Seuss's little creatures. *Oh, Kayla, please learn to be a good mother. Adam needs so much.*

Doug wandered in and sat on the vanity bench, and as she finished the story, Adam laughed. She and Doug glanced at each other. Neither spoke. It was the first time they had heard Adam laugh, and it must not be the last time. The phone rang three times before either of them realized it.

Doug dashed out into the hall to pick up the extension. Beth closed the book and got back to the bed-making, with Adam watching her soberly from the depths of the big chair. She smoothed the spread over the plump pillows and stood up, stretching a little. Doug stood in the doorway. Something in his face alerted her.

"What?" She couldn't keep the alarm from her tone, and Adam frowned.

"That was Bessie, down at the church," Doug said, and added, "I'm so sorry, love."

"Cyrus?" *Oh, no—not yet!*

Doug nodded. "Yes, he died. Quietly. In his sleep. The floor nurse knew right away, of course, because of that little blip screen. He apparently went...peacefully. Do you want a minute?"

I must not break down in front of Adam. It will make him afraid. She nodded and turned away, hearing Doug with the boy.

"Okay, sport. It's time to go downstairs again."

In their own bedroom Beth gave way to an onslaught of grief, longing for Doug to be with her but knowing somebody had to tend to Adam.

She recovered as quickly as she could. *Oh, Cyrus, you were so good to us. Did I ever really thank you?* Yet Cyrus wouldn't have wanted or needed thanks. He had just been doing his job. "Part of my job description," he would have said.

When she was more in control, she called Bessie at the church, but had to try three times to get through. Bessie, thick-voiced, brought her up to date. Cyrus's son and daughter were making plans. The funeral would be Wednesday afternoon, which allowed time for Cyrus's sister to get here from another state. Beth hung up the phone, feeling desolate.

Suddenly she recalled that Wednesday afternoon was Adam's appointment with Dr. Fletcher for his exam. She quickly dialed Jill's number. Jill and Greg lived on the other side of Seattle and went to a different church. Jill might not be planning to attend Cyrus's funeral.

Yes, Jill would be glad to leave her smallest daughter with a friend and take Adam to his appointment. Good. She thanked Jill and hung up, realizing that she had a very bad headache.

"You okay?" Doug stuck his head in the doorway.

"Where's Adam?"

"Sitting in his favorite place, the window seat, observing the world go by."

"I've got a headache." And she had the comfort of Doug fetching aspirin and water for her, and another crying spell as he held her close in his arms. Then Doug had to check on Adam again and the beds weren't finished yet and she must call Kate. *Get a grip, Beth. Do what you have to do.*

She got in a hurried call to Kate, assured herself that her older daughter was all right, so *Finish the beds, Beth.*

Somehow or other she got through the rest of the day. By the time the evening's guests arrived, the bedrooms were ready and all appeared serene. Travel itself was stressful enough and guests didn't appreciate extra confusion.

In the middle of her hard-won calm she suddenly recalled that Doug hadn't done any painting for several days. He had accepted a commission for a landscape painting of Shilshole Bay for the local bank to hang in its entryway, and didn't seem concerned about it. They almost snapped at each other again.

"But you know you don't like to hurry with a painting," she reminded him.

"Quite right, my love, but as they say in books, events have overtaken us and I just haven't had the time."

Don't say, 'The sky will not fall,' Doug. He hated it when he had to hurry with his painting but sometimes he *would* procrastinate.

"Listen up, Beth, the sky will not fall today."

Almost gritting her teeth, Beth stopped herself from answering back.

Tuesday wasn't much better. It was cleaning service day, which meant four young men came in with all their special high-powered noisy equipment as soon after eleven as they could. They went through the house like a hurricane, scrubbing, vacuuming, flipping cushions over and back, dusting, and polishing, their various machines roaring. Adam hated them on sight, and stood guard at the bed-sitter door. He seemed to view them as some sort of invasion. It exasperated Beth, even though she understood that Adam's uncertain life so far had made him always see anything new as a threat.

"Leave the bed-sitter today, Keith," Beth told the one in charge.

"Okay, whatever, but I can't take it off the bill. I mean, I would if I could but I'm not the boss, you understand?"

"Yes, of course. That'll be fine, Keith. Just carry on with the rest." So the house, except for the bed-sitter, was immaculate again. Except that the bed-sitter *should* have been cleaned. There had been that dust lint on that broken cookie from behind the sofa bed. At this recollection, Beth's exasperation with Adam melted and she had to pick him up and hug him.

"See? It's all right. The men are almost finished."

On Wednesday Jill arrived about noon to pick up Adam for his medical appointment. After an initial tantrum, Jill persuaded him to come with her, and they left. Beth and Doug looked at each other in relief as soon as the door was shut behind them.

"Do you hear something strange?" Doug whispered.

"No, what?"

"Silence. Quiet. Peace. No crisis. Just for this one moment in time, no crisis. Let's concentrate on appreciating."

Beth had to laugh, and it eased the tension a little.

* * *

Later, at the familiar old redbrick church where she had worshiped for so many years, sadness pervaded her. She looked around, picking out all those she knew and loved. There was Kate with Ian and their children, all in their Gilmartin Academy uniforms. And there were the frail, gray Gilmartins, in whose son's memory the school had been named. Beside them was dear old Mrs. Hyslop without the gentle, confused husband she had cared for so faithfully until his death. And there was Bessie, the church secretary.

A single spray of bright spring flowers lay on top of the casket. How many people had Bessie called, saying, "No flowers, Pastor Ledbetter's request. Any offering should go to the school sports fund." How like Cyrus. She could almost hear him. *"Look, if the kids are willing to sweat out the math and science, they should have some of the fun stuff, too. And nothing but the best, mind you, and for that we need money."*

The beautiful strains of "Old Rugged Cross" and "Abide With Me" filled the church now. And who was that? Not Flip Cooper. Not that sober young man in a dark suit, speaking so seriously. He had done his homework, too, taken a lot of trouble to learn about Cyrus and his work so he could speak from knowledge and obvious deep respect for Cyrus and his doing of God's work here. Beth felt Doug press her hand. She managed to hold back her tears until the choir got to the line, "Oh, Lamb of God, I come, I come," in the hymn "Just As I Am." Then blessed Doug pressed his handkerchief into her hand.

After the interment at the cemetery, they went home. Beth was drained. She felt a vast vacancy inside her. Somehow she'd have to deal with it. They would just have a snack supper and, oh yes, set the table for breakfast. Three guests would check in about four.

Jill was waiting for them. Apparently she had won Adam over; he seemed quite at ease with her now, and his chin was slightly smeared with chocolate. After they had told her about the funeral, Jill reported on the doctor visit.

"He's underweight by almost four pounds, and on that small body that's a lot," she began practically. She was checking through a list she had made. "They took a blood sample for testing, and, for your information, Adam does not like being stuck with a needle. He was quite outspoken about it, just in case you hadn't guessed that."

It was a relief to laugh a little.

"Dr. Fletcher says he is malnourished, and she'll call with other test results tomorrow. The malnourishment requires a special formula, which, happily, he can take in his milk without noticing it. Then, let's see, his left ankle pronates."

"His left ankle what?" Doug asked.

"Pronates. That means turning downward or, in this case, kind of inward. Haven't you noticed that he walks pigeon-toed with his left foot?"

"Yes," Beth said, "but I thought it was kind of cute."

"It may be cute at three, but Dr. Fletcher says it should have been corrected before. But she thinks a few months in high-topped shoes might fix it. Otherwise, if it doesn't straighten out, the ankle will continue turning, and when he's older, say a teen, he'll have a hard time walking straight. Which he will want to do if he dates and wants to dance at the local clubs. Not to mention sports when he gets in school. He'll need to start with two straight feet."

"Well, if he's like any other kid, he'll want to join the team," Doug said.

"What team?" Beth asked.

"Any team, love. A kid wants to join a team. That's part

of normal growing up." They looked at each other, Beth remembering that Adam's father had been a loner, an outsider. That was not good enough for Adam.

"And I guess that's it," Jill was saying. "Here, keep this list. That's the name of the formula and the place to get the special high-topped shoes. I hope this doesn't cost you a fortune."

They both thanked Jill, and Adam waved to her from the doorway as if he had made a friend for life.

He's *not* a loner, Beth assured herself. Adam will have a good life!

Thursday's breakfast went rather smoothly, since they'd made themselves work quite hard the night before. And when the last bed had been made and everything organized, Beth took Adam shopping. The doctor's office had called and said that the tests showed nothing else seriously wrong.

Beth used her charge card with abandon. She bought Adam the new clothing he needed and, in the children's department, got him a rather grand potty-chair which he personally chose from a selection of several. Plus a car seat that, bulky though the package was, she carried with them. A children's closet arrangement, which would need assembling, was to be delivered. She'd need to call Greg again. Adam would be able to reach his things himself. When it was all purchased, she recalled Jill's success with Adam and chocolate, and paused long enough to get chocolate sundaes. Adam was delighted.

There was one more place to go—the store that sold the special high-topped shoes. Here Adam's pleasure evaporated and the scowl came back.

"Red shoes," he protested. "Adam's red shoes!"

Rather than cope with a tantrum in the shoe store, Beth had the salesman wrap up the white high-tops, and Adam wore his red sneakers home. Suddenly Beth was tired. How in the world had she raised her own two children? She had forgotten how demanding a job it was. Motherhood was certainly not for sissies.

Adam was tired, too. When they drove into the driveway, he was asleep in his new car seat, his fair head drooping over his thin little chest. She wasn't really sure the car seat was in correctly; she'd have Doug look at it. Well, at least Doug would come out the back door to carry in the parcels.

She beeped the horn twice. Gently. No Doug. She beeped again, which woke Adam up. Still no Doug. Surely he was home. Well, obviously he wasn't. Wearily she got out of the car. Unloading the car took two trips. Longer, because Adam wanted to help her and she hadn't the heart to refuse him. She had always encouraged her own children to help. It was a way for them to learn, to more closely bond with the family, to accept responsibility. If only she hadn't gotten so tired.

On the refrigerator was Doug's note:

Beth, my love,
I took your advice. When you read this you'll know I'm at Shilshole putting it on canvas. I'll work as long as there is light. The weather guy says sunset comes at five-ten today.

Love,
Doug

You *told* him to get on with the painting, Beth reminded herself, as she put Adam down for a late nap. She flipped on the child-monitor system and was starting upstairs when the front door chimes rang. *Oh, no! Go away whoever you are,* she thought as she went to open the door. It was Pastor Cooper. She stared at him for a full thirty seconds without speaking.

"Is this a bad time for a pastoral call?" he asked.

"Of course not," Beth said quickly. Whatever had happened to perfect hostess? Embarrassed at herself Beth invited him in.

Well, at least he'd got the message about the cutoffs. He was dressed like a pastor making a call on one of the flock.

"Actually, your timing is good. I just got home, but Doug isn't here. He's out working on a new painting. Would you like tea or something?"

"No, thanks. Do you mind if we don't have anything to drink? I just had coffee at two places. That happens when a guy—when a pastor—makes calls."

"Why don't we go in here?" she said, leading him into the living room and sitting down in the first chair she came to.

"You look tired," he said, sitting down opposite her.

"Well, shopping does that. I'm not as young as I was, but our grandson needed some things." She found herself telling him about Adam's physical. Pastor Cooper was really rather nice. Maybe there was a lesson here on how not to prejudge people.

"You and Doug are right to get Adam's ankle straightened so he can be part of sports in school. And speaking of sports for kids, Cyrus taking care of others until the last moment is paying off. Money is pouring in for the Academy's sports program. I don't think he had any idea how many people loved him. Our kids will have the best sports equipment for years to come."

At the mention of Cyrus, Beth felt a flood of grief so intense that her eyes filled with tears.

"I'm sorry," Flip Cooper said. "Maybe I said the wrong thing."

"No. Not really. I wanted to know. How like Cyrus. Excuse me a minute." She fled to the kitchen for the box of tissues she kept there.

She was feeling better about Flip Cooper all the time, young as he was to be a pastor.

"Speaking of Adam," he continued, "how is his mother? I met her briefly the first time I stopped here. Doug said she was a widow. Her name is Kayla, right?"

"Yes, she's Doug's daughter from his first marriage. You knew, didn't you, that I was a widow when I met Doug over a year ago? He was retired and concentrating on painting. He does landscapes. He had his first gallery showing when we began raising money to start Gilmartin Academy at church."

"I think Cyrus mentioned that," Pastor Cooper said. "Am I looking at one of Doug's paintings now?" He indicated the painting of a part of Seattle Center with the carousel.

"Yes, that's Doug's," Beth said, pleased.

"It's very good," Pastor Cooper said. Then he added, "About his daughter, Kayla. Is she holding up all right? Being that young, and a widow, it must be difficult for her."

"She…isn't really doing too well," Beth said. "I mean…Kayla has some problems." Perhaps it was his kindly interest that encouraged her, but Beth found herself telling him about Kayla's drinking problem and where she was in her efforts to overcome it.

He was serious. "That's really too bad. Addiction, of any kind, is hard for everyone concerned with it, especially the addict. Please let me know if I can help in any way. I have worked with addicted people before. You said that she herself began this present effort?"

"Yes. Going into rehab was Kayla's idea."

"That's a good start. There's no way out of addiction until the addict admits he or she needs help. And please remember, if I can help in any way, give me a call."

He rose to leave shortly after, and Beth saw him out. She

noted that he wasn't riding his bike today but was driving
the old church station wagon that Cyrus had always used.
He seemed to be doing his best to fill Cyrus's place, but,
as Doug had said, Cyrus was a hard act to follow.

She had about half an hour to herself before Adam wandered in. He had dressed himself in one of his new shirts
with the price tag still on it and a pair of cotton briefs from
the rummage sale collection. Sighing, she got up.

Doug got home a little after five, rather happy with himself. During a quick supper in the kitchen she told him
about her shopping trip. Adam joined in, which pleased
them both. Adam was beginning to fit in, becoming one of
the family. When they finished dinner Adam showed Doug
his new clothes, so Beth cleared up the kitchen by herself.
Having a small child certainly increased the work and de-
creased the privacy. Well, so be it.

The expected guests came in just after six and had to be
settled in their rooms, given city maps and directions on
where they wanted to go for their first evening in Seattle.
Doug was very good at this, but he was still in the bed-
sitter with Adam, so Beth took care of it.

When Kayla returned in three months, in control again,
it would be a relief. Wouldn't it? Beth paused, torn two
ways. Did she really want Adam back in Kayla's care?
Please, God, she prayed again, *make Kayla a better mother.*

She didn't think to tell Doug about Pastor Cooper's visit
until they were ready for bed. They had worked until quite
late, getting all the breakfast preparations finished. It should
go well in the morning.

"You told the pastor about Kayla's drinking problem?"
He was annoyed. "You shouldn't have done that!"

"I-I'm sorry," she stammered. "But it just kind
of…came out. With a pastor, one tends to unburden—"

"Yes, well. He really didn't need to know. It's a violation of Kayla's privacy. She's not proud of her life, Beth."

"I'm really sorry," Beth said, and they left it at that. But Doug was angry and she felt it. She held back a sharp response, willing herself to stay calm. She and Doug never quarreled and she felt shaken by it.

Deep in sleep they thought the ringing was the five o'clock alarm. Actually it was 4:00 a.m. and the phone. Doug picked it up as quickly as he could so it wouldn't waken any guests. He flipped on the overhead light.

"This better not be a wrong number." He frowned. "Hello?"

Then he was silent for a time. "Is she all right? You. She's right here." He turned to Beth, who was sitting up now, and handed the phone to her. "It's Ian. He's calling from Swedish Hospital. Kate's okay. He said that first. But she went into false labor. Here, he wants to talk to you."

Beth almost snatched the phone. "Yes? Ian?"

"I'm sorry to wake you both up, but I knew you would want to know. Kate had a problem, but she's okay now. Really. I got the nine-one-one people out and we got her to the hospital as fast as we could. Had to leave the kids home alone, but Ray's pretty mature." He was speaking of their eldest, a fourteen-year-old.

"But Katie's all right? And the baby's all right?" Beth couldn't keep a note of panic out of her voice.

"Yes and yes. We didn't lose our baby. But it was close. I think all the upset about Cyrus's death got to her." Ian paused, and Beth knew he was almost crying. *Oh, dear God, please help Kate.*

"Do you need money?" Beth asked. "Are you—"

"No. We're fine. Good medical coverage is one of my fringes at work. Everything's covered, but thanks for the thought. They're going to keep Kate here for another twenty-four hours just to be sure. I'm staying the rest of the night, but I've got six guys coming in for a conference tomorrow, so could you come over for a while? I don't want her to get depressed or anything.''

''Yes. Absolutely. I'll be talking to Jill and we'll work it out.'' After they had rung off she told Doug and he held her close.

''Don't worry about anything here while you're gone. I'll look after Adam and check out and welcome any guests. That's the magic about family,'' he said. ''When one is at risk, they all rally 'round. Tonight I thought my little grandson was getting the hang of 'family,' the way he wanted to show me his new clothes. I don't know if it's my imagination or not, but he seems to be talking better. He even told me about his hot fudge sundae.''

''He loved it,'' Beth said. ''I don't think he's had a lot of treats. He seems to be settling in, becoming part of things.''

''Kids are resilient, if you give them half a chance. I wish—''

Beth knew he was regretting the past again, so to change the subject, she asked, ''Did you make any progress with the high-topped white shoes?''

''Nope. Struck out there. I have no idea what to do. He's fixated on those red sneakers.'' Then he started laughing softly. ''I think I've got it. I'll have the high-tops dyed red. They do dye shoes, don't they?''

And Beth had to laugh with him. ''Perfect!'' On this note they decided to get up early and get started on the breakfast. The morning went well, and she sent Doug off to Shilshole Bay to work on his painting. She was upstairs making beds when she heard Adam's piping little voice.

''Mommy come back!'' He was shouting. ''Mommy come back!''

She could hear him running, and went to the head of the

stairs. "No, Adam. Not yet," she called. "Mommy will come back later."

"Mommy! Mommy!" He was at the front door, trying to reach the doorknob.

Beth started down, knowing he couldn't reach it. He'd apparently seen someone outside from his window seat. The door chimes rang out as she reached the lower hall.

"Not yet, Adam. Mommy will come home later." She reached the front door and opened it.

It was Kayla.

They both stood silent for a moment, staring at each other. Adam rushed past Beth. "Mommy! Mommy!" He grasped her around the legs.

"Hi, baby," Kayla said in a dull voice. "Hi, Beth."

Beth stepped back and Kayla came slowly in.

"Sorry, Beth. I just couldn't hack it. Is Dad here? I've got to break the news to him. I just couldn't...I quit the rehab place. I..." And she started to cry.

Chapter Six

"Come in," Beth said, leading them into the living room. Kayla collapsed into a chair.

"You gotta tissue? I'm such a mess." She was blotting at her eyes.

"Mommy, I got new shirts. I got new pants." Adam dashed out into the hall headed for the bed-sitter.

Beth hurried into the kitchen to get the box of tissues.

Kayla took them gratefully, muttering, "I'm so sorry. I'm so sorry."

Beth sat down opposite her. "What happened? Can you tell me?" She made an effort not to sound impatient. Really! This was too much!

"Well, nothing to tell. I blew it again. I just couldn't stand it. All those rules. Rules for this and rules for that. And the group things. The group discussions where you're supposed to bare your soul and spill your guts. I just…hated it. I had to get out. Please understand, I had to get out." She started crying again.

Adam trotted back in, his arms full of new clothes, some still in their plastic wrappings. "See!" he said excitedly.

"My new shirt. My new pants." He dropped some and tried to retrieve them, dropping others as he did so, stumbling in his eagerness, his little face radiant.

"What? Oh, Adam, shut up, baby. I'm trying to talk to Beth. Go away."

"But I got new pants. I got—"

Suddenly out of patience, Kayla screamed, "Adam, shut up!"

Adam froze, his arms clutching his things, and Beth recalled his silence when she first met him.

"Kids take advantage if you don't lower the boom," Kayla said tiredly. "He'd throw a real tantrum if I let him. But with kids you have to show them who's boss. No, Adam, go away. I want to talk to Beth."

"Kayla, take a minute to look at his things," Beth said firmly. "He was so pleased at getting new clothes."

"What? Oh, really. Did you buy him this stuff? Beth, you really shouldn't have. You've done too much already. Okay, here, Adam, lemme see that." Kayla reached out her hand and took a small shirt. "Oh, my, that's nice. Beth, that was really nice of you. Now, go away, honey. Put the stuff back where it was. Beth, is Dad here?"

"No, he's out painting."

Adam approached carefully and laid another of his new shirts on her lap. "See?"

"Yeah, that's nice," she muttered. "When do you think Dad will be back? I have to break the news to him that I blew it again."

"I can call him on his cell phone if you want me to."

Kayla leaned her head back against the chair. "Yeah, I guess you'd better. We ought to get it over with."

Beth's mind was beginning to come out of shock. What were they going to do now? If rehab wasn't the answer, what was?

"The rehab center didn't call, Kayla. Did you explain to

them…or anything? Do they know you're gone?'' She tried not to sound exasperated.

''No, I just cut out. They'd only have tried to talk me into staying, and it was no use. I knew a couple of days ago. And finally I just did it. I left. I hope Dad doesn't lose too much money on the deal.''

''How could he lose money?'' Beth asked in sudden alarm.

''How do I know? He paid a lot up front, I know that.''

''I'll call him,'' Beth said quickly, hurrying into the front hall. His cell phone rang several times before he answered.

''Beth? It can only be you. Sorry, but I had a brush full of an exact shade blend and had to get it on the canvas. What's up?''

''I think you should come home. Kayla, uh, came back. I'm sorry, but she felt she couldn't stay in that place.'' She kept her tone even.

Kayla's voice came to her from the living room. ''Tell him I'm going to try AA instead. Tell him that.''

''She says she wants to try Alcoholics Anonymous,'' Beth said into the silence at the other end of the line. Then she heard him sigh.

''I was afraid of this.''

''Kayla was…worried that you'd lose some money. Since she's not going to complete the program, don't you get a refund?''

''Not really. I had to pay half the cost up front. We can talk about it when I get home. I guess I'd better come home soon.''

''Yes. Kayla's pretty upset. Why wouldn't they give you a refund?'' Beth persisted, knowing she shouldn't. It was his money.

''They explained that, and it made sense, more or less. A lot of people who pay their own way want to drop out. It serves as a deterrent if they know they've lost their up-front money. If I can talk Kayla into going back before a certain time—I'll have to look at the contract fine print—I won't lose it."

"Well, you'd better check it out. Are you coming home now?"

He sighed again. "Yes. But the painting is coming along fine and..."

"And what?"

"And the bank is paying me a hefty price, but not until I deliver it. Maybe tomorrow I can work on it again."

Beth started to tell him to stay and work on the painting, but stopped herself. Was she becoming a nag? She had never nagged Ralph. But then, with Ralph there hadn't been any Kayla problems.

Doug came home immediately, and Beth, to prove to herself that she wasn't an interfering nag in his business with his daughter, decided to use the time to run Adam's new clothes through the washer and dryer. Adam was fascinated by this and stayed with her on the service porch; then he insisted on helping her fold his laundered garments, so she wasn't finished by the time she had to leave for the hospital to see Kate.

It was a relief to get out of the house. Doug and Kayla were in the bed-sitter with the door shut. Could he really persuade Kayla to go back into rehab? She hoped so. She rapped on the door and called that she was leaving. Could they look after Adam?

"Okay. Fine," Doug called back. He sounded harassed.

He *must* get Kayla to complete the program. En route to the hospital Beth decided not to tell Kate. Kate had enough problems at the moment.

She met Jill coming out and they embraced briefly. She'd better not mention it yet to Jill, either. With a sigh, Beth settled down in the bedside chair beside Kate.

"Mom, you really didn't need to come down. I know how busy you are with the B and B—and now little Adam. How's he doing?"

"Never mind Adam. He's doing fine. How are you, Katie?"

"False alarm. But scary. I think poor Ian was sort of overwhelmed, but he came through like a trooper. The OB doctor says I have to keep off my feet as much as possible. He didn't say how I was going to do that with three kids. Ian was going to have his secretary call an employment agency this afternoon for household help. Then I got a rather nice surprise. Pastor Cutoffs called this morning to see how I was. I guess he has the same church grapevine that Cyrus had. Anyhow, he's putting it out to the women's guild, and they are going to take turns to come over and help me. I thought that was nice of him. Now, tell me how Adam's really doing."

Beth told her about the shopping trip and how pleased Adam was with his new clothes.

"I'll bet you spent a fortune. Kids are expensive and little Adam's needs are..." She let it rest there.

More than you know, Beth thought, and did not mention Kayla's return. "And incidentally, don't poke fun at Pastor. He's really rather nice."

"I know," Kate admitted. "I'll quit that. I promise."

They had a pleasant visit and Kate seemed so well that Beth was almost happy when she left. She thanked God that neither of her girls had any big problems. She wished that Kayla— *Don't think about Kayla.*

When she got home, Doug and Adam were on the service porch and Doug was supervising Adam in the folding of his new clothes.

"Hi, love," Doug said, kissing her lightly.

"How's Kayla? Is she all right?"

He shrugged. "Dead tired, poor kid. Too much emotion can do that. She was so disappointed in herself. One more failure."

"Yes, I got that feeling, too," she said. She must *not* ask him if he was successful in getting Kayla back into rehab. Then almost instantly, she added, "Is she willing to go back?"

Doug took a moment to reply, concentrating on Adam, half turned away so she couldn't see his face. "Well, we think maybe AA won't be so difficult. She knows people who have succeeded with it. And I've heard it's very successful. She could live here, and I think things would be...easier for her."

Beth's heart sank. No. She didn't want Kayla here.

"Has she tried AA before?" *Bite your tongue, Beth.*

Again there was a pause. He was uncomfortable and she was causing it. "She mentioned it," he said finally. "I don't think she's actually tried it before."

Beth did not press the matter further, but it took some effort.

"It is okay if she stays here for a while, isn't it?" He asked it so humbly that Beth felt ashamed.

"Of course," she made herself say warmly. "Where else would she stay?"

There was more to that than she wanted to admit to herself. The idea of Kayla walking out the door with Adam was frightening. As long as Kayla stayed, Adam stayed. She had the fleeting sensation that some sort of trap was closing over her.

"Did you leave Adam's high-tops at the shoe place?"

"Yes, I did," he said, almost too eagerly. "They'll be ready day after tomorrow."

"Good," she said, just as the phone rang.

"Don't forget," Doug cautioned. "We're not booking fully."

"Right," Beth said. She had privately decided to refuse any more reservations for now, until things worked themselves out. Somehow.

The next morning Kayla didn't seem so exhausted and made an effort to be helpful at breakfast. It was rather pleasant. Beth was pleased with herself because she refrained from asking Doug how much money he had lost since Kayla wasn't going back into rehab. Things would have to work out. Doug was her life.

She managed to break the news to both Jill and Kate about Kayla's new plans. Neither girl was happy, so Beth tried to make light of it, pretending it didn't matter. But it did matter. She hung up the phone both times knowing that the girls didn't believe her. She didn't believe it, either.

It was a relief to attend church on Sunday and leave Adam at home with Kayla. Kayla was chastened and deeply sorry for her failure. She also tried to be patient with Adam.

"She's not drinking," Doug said hopefully. "I mean, at least she hasn't started again."

After the service Beth was enjoying visiting with old friends. She was pleased also to get a moment alone with Pastor Cooper.

"Another good sermon," she could say honestly. "I enjoyed it." She wished she hadn't been so quick to judge him because he wasn't Cyrus.

"Thank you. Is everything all right at home?" He paused. "I heard that Doug's daughter is back." He said no more, but was looking at her keenly. She had the sudden conviction that it was really important to him to know.

"Yes, things are fine," Beth said too quickly, looking around for Doug. Pastor Cooper was sharp. He didn't miss a thing.

"Is Kayla trying some other method to deal with her problem?" he persisted.

Where was Doug? Kayla was his daughter, after all.

"I just wanted to mention," Pastor Cooper was adding, "that I've done a lot of work with addicted people. Addiction is difficult for them to conquer. If you need my help—anytime, Beth—let me know."

"Thank you," she said awkwardly.

"Good," he said. "And perhaps I should mention also that I've encountered similar situations before—yours and Doug's, I mean."

"What situation?"

"A grandchild in the care of the grandparents. Sometimes there can be…misunderstandings, disagreements. It might be good to know where you and Doug stand in this state if there are, shall we say, differences of opinion."

"I don't know what you mean."

"I mean, I'm sure things will work out fine for Kayla and Adam, but sometimes things don't work out. Then the grandparents need to know what their rights are in relation to the child." He waited a moment, and suddenly Beth understood.

"You mean a disagreement about what's right for Adam?" She had a sudden hollow feeling in her stomach.

"Exactly. Different states have different standards. I'm not sure what Washington has. It might be well for you and Doug to look into it sometime."

"Yes," Beth said, "of course," and with a sense of relief she saw Doug coming across the room.

Pastor Cooper was wrong. He had to be. Surely Kayla was going to be all right. Surely Adam would be all right.

But the hollow feeling didn't go away. No way could they depend on Kayla. She had better face that fact.

When they got home, Greg, Jill's husband, was there and Beth immediately felt better.

"Hi. Jill told me Adam's stuff had been delivered so I came to fix his closet."

Kayla was in the bed-sitter reading the funnies to Adam, and Beth felt a little hope. Maybe Kayla could be a good mother if she just gave up drinking. Beth felt she was clutching at straws, but for Doug's sake she had to try. She had taken Adam shopping for new clothes, so maybe she should do the same for Kayla. Maybe Kayla's self-image would improve if she didn't need to wear castoffs. She had to make the effort, for Doug's sake.

With this in mind, Beth asked Greg to modify Adam's closet assembly to fit into half the closet, leaving space for Kayla.

After Greg left, Adam spent some time admiring and rearranging his new clothes in his half of the closet, where he could reach everything. Beth tried not to miss too much of the precious private Sunday afternoons she and Doug had enjoyed during the first months of their marriage. Sometimes they'd had a picnic lunch in the back garden, just the two of them. Well, she couldn't think about that now. Two new guests were arriving soon, and tomorrow or the next day she'd need to get Kayla's wardrobe in order.

She talked to Doug about it that night and, he was so pleased. She was sorry she hadn't thought of it sooner.

"Well, I'll pay," he insisted. "I'll pay for Adam's, too. How much did you spend?"

"Let's share it," Beth temporized. "I'll let you know what your half is," and he agreed. Beth was relieved at this, as she had quite an emergency fund and men never did understand how much good women's clothing cost. She was grimly determined that Kayla would have quality garments. She had tried to bring up both her daughters so they dressed tastefully. She had succeeded well with Jill—but Kate? Well, Kate had other qualities.

* * *

It wasn't until Wednesday that Beth could take Kayla shopping, and it was a little inconvenient to arrange for Adam's care. Doug had simply assumed that the women would take Adam with them.

"No, Doug. We can't possibly. We're going in and out of several shops, and taking along a three-year-old would be too much. Can't you look after him? Just while we're gone?"

"Have you looked out the window, love? Today is one of the most beautiful weather days I've seen in Seattle for a long time. I thought I'd work on the Shilshole Bay painting." He looked over at Adam. "I wonder if he'd like to play on the beach."

"You mean while you're painting?" Beth asked doubtfully. "When you paint, you concentrate on that and you pretty much block out everything else. Suppose he wanders away or something?"

"I'll look after him. I promise," Doug said. He turned to Kayla. "Has he been on a beach before? I thought he perked up when I mentioned beach."

"Yes. We were in Florida for a while. Adam liked that."

Adam was nodding. "Beach," he said. And Beth looked at him fondly. He was feeling more and more secure with them. *Adam will have a good life.* She pushed away the idea that Adam should be talking more fluently than he was. Her own children had been chatterboxes at that age. On the other hand, you had to talk *to* children, and wait for answers, to start them talking. Who had there been to talk to Adam? Certainly not Kayla.

Beth had always enjoyed shopping and was good at it. After first demurring, Kayla couldn't contain her enthusiasm. Beth wondered how long it had been since Kayla had shopped anywhere but a thrift shop. That awful green print dress she had arrived in had a definite thrift-shop look: old, out of style, the wrong size. Kate had been a thrift-shop customer during her widowhood, so independent that both she and Jill had had difficulty helping her, even when she needed help badly.

Kayla was a pleasure to shop with once they got started. She seemed to have innate good taste. This was a relief to Beth, although it was costing more than she had anticipated. Well, that was the price she was willing to pay to make this work out. She realized she was trying to find reasons to like Kayla. It seemed only fair. Doug was so fond of Jill and Kate.

They had made a list, and Kayla surprised her by being quite sensible and practical.

"Now that I'm on the wagon," Kayla said, "I want to get a job of some kind. I want to pay my own way."

"What kind of job do you have in mind?"

"I've worked in a lot of places, and, since you and Dad took Adam and me in, I really want to get started earning again."

"Can you do that and go to the AA meetings?"

"Oh, sure," Kayla said confidently. "I'll be going to the meetings evenings, and working days. It'll keep me out of trouble."

Beth was impressed in spite of her reservations. This seemed like a good beginning, even if the rehab place hadn't worked out.

"I only need a few separates," Kayla told her. "Things I can go to work in. Skirts. Blouses. Some decent shoes."

By noon they had bought casual and workplace shoes, panty hose, underclothes and blouses. They were in another department store now, and had stopped for lunch in the store restaurant, each carrying a tote bag with packages in it.

"I do enjoy shopping," Beth said, picking up her menu.

"This has been fun." It reminded her a little of when she had taken her own daughters shopping. "I wonder if they still have that soup and half-sandwich special here."

"Yes," Kayla said. "And the soup of the day is split pea. Do you like that?"

"Yes," Beth said, putting down her menu. Kayla was certainly being pleasant. Well, she was Doug's daughter. She'd have to have inherited some of his good traits. After lunch they lingered over a second cup of coffee.

"Do you have any special job skills, Kayla?" Beth asked, remembering that Kayla had once told her she had been a maid in a motel.

"Yes. I didn't finish college, but I did complete a business course. I made out okay in that somehow I've done office work." She paused, frowning. "I'll need to think about who I can give as references. Sometimes I've blown it at work. I've been…fired a few times," she ended lamely.

Beth had been about to suggest that either of her sons-in-law might help, but stopped herself. Better not involve them. Kayla was too unstable.

"I was thinking about going to a temp agency," Kayla said. "See, Beth, I've been down this route before. It's best if I temp a while. I'll work a few weeks here, and a few weeks there. I've found in temping that if I do a good job, don't screw anything up, I'm asked to stay on as a permanent employee. That could work out."

"Good," Beth agreed. She was beginning to feel more hopeful. Maybe this could work out, after all.

"I—" Kayla started to speak and then stopped, seeming embarrassed. "Well, I might as well tell you. I think you'll find out anyway. I owe a ton of money. That's why I had to skip out quick and come here. Maybe if I can get working and stay working, I can start paying up. Get straight with everybody."

"Who in the world do you owe money to?" Now what?

"Frank. That's Frank Hughes, my first husband. Becky's father."

"Why? Did he lend you money?"

"No. But he got child support when he divorced me. Frank…kind of lost patience with me. With the drinking. Finally he just gave up." Kayla had bowed her head so she wasn't looking at Beth. "My fault. Anyhow, when the marriage went kaput, it went out with a bang. I never dreamed Frank could be so mean, but he could."

"Mean in what way?"

"Well, first thing, I was served with papers. He hadn't said a word about divorce. It came just out of the blue. And he demanded custody of Becky. That hit me hard. I wasn't that terrible a mother. Anyhow, he moved out and took Becky with him."

"He took your child?" Beth went cold. What an awful thing to happen to any mother.

"Just like that. He was gone. Leaving me with nothing. I wasn't working then. I couldn't even pay the rent. They went to live with his sister, Nell. She was over the moon with joy when he dumped me. Nell and I never did get along. Anyway, his lawyer told him he had to get Becky into a better home situation. Like I wasn't a good mother."

"What in the world did you do?"

"Sobered up. Got a job. Got a lawyer. What else could I do? But I couldn't afford much. I think he was, like, six months out of law school. I guess he did his best, but I lost custody of Becky. Frank got his divorce, and was no longer responsible for my debts, stuff like that. Then they fixed me good. Frank got custody of Becky and demanded child support, knowing that I probably couldn't pay it. And— owing him all that money—I don't even dare to try to see Becky."

"I don't understand a woman having to pay child support," Beth said uncertainly. What a horrible story! "How terrible that you can't even see your own child." Even for a haphazard mother like Kayla that must be very difficult for her.

"Welcome to the real world, Beth. He and his sister really socked it to me. I had a history of working, of holding a job. Time when only men paid child support is past history. Women are more than half the workforce now. And when divorce happens, more and more fathers are given custody. So, get it? Whichever parent *doesn't* have custody pays the *other* one child support. Lots of women pay child support to husbands now."

"But why couldn't you just *see* Becky?"

"You still don't get it. They did it on purpose. Knowing my problems, they figured I could never pay up. So if I don't pay, I don't see my kid. It's that simple. They wanted me out of Becky's life—I was a bad influence. Okay, I'm out of Becky's life." There was infinite bitterness in Kayla's voice.

"Well, do you— Do you know how much you owe?"

Kayla shrugged hopelessly. "Have you got a calculator? It's been five and a half years. I paid some, but I never could keep up. Especially after I married Mitch and Adam came along. Then Mitch died…"

Her voice trailed off and her gaze was fixed on something in the far distance, but Beth knew she wasn't really seeing. What a dismal mess poor Kayla had made of her life.

"Please don't tell Dad," Kayla said, seeming to come back to the present.

"Oh, Kayla, I really don't like to keep things from Doug."

"But I don't want him to know. He'll think he has to pay it. But first he'll get mad and yell at me."

"I can't imagine Doug yelling at anybody."

"Well, you never pushed him as far as I have," Kayla said simply.

"Really, I don't want him to know. At least, not yet," she added, and Beth knew Kayla could see the reluctance in her face.

Beth and Doug had been open and honest with each other. Keeping secrets from him, especially about his own daughter, was dishonest. They were already at odds about Kayla's "problem." She didn't want to complicate their relationship any further.

"All right," Beth said after a moment. "But just for now. You really must tell him yourself. And soon, please." That was the best she could do. Kayla was vulnerable, but she was trying. Beth disliked adding stress to Kayla's makeshift life by putting any more pressure on her, but the line had to be drawn somewhere.

They left to resume their shopping, but for Beth the pleasure had gone out of it. Their curfew for getting home was three-thirty since check-in time for new guests was four. They found Doug had gotten home before them. He was carrying suitcases up the stairs for the expected Mr. and Mrs. Crandall from Fresno.

Doug was in high spirits, and well he might be. He hadn't baby-sat Kayla all day. When the Crandalls had settled in, he joined them in the bed-sitter with Adam. Beth felt her heart soften. Doug was Doug, the love of her life.

She had felt sand under her shoes when they came in. Next Tuesday they'd really need the cleaning service in here, whether Adam wanted it or not.

"Adam loved the beach," Doug said. "Let's sit here, love." He slid his arm through hers and they went to the big couch. The familiar feeling of contentment filled Beth.

"Got this," Adam said, showing her a little sand bucket and shovel. So that was where the sand had come from.

He was slightly sunburned and beaming with pleasure from his afternoon at the beach with Doug.

"Daddy, I want to show you my new things," Kayla said happily. She began to take her new garments out of their wrappings. Beth watched as she showed off their purchases. Doug looked pleased and relaxed. Well, maybe all her efforts were worth it. She moved slightly closer to him, taking his hand in hers.

When Kayla finished, she said, "And Beth, you're not doing another thing today. I'm going to fix dinner for us. Come on, Adam. Help Mommy fix dinner. And don't you two move a muscle," she commanded, picking Adam up from the window seat and hugging him.

Things were going to work out, really they were, Beth assured herself.

"Guess what," Doug said, as Kayla went out with Adam.

"What?"

He kissed her lightly. "I think one more session and Shilshole Bay plus the across-the-water skyline, plus the houseboats and the beach, and the painting will be finished."

"Wonderful. You're doing such a great job with that."

"Yeah," he said contentedly. "I feel good about that picture. I think it may be one of my better efforts. And Adam was a great little companion, too. He stuck around and didn't wander off. I had to stop now and then to admire his sand bucket or some shell or rock, but he really got a kick out of being at the beach. And guess what else."

"What?" She laughed.

"I met our pastor. He was out running. I guess that's how he stays so lean. Anyhow, he stopped—you know how runners are. He was stretching this way and that while we talked, and I invited him to dinner here Sunday night. Was that okay?"

"Of course it was okay." She laughed again with sheer happiness. Being with Doug made life so perfect.

"And you know what else?" Doug asked, sounding smug.

"No, but you're going to tell me."

"Yep. He asked about Kayla and wanted to know how she was doing. So I said, so far so good. I explained that she was going to start AA. And he said a few things that made me think he knows something about substance dependency."

"Well, he mentioned to me that he had worked with addicted people before he came here," Beth said, lifting Doug's big hand to her lips for a moment. Oh, it was so good to be alone with Doug at last.

"And I got the very distinct feeling while I was talking to Pastor Cooper that he's interested in Kayla." He paused impressively. "I mean, not only helping her if he could, but *interested*. Like in boy meets girl. What do you think of *that*?"

"Oh, Doug, no!"

"What do you mean, 'Oh, Doug, no'?" He straightened and withdrew his hand, looking annoyed. "Kayla is a lovely, unmarried young woman and he's a nice, decent, unmarried guy. What's wrong with that picture?"

Beth, go carefully here, she told herself. *He's defensive and protective.* She paused a moment, trying to collect her thoughts. How could she say this kindly?

"I suddenly remembered Cyrus's wife before she died some years ago," Beth said carefully. "She came with him to our church and they worked together, but it was her supporting *him*, in the background. Ours is a medium-size congregation. Cyrus's wife worked full time helping out, always sort of behind the scenes. A minister is coping with a dozen different things every day, Doug. That's a stressful job, but their wives can't afford to be stressed. In a church congregation there is always something going on, something brewing, one group in disagreement with another...about many things. I'm just saying that Kayla is vulnerable.''

She tried to choose her words carefully, because Doug's face had become closed and remote. Was he angry? Was he rejecting everything she said? She swallowed her impatience and went on.

''Please understand I'm not saying anything negative about Kayla. I agree, she is a lovely person, but she's a lovely person with a serious problem. She's got more than she can cope with right now. Don't you see? A demanding relationship that might end in another marriage would put too much strain on her. And it wouldn't be fair to Pastor Cooper, either. She's made a beginning. She's trying. I saw that today.'' His face remained blank. For an intelligent man he did have his blind spots. Hurriedly, she continued.

''She was so excited about her new clothes. She immediately told me she wanted to start looking for a job. She wants to work, to be self-sufficient. That's certainly good thinking. I was impressed.''

''What kind of job?'' he asked, getting up from the couch and going over to the window, looking out, with his back to her. She was at a disadvantage now, not being able to see his face, but she went doggedly on.

''She's qualified for clerical work. And she had such a good, positive attitude. She says she will register at some temp agency, taking only temporary jobs first, not committing for a long term. She knows she isn't ready to plunge into any long-term commitment.'' She got up and followed him to the window and slid her arm through his. ''Don't you see? Don't you think that's a good idea? About getting a job? But one thing at a time.''

''No.''

''No, you don't think it's a good idea? Why on earth

not?'' It took an effort to keep her voice calm. This was a side to Doug she hadn't seen before.

''Because here at home she has some supervision. But going out every day? Meeting people? Coping with job hassles? Beth, Kayla is an alcoholic. That means she can't even take one drink without losing control. What happens if there is an office party? I know my daughter. It's best she stay out of the workplace. For now, anyway, away from any job pressure. Pastor Cooper is a good man, steady, dedicated. If he is interested in her, this may be her one chance at salvation, and I don't mean that in a religious sense. I don't know why you can't see it.''

''I don't see it because it isn't there,'' Beth said evenly, trying to hold back sudden anger. How could he be so dense!

''And Pastor Cooper has had experience dealing with substance dependency. He'll know how to proceed. He'll understand her difficulty,'' Doug continued, seeming to ignore what she had just said.

Beth looked up into his grim face and mentally counted to ten. Then twenty. When Doug had first come to the Pacific Northwest to follow his passion for painting beautiful landscapes and had chosen to stay at her B and B, he hadn't been inside a church for years. He was just now coming to see and appreciate faith as part of his life. He hadn't known Cyrus and his late wife, Adelaide, when they first came to lead the congregation. He didn't know—couldn't know—the constant demands on a pastor's time, on his wife's time. The pastor and his wife did a constant balancing act, serving the people in the church. She could hear in her mind quite plainly Adelaide's laughing comment one hectic day: *''When the church hires a pastor, it's getting two for the price of one.''*

They—both of them—had to be there, for helping, for

counseling, for comforting, for simply lending a hand as needed when anyone was in trouble.

Memories crowded into her mind—when Ralph died and she felt so guilty because she had never loved Ralph as he had loved her. And when Katie, right after her first husband died, cried, "Why did God do this?" Cyrus, and Adelaide, had been there to help Katie through it. *A pastor's wife cannot be a woman with a problem.*

"Doug, has Kayla ever even *been* in a church? What is her faith? Has she *any* faith?" These questions came tumbling out, and even as she said them she knew they were the wrong questions. She was making Doug angry, and she really didn't care. He was wrong and he should have sense enough to know it.

"I doubt if Kayla has a 'faith,' as you put it. Her mother and I were never churchgoers." He spoke stiffly. "Do you see this as a problem?"

"Yes. If," Beth said in an icy tone, "she begins a relationship with a man whose whole life is his faith. Then, yes, I see it as a problem. I see an endless *list* of problems. And if you weren't clutching at straws, you'd see it, too. A pastor's wife has to be stable, Steady. Wise. And I mean steady in the real sense of the word. Strong. Patient. All the things that Kayla *is not*." She could feel herself beginning to shake, she was so angry. "Don't you see it? The best thing Kayla can do is what she herself suggested. Get a job. *That* could be her salvation. *That* could be the best stabilizing force for her." The sudden change of expression in Doug's eyes stopped her, and she turned around.

Kayla, carrying Adam, was standing in the doorway. She looked stricken. Beth felt a quick rush of embarrassment. That she had lost her temper, and that Kayla had heard it. It really wasn't fair. Kayla had enough to worry about without learning she had caused a quarrel.

"Look, Kayla," Beth said. "Don't pay any attention to

us. Sometimes we have these little domestic rows. It means nothing. Don't tell me you've got something to eat already."

"Yes," Kayla said diffidently. "Between your freezer and your microwave I've put together a pretty good spread. Come on. I've laid it all out in the kitchen."

"Fine. Thanks," Beth said. The look of complete defeat in Kayla's pretty eyes made her feel guilty, but guilty with an underlying anger that she felt guilty at all.

"Come on, then. Let's eat," she said brightly, feeling she would probably choke on whatever it was.

Chapter Seven

She hugged Kayla briefly. Doug picked up his cue and came forward, too.

"Great. Beth and I have our little disagreements. Come on, let's eat." He reached out for Adam and Adam came to him. Together they all went into the kitchen.

"I, uh, hope you like what I fixed."

"Fine," Beth said. She would have agreed to anything to relieve the tension. Now, how in the world would she break the news to Kayla that Doug didn't want her to look for a job? Doug took the matter into his own hands after they had finished the meal.

"Kayla, Beth was telling me about your job idea. Do you really think you're ready for that?"

"Ready for it?" Kayla echoed. "I guess so. Do you think I'm not?"

"Well, you'll be starting with AA. I think it's a good idea at the right time, certainly. But why don't you wait awhile longer? Say, a month or two? Maybe when you feel you've gotten a good grip on things, when you feel more confident. What do you think?"

Beth gritted her teeth but kept silent.

"Well," Kayla said uncertainly. "I guess maybe you're right. So far I have a perfect score in making wrong decisions. Maybe I should wait awhile. I could help out here?" She made it a question and looked at Beth, anxiety in her expressive eyes.

"I could use the help," Beth said carefully, "since Doug thinks you shouldn't take on a full-time job yet." Or was that the wrong thing to say? Maybe she'd better talk to Pastor Cooper, get some background on what to do. Maybe Pastor Cooper would agree with her and could convince Doug. Maybe they should *both* talk to Pastor Cooper. They might get the chance when he came to dinner on Sunday. In the meantime Beth didn't offer any more advice on helping Kayla—since Doug was being so pig-headed. Kayla was his daughter, after all. She had to ask herself how she would have taken it if Jill or Kate had a problem and someone else offered advice. Doug seemed willing to smooth things over, too.

Thursday morning Kayla helped with the B and B housekeeping tasks as she had before. The first little flaw came when Doug picked up Adam's dyed, red high-topped shoes and brought them home. He had almost finished the Shilshole Bay painting, too, and was pleased about that.

Adam liked the color but much preferred his red sneakers. He apparently didn't like the way the high-tops felt.

"How come you got him these?" Kayla asked, taking them off him to put on the regular sneakers. "He says he wants these."

Beth told her what the doctor had said about his pronated ankle.

"How come you took him to the doctor when he wasn't sick?"

"I thought it would be good for him to have just a routine checkup," Beth said. Then she went on to tell Kayla what else Dr. Fletcher had said, trying not to imply any criticism, but Kayla inferred it.

"I guess I'm a lousy mother," Kayla said dolefully. "I didn't realize he was underweight. I just figured that little kids are, uh, little. I guess I get too involved in my own problems to get too uptight about his. I guess I never should have had kids in the first place." After a long pause, she added, "I miss Becky sometimes. I sure blew it there."

Reminded of her difficulties with her former husband, Frank Hughes, Beth asked, "Have you told your father yet about the money you owe? On that child support?" She didn't want to start another quarrel with Doug.

"Oh, Beth, don't. Not yet. I will. I promise."

And Beth didn't say anything else. She had to talk to Pastor Cooper. She had to talk to *somebody*. She was completely out of her depth with Kayla and Doug.

When she got a spare moment she called Bessie at the church, only to learn that Pastor Cooper was involved in a series of meetings with the Elders and others about his new ministry. They were discussing his supervising the church school, Gilmartin Academy, of getting settled in his new apartment, of helping Cyrus's relatives with Cyrus's small estate matters and the many things that take up a pastor's time. She couldn't bother him yet with their problems. Perhaps a little later. Or perhaps when he came to dinner on Sunday. Yes, definitely, she would speak to him on Sunday whether Doug wanted her to or not.

On Thursday evening Beth could hear clear into the kitchen that Doug and Kayla were having an argument in the bed-sitter. She went as far as the front hall. They had three guests, but thankfully they were all out for an evening. She paused there uncertainly. Should she go in? Or not? Then she realized Adam was sitting in the corner of the hallway behind the desk, struggling with something. She went to lean over the desk and look at him. She thought he was hiccuping and then realized he was crying. He was struggling to put on one of the new red high-topped shoes. His little fingers were fumbling uselessly with the laces. Lacing up high shoes was beyond him. She knelt down before him.

"Adam, can I help?"

"Adam good boy," he said, still working desperately with the tangled laces. "Adam good. Adam okay."

"Here, let me," she said gently. He had on just his small cotton briefs. Apparently Kayla had been getting him ready for bed when the quarrel with Doug started. What was it like to be three years old and not understand what the big, angry people were shouting about? And like children everywhere, had he assumed that it was somehow his fault? What bad thing had he done to make it happen? He had refused to wear the red high-topped shoes. So now he was doing his three-year-old best to make things right again.

Willing herself not to fling open the bed-sitter door and give both Kayla and Doug a piece of her mind, and willing herself not to cry, she calmly took Adam's small hands from the laces, untangling them and then lacing up the shoes, talking gently to him all the while.

"Of course you are a good boy. I was just saying today that I didn't know any little boy as good as Adam. And I'll tell you what. I forgot to get some fresh flowers from the garden for the breakfast table. Can you imagine that? Forgetting to get fresh flowers? But it's still fairly light outside and I'm just going out now to get some. Will you come with me? I need someone to hold the basket."

He looked up at her with his wide, wet, blue eyes. "Yes," he said. "I c'n help. Adam c'n help."

"Good," she said briskly, ignoring the angry words coming from the bed-sitter.

"You said you'd call AA! Have you done it yet?"

"Okay! I'll call them! Are you satisfied?"

Beth picked Adam up and took him toward the back of the house, trying not to hurry. Let them fight it out. Adam didn't need to hear it. She reached the back service porch and, with one quick motion, took the flat basket from the shelf, pushed open the door and was down the back steps before she realized she was holding her breath. She let it out with a sigh, and put Adam down.

"Now, you take this basket." She really should have put Adam's pants and T-shirt on, but it was a warm spring evening and the backyard was empty. If anybody was looking out any window, well let them. They would see Mrs. Colby picking a lovely array of early daffodils with her small grandson assisting by holding the basket, wearing only his cotton briefs and red high-topped shoes.

It was almost dark when Beth thought she had enough flowers. When she went to the back door the house seemed eerily silent. Was it safe to go back in yet?

Doug answered for her by coming out the back door.

"Oh, there you are," he said. "I was wondering—" He stopped because he saw Adam following her around the corner of the house carrying the flat flower basket full of daffodils.

"Don't say a word," Beth said through her teeth, and had the satisfaction of seeing Doug shut his mouth and come quietly down the steps.

Adam, quite happy now, held out the basket. "Adam helping," he said proudly.

"Well, you certainly are," Doug said heartily. "Good for you. Can I give you a hand with that?"

"Nope. Adam do it."

So Doug stepped back and let Adam struggle up the

steps, the flower basket tilting dangerously. But he made it onto the service porch.

"Thank you, Adam," Beth said, reaching for the basket, which Adam graciously let her take.

She couldn't talk to Doug until Adam, sitting on the high kitchen stool, had watched her arrange the dining room flowers and refresh himself with a cookie and a cup of milk. Then he decided that, yes, he was ready for bed.

"Is Kayla in bed?" Beth asked Doug, keeping her tone remote and cool. She could see Doug trying not to smile as he answered.

"Probably not this early, but she's in the bed-sitter. My daughter and I had a little discussion."

"We heard," Beth said coldly.

"And when I left her, we had reached a decision. Shall I take Adam in?"

"I'll take Adam in," Beth said, still cool. "Okay, Adam, let's go now." She picked him up from the stool and took him into the bed-sitter.

Kayla was sitting on the window seat in the semi-dark room. She hadn't bothered to put on the light.

"Adam's ready for bed, Kayla."

"Oh? Yeah. Thanks," Kayla said absently. Her eyes looked puffy so she must have cried at some point.

"I'll help you put the sofa bed down," Beth offered, and together they unfolded it.

"We got flowers," Adam said in his piping voice.

"Did you? That's nice," Kayla said vaguely. "Come on, then. Time for you to hit the sack."

"Big shoes," Adam said, calling her attention to the high-tops. "Put on big shoes."

"Great. You're a good boy." Kayla's voice was listless but it satisfied Adam. His little world was right again.

Sighing softly, Beth kissed Kayla and Adam good-night

and went out, closing the door softly behind her. Where was this all going to end?

Back in the kitchen Doug was working away at the breakfast preparations, and she found she wasn't angry at him now. Cutting the flowers, she had rehearsed a really excellent commentary on protecting vulnerable little children from the anger of adults who couldn't control themselves. She had fully intended to hurl it at him. Now it seemed a waste of time. She sat down at the kitchen table, enjoying, as usual, the sight of his big gentle hands working so deftly.

"Thanks for starting the breakfast work."

He turned. "Why do I think that's not what you had in mind to tell me?" He was looking at her quizzically and she couldn't help but smile and reach out. He came to her in one stride and took her in his arms.

Later, when they had gone upstairs, she spoke to him about Pastor Cooper. "I think when the pastor comes Sunday, we should talk to him. I'm really at sea with Kayla. I don't actually know what to do—how best to help. Maybe I'm doing the wrong thing, with the best of intentions."

"I agree," he said soberly. "I'm not sure what I'm doing, either. Always before, when Kayla was in trouble, I concentrated on being elsewhere. I pinned her down tonight—right or wrong—and told her if she was going to try AA she'd have to start. If she's going back into the rehab center, it has to be within a thirty-day period from the time she walked out. I guess I kind of laid it on the line. I'm sorry but I forgot about Adam. Where was he?"

"He was in the hall. He must have heard part of the row and got upset." She let it rest there—no point in making him feel worse.

Friday went well. Kayla was quiet and unsmiling, but she helped diligently. She was obviously very troubled.

One guest left and two others arrived. Beth hoped the roof patch would hold as they had a full house through the weekend. The forecast was for continued fair weather, but a storm front was moving in Tuesday. In Seattle one never knew. As old-time Seattleites said, "If you don't like this weather, wait a few minutes."

Beth didn't think to tell Kayla that Pastor Cooper would have dinner with them Sunday until about noon on Saturday. She was astonished at Kayla's reaction.

"Oh, no, not the preacher! Beth, no offense, but I'm just not into organized religion. I'll have to sit this one out. As I recall he's a very attractive guy. Probably very full of himself."

The three were in the backyard. It was a lovely day. Doug had finished the Shilshole Bay painting and was framing it in the basement workshop. They were sitting around the round white table under the faded blue umbrella. One good thing had come of Doug's quarrel with Kayla. Adam was dutifully wearing his red high-topped sneakers now without argument.

"Well, he's not coming to preach," Beth said, laughing. "He's just coming to dinner. Yes, I agree he's quite good-looking."

"Yeah. I like that tall, lanky kind of guy, but wow. I don't know, Beth. If only he wasn't a preacher." She shook her head. "Dad's been on my back about calling AA," she added, changing the subject.

And before Beth could stop herself she said, "Maybe you should."

"The point," Kayla said, "is that I *did*. I already talked to this guy, a very nice guy, and he told me all about it in detail. I didn't really know a lot, see? I just had heard that people going through the program could stop drinking. But I—" She looked off into the distance.

"Have you told Doug this?"

"No. Not yet. I haven't had the guts. Beth, it's like this. AA is all wound up with religion. I'm just not into religion. This nice guy says I don't have to be into religion myself. AA can help me even if I'm not, but—" She paused a long time. "There's so much to it."

"What do you mean, so much to it?" Beth asked, but Kayla shook her head warningly. Beth heard Doug coming so she didn't pursue it.

For the rest of the day she kept thinking she should talk to Doug about it, but couldn't decide. Somehow or other she would ask Pastor Cooper on Sunday evening. Maybe Kayla would feel differently about it when she had had a social evening with him.

But Sunday after church, she and Doug found to their dismay that Kayla wasn't home. The big house was empty. Beth tried to quell her panic. *Adam, where are you, dear child?* Then she heard Doug's grim voice from the kitchen.

"She left a note on the fridge."

Beth ran into the kitchen. "What does it say? Where have they gone? I was afraid of this!"

"She'll be back—she hasn't gone for good," Doug assured her quickly, taking the note from the refrigerator door. Beth could see it was a half sheet of house stationery with scrawly writing.

"She wrote, 'Dear Beth and Dad—Cold sober I can't take an evening with the preacher so Adam and I are eating out. Will be back later. Love, Kayla.'"

Beth felt a surge of relief that Kayla had sense enough to avoid an evening with Flip Cooper since she found him attractive. Getting involved with a clergyman offered pressure that Kayla didn't need and couldn't handle.

"Does she have any money?" Beth asked.

"Apparently. I gave her some pocket money when she

went into rehab. I guess she still has it. I hope she doesn't decide to drink her dinner.'' He handed the note to Beth.

''Well, she wouldn't do that,'' Beth said. ''She says she's cold sober.''

''When she wrote the note she was cold sober,'' Doug said uncertainly.

''All right,'' Beth said briskly. ''It isn't time to start dinner yet, so why don't we do some gardening? The weeds are thriving.''

''Weeding it is,'' Doug said, sounding grateful. Like a lot of men, when he was disturbed he wanted something to do.

In comfortable jeans they spent a productive hour outside, weeding, trimming, raking and gathering up the bits of refuse that persistently clutter the best of gardens. By midafternoon they had had enough physical action, and settled in lawn chairs in the back garden. Both became aware at once that the house phone was ringing, but Doug didn't make it into the house in time to answer. He came back with the portable phone and a note, which he handed to Beth.

''There was a message on the machine from Pastor Cooper. He's stuck at the hospital with a sick parishioner and begs off dinner. Says to call him if we want him to stop by later in the evening. That's his cell phone number.''

''We do,'' Beth said immediately, her eyes meeting Doug's. ''Don't we?''

''Yes,'' he said, sitting down and handing her the phone. ''I think he knows what he's doing and we don't—that's fairly clear. Yes, I think we'd better talk to him, I mean, listen to him.''

Beth dialed the number and Pastor Cooper answered immediately. ''I'm sorry you can't make it to dinner,'' Beth said. ''But we certainly understand. A sick parishioner takes precedence. But both Doug and I would like to talk with you later, if you aren't too tired.''

"Fine. I'll be there," Pastor Cooper said. "It may be late. How late is too late? Would sometime between nine and ten be okay?"

"Fine," she said, so it was settled.

Beth felt a sudden lilting happiness. Nobody was checking in tonight, so she and Doug would have this time to themselves. They would get rid of the sense of strain that had existed between them since the quarrel.

Pastor Cooper arrived a little after eight. He looked tired, and Beth wondered about the stress of his afternoon. Cyrus had been so strong, but comforting the bereaved, giving hope to the hopeless, trying to encourage the defeated took strength, and she wondered what he had already dealt with today.

"Why don't we sit out here?" Doug suggested. "It's a nice evening. I think in Scotland they call it the 'gloaming.'"

"Lovely word," Pastor Cooper said, sitting down.

"Did you have dinner?" Beth asked. "I could fix you something."

"Nothing, thanks. I picked up a sandwich at the hospital cafeteria. I'm fine."

"We probably should let this go until later," Beth apologized, "but we're both worried about Kayla. Since it's late and you've already had a full day, I'll get right to the point. Both Doug and I are confused. Kayla was in the rehab center but left it. She decided to try AA. Now she seems to be reluctant to start that. We don't know what to make of it."

She could sense him focusing in on what she was saying, putting aside that which had engaged him all afternoon.

"What did Kayla say about it? About going to AA?"

Doug answered. "Not much to me. I handled it badly, I'm afraid. I quarreled with her, sort of backed her into a corner. Did she talk to you about it, Beth?"

"A little. She said she had actually called them and talked to a 'really nice guy' there. He apparently filled her in on the details. And she said—" Beth paused, wanting to be precise. "What she actually said was that it was all wound up in religion first. Before that, she had said she was not religious. I got the impression that was pretty much carved in stone. Then, about the AA program, she said there was 'so much to it.' We have no idea what she means by that."

"I do," Pastor Cooper said thoughtfully. "She's only half right about the 'religion.' The whole program is based on a person accepting that there is a—what can I call it?— higher power. That we are not really in control, but that higher power is. The program itself can be used by people of any faith, or no faith. It can be effective for all. And she said there was 'so much to it'?"

"Yes. What could she have meant?"

"My educated guess is there's more to it than she realized. Has she been an alcoholic for some time?"

Doug answered. "Yes. I first realized she was drinking when she was a teenager, so it's been more than ten years."

Pastor Cooper nodded. Beth wished she could see his face more clearly in the dusk. "Then, she's probably had some hard times," he said. "Probably done some things she regrets—all people with a substance dependency have. It's what happens when these people lose control of their lives. They hurt other people."

"Well, she's done that," Doug said bleakly. "Her mother gave up on her years ago. I…defaulted in my parental responsibilities, I'm ashamed to admit. Kayla was on her own a lot, when she shouldn't have been. She's had two failed marriages. That is, her first marriage ended in divorce, and her child, Becky, is now in the father's custody. Then there was a brief second marriage to Adam's father. He died, but from what she's said, I gather they were both pretty much basket cases. I doubt that marriage would have lasted. It all sounds like a grim litany of failure, which I guess is what it has been...." His voice dwindled away.

Pastor Cooper was quiet for a moment, then he said slowly, "Without speaking to Kayla herself, I believe, then, the part of the AA program that's put her off is probably steps eight and nine. It's a twelve-step program. And the recovering user needs to work his or her way through all twelve steps. One at a time. It takes guts and perseverance and strength. Maybe that's what frightened her off."

"What are steps eight and nine?" Doug asked.

"To make a list of every person your dependency has harmed. Then make amends to each of these people whenever possible—unless making amends now will injure them or others. It's a tall order. Do you know of anything in her life so far that she can't consider going back to? To try to make amends?"

Beth gave a small gasp. Both men glanced over at her.

"You've thought of something?" Pastor Cooper asked.

"Yes," Beth said hesitantly, "but Kayla asked me not to mention it. If I do, I'm breaking confidence." She paused for a moment, then decided. Kayla's life really was out of control. Doug was her father. Pastor Cooper was here now, and, busy as he was, she wasn't sure when they could talk to him again. Doug would probably be annoyed, but...

"If Kayla is disappointed or angry that I'm breaking confidence, I'll just have to deal with it. My guess is that it would be her first husband Kayla would be reluctant to—"

"Frank Hughes?" Doug asked, puzzled.

"Yes. It was Frank who wanted the divorce. He demanded custody of their little girl. Kayla said he ran out of patience. I gather he had tried to help her but...it hadn't been successful. Anyway, he got custody of Becky. Kayla says that the court awarded him child support, which Kayla has never paid. Her life was in such a shambles that she couldn't. I'm afraid that's the situation she's avoiding. She owes— I don't know how much. But that's the reason she ran away from…wherever she was.'' Beth tried to recall exactly what Kayla had said. ''She was frantic, desperate. She just took Adam and ran. And I think she said they had 'found' her. Apparently there's an ongoing process to locate noncustodial parents who owe and don't pay.''

''Yes, there is,'' Pastor Cooper said quietly. ''Usually it's the male parent who defaults because the courts used to give children to the mother, but now fathers are often granted custody. So it works both ways.''

Doug was silent, which worried Beth. She could sense his resentment that she had kept Kayla's confidence and hadn't told him.

''Poor Kayla,'' Pastor Cooper murmured. As he said it, they heard the back door shut.

''Hi. Anybody out there?'' It was Kayla. ''Is the preacher gone?'' In the dusk they could see Kayla coming toward them. She looked like a lovely wraith in the semi-darkness, wearing one of her new outfits, a casual swishy skirt of light green jersey topped by an embroidered sweater in the same shade. She was talking easily. ''Adam zonked out so I left him asleep in the bed-sitter. We had burgers and I took him to a park and…'' Her voice trailed off.

Pastor Cooper and Doug stood up.

''I'm afraid the preacher is still here,'' Pastor Cooper said, not quite smiling, his eyes on Kayla.

''You've met my daughter,'' Doug said awkwardly. The derision in Kayla's tone at the word ''preacher'' would have been hard to miss.

''Oh,'' Kayla said, ''I think I've offended the clergy. What do I get for that? Fifty lashes or being burned at the stake?'' She was quite drunk. ''And you know what else? I have this strange feeling that if I don't sit down I'm gonna fall down. One of you guys will have to give me a chair.''

''Sit here,'' Doug said grimly, and Kayla went unsteadily to Doug's chair and sat down.

''Lovely feeling, sitting down. Lovely evening.'' She leaned back against the headrest, looking dreamily at the evening sky. ''One nice thing about Kayla,'' she added, ''is that Kayla is a *happy* drunk. We went to this nice park, see. Adam and me. Seattle is full of these little neighborhood parks. And I pushed him in a swing. He was so thrilled, and pretty soon I got tired and when I get tired I get thirsty and there was this nice vendor who was selling cold beers.'' She closed her eyes, ''It only takes one these days.''

''I'm sorry,'' Doug said to Pastor Cooper.

''Doesn't matter. She said it all, Doug.'' Pastor Cooper's voice was gentle. ''She said 'happy drunk.' When people need happiness badly they take it any way they can. Let's not pass judgment. It's not our place.'' He didn't need to speak so softly because Kayla's eyes had closed and she seemed to have fallen asleep.

Beth glanced sharply at the pastor. Doug had been right. Pastor Cooper *was* attracted to Kayla. The expression on his face seemed to say that clearly. *Oh, surely not!*

''Now what?'' Doug was asking.

''I think I'll get Kayla inside,'' Beth said. ''It's getting chilly out here. Kayla, come on, honey. I'll help you.'' And she roused Kayla from Doug's chair.

Kayla awoke at Beth's touch. ''Okay,'' she said agreeably. ''Okay. Good idea. Beddy-bye sounds fine to me.'' Standing, she turned to Pastor Cooper. ''Sorry about my goof,'' she said. ''No offense, okay?''

''None taken,'' Pastor Cooper said softly. ''Good night, Kayla.''

*   *   *

Once inside it took Beth half an hour to get the sofa bed down, and both Adam and Kayla in it. She was a little breathless when it was done. *When will this end, Lord?*

She found both men in the living room, deep in conversation. She sat down on the settee beside Doug.

"Flip was just giving me some good advice. You've heard the phrase 'tough love'?"

"Yes, of course," Beth said, looking at the pastor.

"It's not easy," Pastor Cooper said, "but in Kayla's situation it may be your best course now. I'll talk to her if you and Doug want me to, and if Kayla agrees. Doug thinks I could help."

"We haven't been doing too well," Beth said carefully.

"If she'll talk with me, I can advise you better," Pastor Cooper said. "Doug thinks she will when she's sober. Tomorrow she'll feel embarrassed, contrite. She'll be eager to make peace, to atone, as it were. It would be a good time to press your point, if that's what you want. Have you noticed that she's been self-condemning?"

Both answered at once.

"Yes," Doug said.

"Very much so," Beth said, and added, "She can't say anything good about herself."

"This is sometimes a ploy for sympathy, but sometimes it can be a beginning, the acceptance of the idea that it's her fault. The fact that she wanted to enter rehab, even if it failed, was the first step. Now that she is resisting the AA program, maybe individual counseling could help. I've had some success before. With dependency nothing can be accomplished without the willingness of the dependent person—if you can get it. Often addicted people vacillate. They hate to lose their one escape hatch."

"I understand," Doug said, and Beth nodded.

After Pastor Cooper left, Doug turned to Beth. "Since when do we keep secrets from each other? Why didn't you tell me about Kayla's money problem with Hughes?'' His voice was cold.

"She asked me not to," Beth answered. "She wanted to tell you herself." She could feel the beginning of his anger. *Not another quarrel.*

"Would it surprise you to learn that she has *not* told me? Look, Beth, Kayla's *my* responsibility. I don't take too kindly to the idea that you and Kayla have these little woman-to-woman talks, shutting me out."

"If Kayla is *your* responsibility, why was I the one who spent half an hour putting her to bed? No, scratch that. I didn't mean to snap. But we weren't shutting you out, as you put it." Beth tried to keep her voice calm when she was feeling anything but. "We were downtown shopping and she just…just spilled it. Then she was sorry afterward that she'd said so much. It occurred to her she didn't want you to know. She did promise me she would tell you. If she hasn't, that's not my problem, Doug."

He didn't answer for a long time, looking stonily down at the carpet. "Okay," he said grudgingly. "But don't do it again. Please. That's probably what's stopping her from going into AA." He looked up. "Maybe Pastor Cooper can help, but that's not what really bothers me. Once again, I've played it my own way. I should have tried to make amends to Kayla. I should have helped her somehow. Instead I just grabbed at this chance for happiness for myself. I had no right to enter into a second marriage. No right at all."

A sudden chill went through Beth. *No! Don't start regretting our marriage! Don't ever regret that!*

Chapter Eight

Beth lay awake long after Doug lay sleeping beside her. Their lovemaking had had a kind of fierce desperation to it, as if it were something they must snatch in passing. Nor did she feel that sense of permanence, of security she was accustomed to feeling. The feeling that she had at last found her true safe haven with Doug. It troubled her deeply, and she strained to see his sleeping face more clearly in the semi-dark room—the strong jawline, the tousled hair.

There was a murmur and rustle from the child monitor that she had turned on in case Kayla, in her alcohol-drugged sleep, did not wake up if Adam needed her. Beth was right, for she had to go down twice to attend to the boy herself.

In the morning she had no idea how much sleep she had managed to get. She was only fifty—she shouldn't be starting the day feeling bone-tired. Fifty-year-old people were in their prime. Weren't they? But she was dealing with the stress of the Kayla problem.

Doug was already downstairs when she hurried into the kitchen. He was busy with the breakfast preparations, and she joined him.

"You look beat, Beth. Maybe all this is too much."

"Not at all," she said, assuming a brisk tone. She wouldn't mention that Kayla was nowhere to be seen.

He answered her unasked question. "I looked in the bed-sitter. Kayla's still asleep, and so's Adam. I'll go get him in a little while."

When breakfast had been served and the guests were all at the table, he slipped away. He came back shortly with Adam, looking very cute in one of his new T-shirts, pants and red high-topped shoes.

Kayla didn't come out until after all the guests were gone. Beth was on her way up to do the bedrooms. Adam followed along contentedly, bringing a bright book from the toy box.

"Hi, Beth," Kayla said, not meeting her eyes. "I'm so sorry about yesterday," she added humbly.

"Well, I guess these things happen," Beth said. She made an effort to be understanding, but couldn't help but wonder how anyone could lose control of her life as completely as Kayla had. "Why don't you go and have some coffee and muffins? There's juice in the fridge. I'm going to do the beds."

"I'll...I'll help you," Kayla said, starting for the stairs. "I can't even think of food yet. Okay?" Then she added, "Where's Dad? I guess he's going to be furious."

"He's going to deliver the Shilshole Bay painting to the bank. I think you'd better at least have some juice and coffee."

"Okay," Kayla agreed listlessly.

She joined Beth upstairs a few minutes later. Beth tried to keep up a friendly conversation, but Kayla only answered absently, and finally Beth fell silent. When the last bed was made, Beth felt a rush of relief as she heard the front door shut. Doug was back.

Kayla gave a deep sigh. "I guess I'll go down and face the music. Was he very mad last night?"

"He was...disappointed," Beth hedged. "But I guess he does want to talk to you." When was this bad dream going to end?

Kayla grimaced. "That's the understatement of the century. Wish me luck." With dragging steps, she started downstairs, and Adam was pulling at Beth's skirt, holding out his book. He had waited patiently through the bed making and tidy-ups for her to read to him. With a surge of affection, she couldn't resist picking him up and hugging him. She chose to read him his story in the big chair in the back bedroom. In case voices were raised again in the bed-sitter, he needn't be upset about it. There was a feeling of contentment and quiet joy in feeling his little body nestle into her lap, intent on the adventures depicted on the colorful pages. He made a point of being ready to turn the page each time she came to the end of one and paused. When the third story had been read, it was past noon. Beth regretfully shut the book.

"We'd better go downstairs now, Adam."

"Okay, Gamma Beff." And he scrambled down from her lap. Had he felt just a little bit heavier this time? Had he perhaps started to gain some weight?

She found Doug in his basement workroom. Kayla was nowhere to be seen.

"Where's Kayla?" she asked, putting Adam down. He scurried over to Doug, watching him intently. He was becoming more secure with them by the day. Doug finished putting away some leftover bits of framing and brushed his hands together.

"In the bed-sitter," he said slowly. "She took it rather well. She agreed to talk with Pastor Cooper. I felt like a bully. That 'tough love' is tougher to apply than I thought. She seemed so beaten. But I stuck to it."

"I suppose that's best," Beth said. "Do you know when she's going to see him?" A brief flash of light came through the basement window, and they both paused, waiting for the distant roll of thunder to follow. Eventually it did.

"I guess the storm front is moving in before Tuesday," Doug said, grinning. "Good old Seattle weather. To answer your question, I called Pastor Cooper, and he has an hour free between two and three. So she agreed, and I'll drive her over to the church. I can keep busy there until they've had their talk, and I'll bring her back." He didn't need to add that, after yesterday, he didn't want to let Kayla go anywhere by herself.

When they left just before two, Kayla looked desperate. Beth couldn't help feeling sorry for her.

"Bye, bye, baby," Kayla said to Adam. "Kiss Mommy goodbye and go wave to me from your window." She bent over to kiss Adam's upturned little face, after which he ran into the bed-sitter and scrambled up onto the window seat, pushing aside the curtain.

Beth felt a sense of satisfaction. Adam no longer cried and had a tantrum when Kayla left, because he knew she was coming back.

This is good for Adam. Adam has a home. Please, God, let this work out for Adam's sake, for Doug's sake, and for Kayla's sake, too.

Adam seemed content for the time being to kneel on his window seat looking outside at the splashing rain, so Beth decided to catch up on her knitting and went to get her knitting bag. Before Adam and Kayla's arrival she had spent one afternoon a week with a group of churchwomen called 'The Pastor's Aid.' They knitted, crocheted and sewed baby layettes for sale at the church bazaar each autumn. All the money raised from this went to the Pastor's Discretionary Fund, so when he needed to spend small amounts of money for this or that charitable purpose, he didn't need to ask the Elders. She missed the friendly gathering and had promised herself that she'd continue with her knitting at home whenever she could, but it was slow going with the increased demands on her time. She glanced over at the small boy, peering out the rain-streaked window. *Adam is worth it.* She had to do what she could for him until they left.

Doug and Kayla came home a little after three, and Doug found Beth in the kitchen. Adam was still down for his nap.

She glanced up. "Where's Kayla?" she asked, then, "How'd it go?"

"In the bed-sitter. I think things went okay. I didn't sit in, of course. But, coming home, Kayla said he gave her a lot to think about, which could mean anything, I guess. But I'm hoping for the best. He said he'd call me later. Can you get along without me for a while? The bank called me on my cell phone."

"Doesn't the bank like the picture of Shilshole?" Beth asked in alarm. She knew Doug already had plans for the large check that he had received. He needed more framing materials and other supplies.

"They loved the picture," Doug said smugly. "In fact, they loved it so much, they want another one."

"You're kidding." Beth fairly beamed at him. It was almost as it had been in the beginning—just the two of them, before Kayla complicated their lives.

"Nope. The branch manager is retiring, and they have collected money to buy him a retirement gift. The gift committee has now decided that it will get him an original painting of the Pacific Northwest as a memento—since he is retiring to Arizona," he added.

"Oh, Doug. That's wonderful!"

"I'm going down to talk to them about possible subjects or places to paint, but don't get your hopes up too high. It's a committee, don't forget, and it may take them ten years of argument to settle on what I'm supposed to paint."

Laughing, she saw him off.

Kayla must have watched him go from the bed-sitter window, because she came quietly out when he had gone.

"How'd things go, Kayla?" Beth couldn't resist asking.

"Let's sit down in here," she said, going into the living room.

"Well, I listened like a good girl to Preacher-man," Kayla said, sitting down beside Beth on the settee. "I kept reminding myself he's a preacher, trying not to think of him as the good looking guy he is."

"He's really nice," Beth said. "I've gotten to know him better now."

"He *is* very nice," Kayla agreed somberly. "No fire-and-brimstone. A really nice guy and nobody's fool. He…he understands a lot. He has an uncanny way of reading between the lines. He's…" She paused for a long time. "He's not somebody who can be conned."

"Well, you wouldn't try to con him," Beth said, hoping she was right.

"No. I wouldn't," Kayla said thoughtfully. She smiled weakly. "It's just that we, uh, drunks usually try a con first. Then, if that one doesn't work, we can usually think of another. Anything to put off the fateful day, whatever that is at that particular time. But you're right. I didn't try to put him off. I don't think it would have worked anyhow. Have you ever noticed how…searching his eyes can be? I guess not. You wouldn't have had occasion to — Is that Adam getting up?" They both paused to listen, but heard nothing more.

"He's not married, is he?" Kayla resumed.

"No, he's not," Beth said cautiously.

"I thought not. He had that way of a single guy on guard, you know what I mean. A single guy who is used to being targeted by lonely single women and doesn't want to be snagged. He's probably got great avoidance skills."

"A pastor is a target. After Cyrus's wife passed away, it took the single women at church a long time to get the message that he wasn't going to remarry in the foreseeable future. Do you think Pastor Cooper was helpful about it— your difficulty?" Beth added, trying to be tactful.

"Very," Kayla said promptly. "He's done his home-work on my particular 'difficulty,' as you call it. He sort of laid out everything for me—what I could do, what was available to me, what was needed from me as a person— that was scary—and what my life could become if I made a success of it this time around. I wish…" She fell silent, looking pensively down at the carpet.

"Well, that sounds hopeful."

Kayla looked up. "It does, doesn't it? Then he wanted me to talk, and I managed to open up. That's not ever easy for me. I've had a lot of practice keeping things to myself." She paused and her eyes seemed wet. She ducked her head. "Anyhow, he's easy to talk to, in a way. I guess he's had a lot of listening practice. I think he…understood a lot of the things I didn't have the guts to say. I guess I probably had the same problems other drunks have had. Maybe we all fit into a pattern. He didn't seem surprised at anything I *did* say. Anyhow…" Her voice dwindled away. She gave a little shiver. "I think I'll need to go back into that rehab place. And I've got to do it in time so Dad won't lose all that money he paid out up front."

"But I thought you'd—" Beth began in surprise.

"You thought I'd be—what's the term?—counseled by Preacher-man." Kayla looked up, meeting Beth's eyes. "No can do, Beth. And I think I'd better level with Dad on this one, too. No way can I keep meeting with your preacher-man like I did today.''

''Why in the world not?'' Beth protested. ''You hated that rehab center, Kayla. You walked out of it. You just said some very nice things about Pastor Cooper, and I wish you'd stop calling him Preacher-man. You said—''

''Oh, Beth,'' Kayla said timidly. ''Don't you get it? I don't want to see him again. Not because he's some sort of religious freak, but because I—because to be brutally frank here, he's too attractive, and it works both ways. I could see that, even if he couldn't. I've already messed up two men's lives. I messed up Frank's life. And, well, I guess Mitch was pretty well messed up before we connected. I'm not good for any man. And in Preach— In Pastor Cooper I kept seeing…you know— Stable. Strong. Good. He's a rock, Beth. And I'm a clinger. I'll want to *depend* too much. I *need* too much. I'm *not* stable. I'm *not* good. I'd be nothing but a burden to a man like that. He's got his hands full with the work he does. When we came out of his office that what's-her-name, that secretary—''

''Bessie.''

''Yeah, Bessie. She handed him a whole stack of those pink message slips. After he found Dad and saw us out, he was going back into his office to start returning calls. He's probably still making them, making appointments to help people…and he was so…nice, in a kind of— What can I say?'' She stopped, her voice unsteady.

''Yes,'' Beth agreed thoughtfully. ''But, Kayla, I think he's had a lot of practice—training, actually—in *not* getting involved with people he counsels. There's always the probability that people who need help can become too attached to the person helping. He'll know that, be prepared for it. A pastor has to walk a kind of tightrope. He has to treat everybody with kindness, consideration, sort of dividing his attention…fairly. But being human, he's bound to like some people more than others. A pastor may even dislike some of the people he ministers to, but he can never let them know that, either. But you're right, he has to keep that distance, he has to stay…apart.'' Beth tried to keep the disappointment from her voice. She had thought this might be the answer for Kayla. Kayla had left the rehab center once. Could she stick with it if she went back? And, despite herself, she rather admired Kayla's common sense.

''Is that Adam?''

Both she and Kayla listened, trying to hear above the sound of the wind outside. This was really a storm. They both got up and went into the bed-sitter.

Adam was up, kneeling in his window seat. He had on his cotton briefs and one of his red shoes. He was staring out the window in fascination at the dashing rain and the wind-whipped trees.

''Look!'' he said. ''Flowers gone!'' He was holding back the curtain and pointing to the blossoming tree in the front. The wind had mercilessly torn off all the bright pink blossoms. They lay on the sodden grass or swirled in eddies in the rushing waters in the street that almost came up to the curb.

''I hate it when Doug is out in weather like this,'' Beth fumed. ''I hope he remembers to keep his headlights on.'' They all watched out the window until the lamp in the bed-sitter flickered off and on again, then off.

''Oh, dear, I hope the power doesn't go,'' Beth said, and they waited, but the lights flickered back on again and remained steady.

They saw Doug's car turn into the drive. The headlights were on. He drove back to the end of the drive, so Beth knew he was coming in the back way. She hurried to the service porch to kiss him hello and help with his wet raincoat. He'd gotten drenched walking from the bank to the parking lot. Little droplets clung to his crisp hair. The moisture had made it curl here and there, the way it always did. She handed him a towel she had picked up in the kitchen, and he wiped off his face after hanging his coat on the wall peg.

"Should have worn fishing boots," he said, smiling at her. "What a day. I don't suppose there's a cup of hot coffee around?"

"Half a minute," Beth said. "Sit here in the warm kitchen. Did you get the commission?" she asked as she quickly pulled out the two-cup pot.

"Yes, I got the commission. The gift committee has definitely decided. The gift is a picture, and I'm to paint it. They just haven't decided what it is. I'm going to attend what they call a 'working lunch' next week with sketches, Polaroids of some of my other Northwest paintings and suggestions. Opinion is divided, as usual with committees. Some want woodsy. Some want water. Some want city. One is even holding out for a picture of the bank building itself. But something tells me that the manager doesn't want a picture of the Seattle bank building he worked in for seventeen years hanging in his retirement condo in Scottsdale. And that is the good news— Oh, Beth, that sure smells great. Nothing like the aroma of hot coffee on cold, wet days."

"It's almost ready. What's the bad news?" She got two mugs from the cupboard. She hoped he wouldn't ask her where Kayla was. Kayla had shaken her head in panic when they had seen Doug's car come in and had stayed with Adam.

"The bad news, my love, is that the wind has ripped off at least a dozen more shingles from the roof. Some are lying on the lawn, and I saw some on top of the grape arbor. As soon as I fortify myself with some coffee, I've got to call that roofing guy."

"Didn't his patching hold?"

"I'm sure his patch held. This is probably some non-patched area. And if Jill calls, don't tell her, because she'll want to send Greg over, and the life of a CPA in April and early May can be hectic."

"I know," Beth said. They had agreed not to call Greg about the ongoing roof problems. Easygoing as he was, he'd want to help. The big IRS push for April fifteenth was past. Now he would be up to his eyes doing taxes for those he had gotten extensions for. It was an old family joke.

"The roof man won't come in this weather. He can't work on the roof in the rain," Beth said, pouring two mugs of coffee.

"He can put on that blue tarp stuff," Doug said, sniffing his coffee. "He's done that before. I'll go up in the attic first to see if there are puddles over any of the bedrooms."

"The blue tarp is hideous," Beth said, sitting down.

"It's better than wet guests. Remember Mrs. Driscoll?" They both laughed.

Only then did he ask about Kayla.

"I...think I'd better let you talk to her," Beth said carefully. "She says she wants to go back into that rehab center."

"You're kidding! I thought maybe just counseling with Pastor Cooper might do it. I have a lot of confidence in him, young as he is."

"Well, she has reservations. As soon as you get the roof problem dealt with, you talk to her." She let it rest there; he was so touchy about what he seemed to see as her intrusion with Kayla.

"All right," he said quietly, the pleasure suddenly gone from his face. "I'll do that."

The afternoon was hectic. There were several phone calls. Beth had to refuse last-minute reservations from individuals and one from a small hotel that had overbooked and was desperately trying to find extra accommodations. Doug was in and out, dealing with the roof problems. The roofing crew came, and Beth stopped everything to give them cups of hot coffee and warm home-made cinnamon rolls when they finished their wet job with the blue tarp. It was only humane, plus they'd been here before and expected it. At least the guests would stay dry tonight.

The six o'clock arrivals got in at a little after four, due to a misunderstanding, and one had taken ill driving. They were Mr. and Mrs. Jessup, a thirty-something couple who ran a large ranch in Montana. They enjoyed city living and the bright lights in very limited amounts. They took a week's vacation every spring in some city. This year was Seattle's turn. They had booked weeks ago but hadn't counted on Mr. Jessup's severe attack of flu, from which he hadn't quite recovered when their vacation time came. Beth did what she had done before in such an emergency. She offered to send up a dinner tray to the room, as the sickee wanted nothing so much as to crawl into a warm bed. Going to dinner in a strange Seattle restaurant in a violent storm was out of the question.

Then Doug made the mistake of trying to convince Adam that the roofers weren't invading their territory, and took him outside in the rain to see the blue tarp from the side yard. When they came back in, Adam had to be completely dried off and his clothes changed.

"I thought you said you'd wrap him up well," Beth said testily as she dealt with the shivering, excited little boy. Adam had been thrilled.

"I thought I did," Doug protested. "Anyhow, he had a good time."

Beth bit back a sharp retort and tried to listen to Adam's chatter instead. Kayla was next to useless. She sat in the deep chair in the bed-sitter and watched Beth deal with Adam. Her eyes were red and puffy. Sometime during the hectic afternoon she and Doug had talked. There was a stubborn set to her jaw. Beth knew she shouldn't ask, but couldn't resist.

"Did you and Doug decide anything?" she asked when she had attended to Adam.

"I'm going back into rehab. He's taking me over in the morning. He called the director and they arranged it."

"And…you're happy with this arrangement?" Beth asked, sitting on the edge of the sofa bed. She felt a surge of relief that Kayla would be out of the house again.

Kayla shrugged. "Beth, forget happy. Happy disappeared a long time ago, if I ever had it. No, I'm not happy with it. But let's say I'm less miserable with this arrangement. I'm going to try to stick it out this time. If I can get dry, get in control, I'll take my kid and you'll never be bothered with me again. Dad and I get on each other's nerves. But he's doing his best."

Beth felt slightly sick at the thought of Kayla leaving with Adam. That was yet another complication. She was getting too attached to Adam, too protective, too fearful that Kayla could never give him the care he needed.

"Don't pay any attention to me, Beth. You've been great. Better than I deserved. And I can't thank you enough for stepping in and looking after Adam. I've got to make it this time. And I'm really going to try. You…you explain it to Preacher-man. I mean Pastor Cooper. He's a great guy, but I can see the handwriting on the wall there."

Beth shook her head. "Kayla, as an unmarried pastor, he's accustomed to—to not letting himself get involved. Just because you may have felt attracted to him…I mean, you can trust him to know how to handle that—" She stopped, wanting to go on but she decided to stay out of it.

Kayla gave a wan smile. "Don't sweat it, Beth. Just look after Adam while I'm gone. Okay?"

"You know I will," Beth said. This she could do, and willingly.

They left it at that, and she went toward the kitchen. There was dinner to start preparing, with two trays to be sent upstairs. The Jessups' vacation hadn't started out very well. Mr. Jessup was sleeping soundly, and Mrs. Jessup, who was fortunately a mystery fan, had borrowed two of Doug's books to read.

In the midst of Beth's dinner preparations, Kate called, which she never did when she knew her mother was busy. This must mean she was upset about something.

"Guess what?" Kate demanded.

"What?" Beth said, reaching over to turn down a burner on the stove. Now what?

"Raymond came home from school, all upset."

"Why was he upset?" Beth asked, suddenly all attention. Raymond was Ian's son from his first marriage, and Raymond and Kate were very close. The boy had been badly affected by his parents' divorce, and Kate had done wonders for the sensitive child.

"You know he loves those school uniforms. Well, Flippy Philip is considering letting the kids wear anything they want on Fridays. And only wear their uniforms Monday through Thursday. Statistics have proved again and again that students in uniform do better than students not in uniform. Sloppy clothes, sloppy thinking. *Cyrus* knew that!"

"Are you sure about that? I am finding Pastor Cooper a man of very good sense." How she wished Kate wouldn't fume about such things. She was far too protective of Raymond.

"Well, not in this instance. Raymond says some of the kids started a petition, and Pastor Cooper's considering it."

"Have you talked to Pastor Cooper about it?"

"I've left a message for him," Kate said grimly. "I will

not have Raymond going to school unhappy. He's doing marvelously well, the way things are. Believe me, I'd be down at the school giving him a piece of my mind, but I can't—I've got to rest about twenty-three hours out of every twenty-four. Can *you* talk to him about it?''

''I—I can, if you think it would help,'' Beth said. Kate must rest, by all means, if she was to have this baby without difficulty. ''Yes, I'll do that,'' she added firmly. ''Please, Kate, calm down and put it out of your mind. Okay?''

Starting Gilmartin Academy had been Kate's idea, and she and Cyrus had worked almost a year to get it established. It meant a great deal to her. Okay, one more thing to do. Beth turned back to the stove.

Between dinner tasks Beth made a quick phone call to Bessie at the church. Bessie was just going out the door and her day was over, so Beth spoke rapidly.

''Bessie, just ask Pastor Cooper to give me a call tomorrow, will you? Nothing earth-shaking, but I do need to talk to him for a couple of minutes.''

''Sure,'' Bessie said good-naturedly. She'd been a church secretary for a long time. ''I'm writing it down on one of his pinks. He'll get it when he comes back in. Have a nice evening.''

Beth turned back to the stove just in time to snatch off a pan before it boiled over. She continued to worry about Kate. Kate was having a difficult pregnancy and she didn't need any extra problems. She had enough to deal with. Beth sighed, and tried to put it out of her mind. One thing about motherhood was that no matter how adult your children were, you never stopped worrying about them. Unless you were someone like Kayla. What would it take to make Kayla into a good mother for Adam? Or was that even possible?

That evening as she and Doug were preparing for bed,

Beth asked how his talk with Kayla had been. He was buttoning his pajama top over his broad chest.

"All right...I think. I know she doesn't really want to go back there, but she's got this bug about Pastor Cooper. I personally think it would have worked out, but she's dead set against it." He looked troubled and sat down on the side of the bed. Beth was brushing her still dark hair in front of the mirror. "You're a beautiful woman, Beth," he added pensively.

"Which has nothing to do with anything," she said lightly. "Did you get the feeling Kayla could make it work at the rehab center this time?" She knew she shouldn't push him about it, but she needed to know.

"I can only hope so," he said.

In the morning, as soon as the breakfast rush and checking out was over, Doug planned to take Kayla back to rehab, but it wasn't that easy.

Beth checked up on the Jessups, only to find that Mr. Jessup wasn't doing very well. Going out in a still-drenching rain wasn't an option. But Mrs. Jessup proved a very competent guest. As soon as Adam started screaming, she took over the task of carrying their breakfasts upstairs, shutting themselves away and letting their hosts solve domestic problems.

"He saw my suitcase," Kayla said helplessly. "Shut up, Adam," she added, turning to the panicky little boy. "See, he knows I'm going again and he wants to come."

"Me, too! Me, too!" Adam was screaming. "Mommy! Mommy! Don't go!" He was clinging wildly to Kayla's skirt. Beth felt sick and Doug looked miserable.

"Look, Beth, can you... Can we leave him with you? I told the director I'd bring Kayla in before noon."

"Yes, of course," Beth said, trying to pick up the struggling little boy. "Adam, listen! Adam! Mommy's coming back! She came back before, didn't she? Listen to me, Adam.''

Finally, Doug just picked up Kayla's suitcase and they left, while Beth held Adam's rigid little form. It took her the better part of half an hour to comfort him. She assured him repeatedly that his Mommy would come back. It was the earlier crisis all over again. It broke her heart to look down into his red, tear-streaked little face and feel the heavy sobs that convulsed his thin body. *It isn't fair. It isn't fair. He shouldn't be repeatedly hurt like this. How much more can he take, Lord?* For a moment she almost hated Kayla for the shambles she had made of her life. And of Adam's.

She carried him over to the basin behind the screen and washed his flushed face, talking to him soothingly all the while. Finally, he said, ''Book,'' and she knew he wanted to be read to. It was a small indication that things were returning to normal.

''Fine,'' she agreed quickly. ''Which book do you want?'' And they went over to the toy box.

They got one story read before the door chimes sounded. What now? Beth put Adam off her lap and went to the door. It was Pastor Cooper. He smiled and said, ''Hi?'' with the slight sound of a question.

''Come in,'' she said, knowing she looked blank.

He grinned. ''You told Bessie you wanted to talk to me?''

Suddenly she laughed. ''Of course. I'd completely forgotten. Please come into the living room. Excuse me just a minute. I've got to get my little grandson settled.'' She hurried back into the bed-sitter.

''Adam, can you play with the toys awhile? Gramma Beth is busy, okay?''

''Window,'' he said, scrambling up onto the window seat and pushing aside the curtain. He pressed his forehead against the streaming glass, looking out into the rain. "Mommy come back?"

"Not right away, but soon," Beth heard herself saying. She paused a moment, but he seemed to be concentrating on watching, so she went back to her living room, leaving the bed-sitter door open.

When she and the pastor were seated in the living room, she mentioned Kate's concern about the school uniforms, and Pastor Cooper grinned easily.

"Tell Kate not to worry. I don't think it's going to go through. Privately, I'd be inclined to let the kids whoop it up on Fridays in anything they wanted to wear, but you'd be surprised how many *kids* don't want to. The principal, Mrs. Lundy, and I are giving them a lesson in democracy. They're taking a vote on it. Each side is campaigning like mad. Posters. Meetings. They're getting good practical experience. The whole enchilada."

Beth laughed in relief. "Well, Kate's a worrier, not like her sister. Jill takes everything in stride. Kate's going to have another baby, you know. That delayed her redecorating her house, and she fumes about that."

"What house?" he asked.

"The little gray frame house next door to where she and Ian live. She lived there before she was widowed. It's vacant now, and she wanted to fix it up, but that got put on hold."

There was a pause, then he asked, "Where's Kayla? I didn't see her when I came in."

"Oh, she isn't here," Beth said. "She's decided to go back into rehab." She didn't continue because of the disappointment that came and went in his eyes. "Didn't you think she would?" she asked.

"Let's say, I hoped she wouldn't. Do you know why? Actually, I should rephrase that. Are you at liberty to say why?"

"Not exactly," Beth said uncertainly. "I mean…"

He waited a moment, then said, "I'm more sorry than I can say. I could see in our interview…that there might be complications, but she needn't have worried. I've had some solid training in dealing with dependent people. It would have been okay."

"I knew it would," Beth said warmly. "But Kayla is so insecure. She doesn't trust herself. She said… She said she couldn't get emotionally involved. She just panicked at the idea."

"I was afraid of that," he said slowly. "I could have handled it, but she wasn't to know that." His voice held a tinge of sadness, and for a moment, his expressive eyes revealed more than he realized.

Poor Philip. Poor Kayla. She extended her hand to wish him goodbye. She hoped her face didn't show what she had just realized. Kayla was the last woman in the world Pastor Cooper should be interested in, but only she and Kayla knew it.

Chapter Nine

Beth was about to go back into the bed-sitter to check on Adam when she noticed Mrs. Jessup waiting at the top of the stairs. She suppressed a sigh. Running a successful B and B was a full-time job and she was stretching herself rather thin these days. She made herself smile up at the other woman, who really was a nice person.

"Oh, hello, I didn't see you. Can I do something for you? How's Mr. Jessup doing?"

Mrs. Jessup started down the stairs. "I'm a little worried," she said. "He insists he's doing fine, but you know how men are when they get sick. Anyhow, I'm going out for a while. Will you help me a bit with this bus schedule?"

"Of course," Beth said, as the other woman reached the hallway. She liked Mrs. Jessup. She liked most of her guests, and hoped she hadn't been neglecting them. Today, to her trim, neat, blond attractiveness, Mrs. Jessup had added a lovely scent, which Beth noticed as she looked at the bus schedule and gave directions.

"It's still pretty rough weather out there," Beth cautioned. "Are you sure you don't want me to call a cab?"

Mrs. Jessup looked out the window. "I just have to get out of the house for a bit," she said, then added, "Well, maybe I'd better settle for a taxi. Otherwise, I'll get soaked."

While Beth rang the cab company, Doug's car drove in the drive, and by the time the taxi had come, Beth could hear him in the kitchen. He was getting himself something warm to drink. As soon as she could, she hurried back to join in. He was seated at the kitchen table, waiting for the coffee. The pot had begun its little humming sound. He looked tired, and her heart went out to him. Things had been so perfect—before Kayla.

With half her mind still thinking she should have checked on what Adam was doing, she reached for his hands, which lay lax on the table. "How'd things go, dear?"

He sighed. "Well, first let's decide which things. If it's how things go with my Kayla problem—as well as can be expected, I guess. I know in my gut she doesn't want to go back into rehab, and from that state of affairs I rather think it's not going to work out this time, either." She could hear the disappointment in his voice.

"Oh, Doug, let's not be defeatist. At least *think* positively." She tried to lighten his mood but hers wasn't any better. Was Kayla going to be a problem forever?

"Then," he continued, "the bank called me on my cell phone, which I wish now hadn't been invented."

"What did the bank want?"

"It's that gift committee. They've decided—against all odds—what they want as a gift for the departing manager. Is the coffee ready now?"

"Yes, I think so. I'll get it." Beth rose, got mugs from the cupboard and poured out the fresh coffee for them both. Was Adam still okay on his own? He had been so crushed at Kayla's leaving again.

"So, what happened about the picture?" she asked. "Why are you down about it?"

"The bank manager is so pleased with the one I did of Shilshole Bay and vicinity that he wants one exactly like that. And you know how I never want to paint anything twice." He tried to take a sip of coffee, found it still too hot and put down the mug.

"You see my problem here, Beth. I traveled the nation selling textbooks for a living, practicing my painting whenever I could. Then I took the earliest retirement I could afford. I wanted to paint the beautiful landscapes of the world. I never actually thought of *selling* any. I was doing this for love, not money. Then I came here, and last year it seemed such a good idea to start selling them—since I had found out people wanted to actually pay for them. We were trying to fund the church school for Kate and Cyrus. It seemed like a great idea. Then I fell into the habit of painting to sell. Now…" He paused, looking off into the distance. "I guess I'm stuck with it. I *want* to sell them. I plan on what I'll do with the money I get. What I've done, my dear love, is I've traded selling textbooks for another *job*, and…that's not what I wanted to do. I absolutely *hate* painting something I've painted before."

Beth had been trying to quell a rising irritation. She had been the one who started selling his paintings when they had had to fund the church school, because she had realized he was more talented than he thought he was. At the time he had been surprised, pleased, flattered that what he had been doing as a hobby was worth so much to others. Now he saw it as a trap. And somehow he made it seem all her fault.

Before she could stop herself she said almost snappishly, "Are you blaming me for this?"

He assumed a look of surprise. "Blaming? Of course not. At the time—when we were all scrounging money for the school—I was pleased to sell them, to get my first showing in a real gallery. No, I'm not blaming you. Or anybody. It's just that…oh, well.''

Beth felt ashamed, but couldn't really forget her anger. He *had* been blaming her. She had heard it in his tone. She searched her mind for something conciliatory to say.

''You were right about our Pastor Cooper,'' she said finally.

''In what way?'' He started sipping his hot coffee again.

''That he's attracted to Kayla. I noticed it when he stopped by here because I wanted to ask him about the school uniforms. So you had that pegged right.''

He grinned halfheartedly. ''Good to know I'm right about something. I still think that's the answer. If Kayla ever teamed up with the right man, I think it would be her salvation.''

''Or his downfall,'' Beth said, then instantly regretted it. ''I don't mean that in a derogatory way,'' she added quickly, but Doug's face had closed into a frown.

He got up abruptly and dumped his nearly full cup into the sink. ''I drink too much coffee. Only native Seattle-ites—which I'm not—can drink six gallons of this a day and thrive on it. I'm going down in the basement for a while.''

Now what have I done? Beth thought in dismay. *Everything was so perfect before Kayla crashed into our lives. What is happening to us, Lord?* Doug had been, at fifty-plus, wandering around the country, painting his beautiful landscapes, lonely, with an unsuccessful marriage and a problem daughter behind him. She herself had been widowed, with a near loveless marriage behind her, running her small business, lonely. And somehow they had come together, found one another and with it their wonderful September love, their second chance at happiness. It had been so…so good, so perfect. Then Kayla had come, with her confused little boy clinging desperately to her billowing green-and-white skirt. And now, somehow—what was happening? They were worried, stressed, snapping at each other, critical of each other.

Oh, dear God, help me. I can't lose this. I can't.

Shaking, Beth got up and hurried down the basement steps. "Doug! Doug!"

He was seated on his workbench, leaning over with his head bowed. "Doug, what are we doing?" she asked, feeling close to tears.

He sprang up and took her in his arms. "Oh, Beth, I don't know," he said, holding her close.

She buried her face in his shoulder. "We can't let this—this difficulty—come between us. I'm sorry. I'm sorry."

"I'm sorry, too," he muttered into her hair. "Don't apologize, Beth. If anybody should apologize, it's me. And no, we mustn't let this come between us. People cope with problems all the time. We can cope. We *can*." There was desperation in his voice. "I've coped with problems all my life. So have you. We can do this—whatever happens—without letting it change our lives."

"No, we can't let it change anything." Beth realized her tone was almost pleading, and she didn't really know whom she was pleading with. She raised her face, knowing Doug's kiss would block out everything else.

Then—from somewhere came the errant thought. *Where's Adam? What's Adam doing upstairs in those big, empty rooms?* Perhaps the same question had occurred to Doug, too, because he released her.

"We'd better go up—at least, I'd better go up. Adam's all by himself in the bed-sitter. He's been awfully quiet," she said.

"I'll come with you. I can't help but feel I'm imposing on you. Kayla and Adam—they're really my problems, and they both *need* so much."

Arm in arm, as if they couldn't let go of one another, they went up to the bed-sitter. It was empty. Some of the toys were on the floor near the toy box, and the curtain above the window seat was askew.

"Adam," Beth called out. "Where are you, sweetie?"

There was no answer. Doug made it to the front door in a split second and tried the handle. "This is tight. He couldn't have gone out this way, anyhow. He probably couldn't reach the knob. Adam?" he called. Then they started to look in all the downstairs rooms.

Self-doubt flitted through Beth's mind. *Can I do this, God? Am I too old at fifty to keep up with a lively, unpredictable little three-year-old boy, and also run my business?* Oh, surely not. Fifty isn't old anymore.

Not having found Adam in any of the downstairs rooms, they started up the big stairway off the entry hall.

"Adam?" Doug called loudly. "I'm glad all the guests are out," he muttered to Beth.

"Well, they aren't," Beth said. "Poor Mr. Jessup is sick, remember?"

"Oh, yes," Doug said contritely. "I hope he wasn't trying to sleep."

"Gamma Beff?" Adam's little voice came to them, and he peeked out the door of the Jessups' room. Oh, he was in with poor, sick Mr. Jessup. Beth felt embarrassed color rising to her face.

Doug gave a soft knock at the door and stuck his head in.

"I'm awfully sorry, Mr. Jessup. It seems my little grandson…" He paused and went into the room, and Beth followed.

"That's okay," Mr. Jessup said in a faint, rasping whisper. "I thought he just stopped in for a social call. Hi," he added when he saw Beth. "But he's not comfortable with chitchat, is he. I said hello, but he didn't answer. Just stood there with that funny little frown on his face.''

Beth looked at Mr. Jessup in dismay. *He's awfully sick,* she thought suddenly. Much sicker than she had thought. He even appeared to have lost weight, and he looked so gaunt. His color was more gray than suntanned as a rancher's face should be. Could his flu have turned into pneumonia?

"How are you feeling?" she asked, going quickly to his bedside. She was aware that Doug had picked Adam up and was holding him.

"Not too good," Mr. Jessup said. It seemed a great effort for him to speak. "Do you... do you happen to know where my wife went?"

"No, I don't. I'm sorry. She just said she had to get out for a bit. I got her a cab. Do you mind if I feel your pulse?" She had taken a first-aid course when she first decided to start a B and B business. Emergencies did happen, and she had wanted to be as prepared as she could be.

"Sure," he whispered. "If you can find it. Be my guest. I'm sorry about all this. I don't want to be a problem."

"You're not a problem. Not at all," Beth said, feeling for his pulse. She paused in silence, trying to count. The pulse was there, but thready. She let go of his wrist.

"Mr. Jessup, don't you think this is more serious than you first thought?"

"Yeah, I'm afraid so. I was hoping my wife..." His voice lost power again, and he was whispering. "I have medical insurance, if you know a doctor."

"Yes," Beth said briskly. "I do. Do you want me to call him?"

"Please. I guess I'm about to give up on this vacation. We'd allowed our regular two weeks. One for driving back and forth to the ranch, and one for our annual big-city event. I sure messed this up..." Even his whisper failed now, and he stopped trying to talk.

"If they want to take you to the hospital, would you go?" Beth asked.

Mr. Jessup nodded.

"Where's your insurance card?" she asked. "In case it has any restrictions."

He gestured to the bedside table, and Beth took up his billfold. "All right if I open it?"

He nodded again. There was a film of perspiration on his face and his breathing was more labored. She hurried out into the hall. As she reached the hall phone, it rang. She did something she almost never did. She picked up the receiver and put it down again quickly, cutting off the incoming call so she could use the line. If it was a potential guest, she was sorry, but her current guest needed medical help and soon. She dialed the doctor's office. She was aware that Doug had stayed in Mr. Jessup's room, still close to the door, talking easily, reassuringly, with Mr. Jessup.

The doctor wasn't available, but Beth explained what she had observed to the nurse. Together they concluded that Mr. Jessup needed to be in the hospital.

"And his insurance card authorizes hospital stays in a strange city," Beth said. "He and his wife are traveling." They quickly made the arrangements, and Beth hung up.

"They're sending an ambulance," Beth said, standing at Mr. Jessup's door. "It'll be here in a few minutes. My husband would have taken you down, but in this weather an ambulance will be better."

"Thanks very much," Mr. Jessup said in his rasping whisper. "If my wife doesn't get back before..."

"Don't worry," Beth assured him. "I'll tell her where you are."

The phone rang again, and, with a gesture of irritation, Beth went to answer it. It was Kate.

"Guess what," Kate said. "Raymond was upset again about the school uniform thing. He said—"

"Listen, Kate," Beth interrupted. Not Katie nit-picking again! This was too much! "I have a sick guest, and we're waiting for the ambulance. Can I call you back?"

"Oh, sure, Mom. I'm sorry," Kate said immediately, and rang off.

Beth sighed in exasperation, then looked at Doug, still holding Adam. At least her girls didn't have the problems that Kayla did....

They heard the whine of the siren outside and hurried downstairs to admit the ambulance attendants.

Fortunately, Mrs. Jessup came back just as her husband was being settled inside the ambulance, and was told of the emergency. She was grateful to Beth.

"How can I ever thank you?" she said, sounding a bit teary. "When I left, I thought he was all right."

"Don't worry about a thing," Beth reassured her. "You go on down to the hospital with him. Let me give you a key so you can get in when you come back—it doesn't matter how late."

When they finally had gone, she and Doug took Adam back into the bed-sitter. She was feeling a small glow of satisfaction. She had never worked during her long marriage to Ralph Bennett. She had started her B and B business after his death, to supplement her widow's pension. She had never known the satisfaction of doing a job and doing it well. It was a good feeling.

"You're looking pleased," Doug said, smiling, as he put Adam down on the window seat.

"I am pleased. I'm sorry Mr. Jessup is sick—it ruined their vacation—but I do like this work. It's always a challenge."

"It suits you," he said easily. "You're a natural hostess."

She sat down beside him on the sofa-bed couch. They were both looking fondly at Adam. He had pushed aside the curtain and was looking out into the still-wet world.

"Mommy come back?"

"Not yet," Beth said. What was she going to do about Adam? How did you explain to a three-year-old child that he mustn't go around into the bedrooms and glower at the guests? Poor little mite. His world was so confused.

"Beth," Doug said, "can we talk about…" He gestured toward the window seat and the little watcher still staring out.

"Of course," she murmured, feeling suddenly hopeful. She had wanted for some time to talk, *really* talk, with Doug about Kayla and Adam.

"I get this kind of sick feeling," Doug said. "I hope… I hope that things go right, but at the same time I…dread the time when, if things do go right, we might see the last of him. I'd hate to not know where he was, how he was doing, if—" He stopped.

Doug was right. The angry, confused little boy had somehow touched her heart, too.

She took his hand. "Me, too. I think we mentioned before, that if things do go right, maybe they could stay here in Seattle so we could…" So they could what? What was she getting herself into?

"Yeah, I agree with that. And if and when the time comes, I'd exert any influence I had to keep them from going off into the world somewhere so we…wouldn't *know* how things were going. I would *need* to know, Beth. How he was doing. If he was okay or not."

So he realized it, too. Kayla's instability couldn't be discounted. Even if she were successful in this new effort, could she *stay* successful? What about Adam? Suddenly Beth couldn't bear the thought of Adam somewhere, frightened, confused, clinging to some thrift-shop skirt as Kayla wandered on.

"I really love that little boy," Beth said thoughtfully. "I don't think I could stand it if…if we lost track of him. If we didn't know he was all right."

"Me, too," Doug said softly, a sigh in his voice.

"I was thinking I'd like to try next Sunday, or the next, to see if he's ready to mix in with other children at Sunday school." Or was this wrong? Was she starting to give Adam a life, only to have Kayla snatch it away?

"You could try it," Doug said without hesitation. "He should learn to be with other kids. Learn to play. I don't think the little guy ever has learned to play."

Beth knew he was right. *What kind of world was it when a child didn't know how to play?*

"He needs that," she said firmly. "It's part of learning. I've noticed that he doesn't have much vocabulary. He should be talking more. He—" She stopped, uncertain how much she could say without offending Doug.

"I agree," he answered. "And I'm sorry I got childish about painting another Shilshole Bay scene. If I have a talent worth money, I should use it and not be such a nitwit. And if I'm right about his highness there, if he gets as far as college, I have a good hunch about who's going to have to pay for it. You do realize, don't you, my love, that I have a responsibility with this?"

"*We* have a responsibility," Beth corrected. "Your life is my life." She would have continued, but the phone rang again. She got up quickly to answer it, instinctively assuming her perfect hostess voice. She loved her small business and nothing—absolutely nothing—would ever take it away from her.

For most of the following week things went smoothly. For one thing, the weather cleared and Doug was able to resume work on another painting of Shilshole Bay. He worked hard at it, and Beth concentrated on preparing Adam for next Sunday's attempt to get him accustomed to being with other children.

In between the many tasks of running her business, she *made* time to talk with Adam, trying to really communicate at his limited level. He was a bright child who simply hadn't had a normal enough life to allow for adequate development. It was a pleasant, peaceful time with Kayla gone. It seemed—somehow or other—things would work out. It seemed—somehow or other—Kayla would succeed in rehab. If Kayla didn't succeed in rehab, then—somehow or other—Kayla would be elsewhere. But Adam would be all right. Somehow or other. Life was too good to waste the lovely spring days on worry.

Mr. Jessup came out of the hospital in time for them to embark on the drive back to their ranch.

"I guess you'll write off Seattle as a big-city holiday," Beth said, laughing as she checked them out.

"Not on your life," Mrs. Jessup said. "We'll try again next year if you'll put us up again."

Beth watched them go with a happy heart. She loved this work. Adam was doing well; he was more secure, talking better and not so restless during the night. Doug was working on his painting. She successfully tackled making the breakfast minimuffins herself because Kate was temporarily unable to do the B and B baking. Using Kate's recipes, she found she could do just as well. Although it meant more work for her, she managed to fit it all in.

Adam came through like a champion at his first entry into social life with his peers at Sunday school. He only got into one battle with another three-year-old. They fought over one of the colorful Sunday school books. Adam did love books.

"Well," Doug said philosophically, "I hope the other

little kid doesn't have a black eye. The flip side is it may indicate that Adam is a potential book lover. That would be good. I mean, I think it would be good.''

Beth laughed. ''Adam's going to be fine,'' she assured him. ''I can see him in years to come. He may be the family's first Rhodes Scholar or something else impressive.''

She felt optimistic about Adam. He was responding, as all children will, to the affection and attention he was receiving. It seemed to center on the bed-sitter, which he considered his home base. He was somewhat possessive about his half of the closet.

Doug had brought up a small bookcase from the basement for Adam's growing collection of books. She and Doug had both bought him books. Beth fell into the habit of rushing through her work on Tuesdays so she could take Adam to the library to hear the storytelling lady. He was fascinated. The top of his bookcase was reserved for his two greatest treasures. They were the card with the gold stars stuck on it to show how many times he went to Sunday school, and his plastic library card. There was one small battle. He had to accept the fact that he had to give books *back* to the library so he could get more. But Beth was able to get him through this little crisis.

Without actually discussing it, she realized that she and Doug were accepting that Adam could become a permanent part of their lives, an ongoing responsibility. She assured herself it wasn't something to worry about.

On Sundays during Coffee Hour, Pastor Cooper never failed to ask about Kayla, and Beth knew, with a sinking heart, that Doug had been right about him.

''Yeah, he's smitten all right,'' Doug said, driving home one Sunday.

And Beth said nothing in response. There was nothing she could say. Instead, she changed the subject.

"How many weeks has Kayla been in the rehab center now?"

"Five. Things must be going well," Doug said contentedly.

"I think you told me she could have visitors and calls after six weeks, didn't you?"

"Yes. I'm planning to go over next week. See if she needs more pocket money or anything else. Have you any ideas?"

"Not really. Give her my best, of course." It was going to work. She felt a great sense of happiness, mainly on Doug's behalf. He would be so disappointed if Kayla failed again.

So it was a double shock on Monday, the beginning of Kayla's sixth week, to get a phone call from Dr. Hanson, the facility's director, asking for Mr. Colby.

"Mr. Colby isn't here. I'm Mrs. Colby. Can I help you?" Beth said, her heart starting to beat faster.

"Yes, of course. And perhaps you'll talk to Mr. Colby when he returns. I'm more sorry than I can say, but his daughter Kayla has left the institute. She wasn't in her room this morning, and her bed hadn't been slept in. I was rather hoping she had gone back to her father. I take it she hasn't?"

"No, she hasn't come here," Beth said, her mouth feeling dry. *Adam. What about Adam?* "What…what do you suggest we do?"

"Do you know who her friends are here in Seattle? Do you know if she would have gone to anyone?"

"No. She doesn't have any friends here," Beth explained. "She knows almost no one. The last time she gave up and dropped out of the program, she came here. And she hasn't," she added, feeling queasy.

"I see," he said thoughtfully. "Will you have Mr. Colby

call me when he returns? Perhaps he'll have some ideas. We try to work with parent or guardian if we can, but since Kayla is over twenty-one, it's difficult.''

"Yes, of course. I'll...I'll talk to Mr. Colby, and he'll get back to you," Beth promised, knowing her voice sounded bleak.

"One other thing," Dr. Hanson added, almost as an afterthought. "She did have a friend here, another patient—also missing. I'm not sure I should mention it, but perhaps it might help, if you also know the person."

"No, I don't. I have no idea who she knows there, or who she has made friends with in the Institute. I suppose you can't give me a name, can you?"

"I'm sorry, no," Dr. Hanson said firmly.

Beth hung up the phone feeling annoyed. It might have helped if Dr. Hanson had told her, but she supposed it came under the doctor-patient confidentiality rules. Everything seemed too complicated.

She and Doug had a bad evening staying near the phone and the front door. Two guests checked in about five and went out for the evening after they'd put their luggage in their room. Doug was pacing. Beth could feel his anxiety about Kayla.

At eight o'clock Beth put Adam to bed and rejoined Doug for their vigil. Where was Kayla? Would she come back? It was maddening. Finally, at about eleven, they gave up and went to bed.

At three o'clock the bedside phone shrilled. Beth felt Doug jerk awake beside her. He snatched up the phone. Why did phones sound so piercing in the small hours of the morning? She sat up, snapping on the bedside light, listening to his side of the conversation.

"Yes, this is Mr. Colby. I can't hear you. Can you speak

up? Yes. Okay. Yes, all right. Who is this? Yes, of course.'' He was silent for a time. Once more he said, ''Please speak louder. Okay, will you repeat that?'' He had begun writing something on the bedside notepad. ''All right. Yes, a light would be helpful. Thank you.'' Slowly he hung up the phone and turned to Beth.

''Was that Kayla?'' she asked, trying to keep the dread out of her tone.

''No. It was somebody called Wanda. Apparently she's the friend Kayla made in rehab, the other patient. It appears they left *together*. This Wanda person called to tell me that she and Kayla decided to abandon the program. And they just took off! She sounded quite drunk. She said she and Kayla are staying with friends. I suppose she means her own friends. Anyhow, she thinks I should come get Kayla. She gave me an address.'' He held out the slip of paper.

Beth looked at it. ''That's not a very good neighborhood, Doug. Why does she want you to come and get Kayla?''

''It was rather garbled. I gather the friendship is being somewhat strained at this point. It seems Wanda had a boy-friend—that's where they are staying. And now Wanda seems to feel that Kayla is…well, it seems that three's a crowd now and she wants Kayla to leave.''

''Didn't Kayla want to?'' Beth asked uncertainly. Now what?

Doug smiled grimly. ''To put it in Wanda's somewhat indelicate manner of speaking, 'Your daughter's out cold. Come and get her!' So apparently they've both celebrated and had a few too many. Well, I'd better go.'' He got up.

''But, Doug, that's a bad neighborhood. Maybe you should call Ian or Greg—have one of them go with you.''

''Nonsense. Your husband may be over the hill, but don't forget I'm a fairly big guy. Thugs seldom attack the big guys. Plus, I did my bit in the military. I can handle a brawl if it comes to that. Don't worry, love.''

Beth sat huddled in the bed, watching him as he dressed quickly. Yes, Doug could probably take care of himself in *any* brawl. Scrambling into her robe, she went downstairs with him in the silent house and saw him out the front door. She shut it quietly behind him, willing herself to remain calm.

She wanted to scream.

Adam! Somehow I must protect Adam's little world. With his books. And his gold stars. And his library card. Dear God, it was little enough.

Chapter Ten

Beth went into the bed-sitter. She looked down at Adam, sprawled in deep sleep in the middle of the big sofa bed. He looked so little. So innocent. So defenseless. There was a feeling of dread in her stomach.

Kayla is coming back.

She should probably feel some guilt about this, because Kayla needed help as much as Adam did, but try as she would, she could feel little sympathy for Kayla. Kayla was a user, a loser. She was a threat to her own child's well-being. And—because of Doug's feeling about the situation—she could be a threat to their perfect life.

No! Never! Nothing must threaten my marriage to Doug! Somehow she would need to cope with Kayla's return. Beth went to the wall phone and quietly dialed the church's number. The office would be closed now, of course, but she could leave a message on the answering machine. When the mechanical sound of Bessie's voice finished speaking in her ear, Beth said very quietly, "This is Beth Colby. Will you ask Pastor Cooper to give me a call, Bessie? Thank you." *Help me,* she was pleading in her mind. *Help me, God.* She went to the kitchen table and sat on one of the stools. The only sound was the ticking of the kitchen clock.

It was almost four, too early to start any preparation for breakfast. Vaguely she thought about going back upstairs to dress, but didn't move. There came the sound of gentle spring rain outside. It was an oddly comforting sound. Good old Seattle night rains. It would be gone before day-light, leaving the streets and sidewalk cleanly washed and the lawns and gardens nicely watered.

Then she heard the dripping sounding on the service porch. Oh, no. Not another leak in the roof!

Hurriedly she got up and went onto the service porch, which protruded from the house, sheltered by its own roof. As soon as she stepped onto it, she felt water under her feet. In one motion she snatched up a bucket and placed it under the leak. It was not exactly a stream, but would be before the day was over. It meant more of the ugly blue tarp, if they could get emergency help from the roofing company. What next? This was going to cost even *more* money they couldn't really afford. Then, suddenly, the rec-ollection sprang into her mind. She had had two offers for the flourishing B and B. And one had been a firm offer—from a middle-aged couple who had taken early retirement and then regretted it. They had wanted—intensely—to have some work to do. *No! Never! Never would she sell her B and B!*

She might as well go up and get dressed, she thought angrily, but going back into the kitchen she was startled to see the guest from the back bedroom, Mr. McCormack. He was an elderly ginger-haired man who had come to Seattle to settle an estate matter.

"I'm sorry," he said quickly. "I didn't mean to startle you. Ah, I see you've got the same problem." He had no-ticed the mop bucket as she shut the service porch door.

"I'm afraid I've got a leaky ceiling. I came down looking for a pot or something." He seemed quite good-natured about it, and Beth felt a flush of embarrassment rise to her face.

"I'm so sorry," she said. "Here, let me get you something. There's another bucket." She opened the back door again to get it. A leak in the back bedroom, too? That was the part not protected by the blue tarp. *We can't afford a whole new roof.*

"Do you mind if I go up with you? I'd like to see what…what damage—''

"I don't think it's real damage," he assured her, reaching for the bucket. "The carpet on that side is soaked, but it's just clean rainwater. Could that do damage?"

"I suppose not," she said, "and I have one of those carpet cleaners that sucks up water, but I can't use it before everyone's up and gone. It's so loud it'd raise the dead, which I don't think anyone would appreciate."

Together they went up to the back bedroom and placed the bucket under the steady *drip, drip, drip* from the ceiling.

"That should do it. I'm a light sleeper or I wouldn't even have noticed it," Mr. McCormack said.

"I'm so sorry," she said again. "I'll give you our off-season discount rate—''

"Nonsense. Don't worry about it. Life's full of interesting little challenges. I'll be fine now. And I'll see that the bucket doesn't overflow, I promise."

Back in her own room, Beth took a quick shower and dressed. Where was Doug? Surely he should be coming back soon with Kayla.

Kayla. Her heart sank. Adam was doing so well. And what would this failure do to Kayla's already low self-esteem?

It was almost five-thirty before she heard Doug coming back. She had just started the breakfast preparations. Breakfast hours were eight until ten. She opened the back door and went down the back steps to meet them. The predawn air was chilly.

"Are you all right? Is Kayla all right?" she asked as she saw them get out of the car. Doug was helping Kayla, who was staggering and weaving.

Doug looked grim. "I guess you could say we are all right," he said. Then to Kayla, he said, "Watch it, dear. There are steps."

"Okay," Kayla said agreeably, "I can do steps." And holding on to her father, she managed fairly well. "Hi, Beth. It's the bad penny coming back. Sorry about that." She looked half asleep.

"I'll get her into the bed-sitter," Doug said, sounding embarrassed and apologetic. "I see we've got another leak," he added, noticing the filling bucket on the porch.

"And one in the back bedroom. Mr. McCormack reported it a while ago."

"Two leaks, huh?" Doug added. "Looks like the beginning of another perfect day."

Feeling helpless and trying to hide her disgust, Beth followed them. In the bed-sitter Adam was still sleeping deeply, and Kayla headed for the broad window seat.

"Love that window seat," she said. "Good old window seat." She collapsed onto the long padded cushion, saying in a singsong tone, "Oh, lovely, lovely, lovely," and promptly fell asleep.

Both Doug and Beth looked at her. In a moment she curled up like a child, her blond hair tousled, her lovely face flushed.

"What do you think?" Doug asked. "Should she just sleep there?" He turned to Beth. His eyes looked so sad and defeated that she wanted to cry.

"Why not? She looks quite comfortable. I'll get a blanket and pillow.'' She did, and covered Kayla, carefully tucking a pillow under her head. Kayla gave a gusty sigh and seemed content.

Since there seemed nothing more they could do, both Doug and Beth went back into the kitchen. ''I'm fresh out of ideas,'' Doug said.

''I am, too,'' Beth answered. ''I left a message for Pastor Cooper to call, but…''

''Maybe he'll have some ideas. She's failed twice at the rehab center. She can't handle the AA program. What else is there? And I—'' He stopped, his head and shoulders bowed in defeat.

''And you what?'' Beth prompted.

''Beth, I can't keep imposing on you with this. It's my problem. I can't turn her out—there's Adam to think of, as well as Kayla.''

''Don't be silly. You're not imposing on me. I'm your wife. If you have a problem, I share it. If I had a problem, you'd share it, without any question. So don't talk about imposing.'' In her sudden panic, she had spoken more sharply than she had intended, and he glanced up, startled.

''I didn't mean to snap your head off,'' she added with a forced smile, and he reached out, took her hand and kissed it.

''What kind of place was it, where she was staying?'' Beth asked.

''You were right. It's a crummy neighborhood. This Wanda—Wilson's her last name. Wanda Wilson had gone to 'crash,' as she put it, at her boyfriend's house. His name is John something—Hull, I think she said. He's apparently unemployed at the moment and living with his parents. I think he may have a drinking problem, too. Incidentally, they didn't seem too pleased at the arrival of two new houseguests. We had an uncomfortable few minutes until I assured them I was there to take one of their sudden houseguests off their hands. Then things lightened up some-what.''

''Oh, what an unpleasant situation.''

''You could say that. It seems that John plans to marry Wanda. His parents had sprung for the price of the rehab in the faint hope that their son's bride would be sober when the big day came around. We were a pretty glum crowd. So I got my daughter and got out as fast as I could.''

They were halfway through the breakfast preparations when Adam came running into the kitchen in his pajamas, his face radiant. ''Mommy's back! Mommy's back! Mommy's by the window! Mommy's back!'' He caught at Beth's skirt. ''Come see! Come see!''

''Not now, sweetheart. When I get through here. Is Mommy still sleeping?''

''Yeah, sleeping.'' Then he ran to Doug. ''Mommy's back.''

''Yep, buddy, I know. How about we go and get you dressed?'' He stooped and picked up the delighted little boy.

Beth suppressed a sigh but said nothing as she realized that she would finish the breakfast preparations by herself. She managed to do so, feeling somewhat harried as the guests started coming down. Were all the salt shakers filled? Did everyone have water? Where was the carafe of pineapple juice that was supposed to be put on the buffet between the orange juice and the tomato juice? Still in the fridge? She rushed back into the kitchen to get it. She hadn't realized how much work Doug had taken over since their marriage.

The rain had cleared before the guests finished breakfast, and as they all started out on their day's adventures, one of Seattle's brilliant spring days had begun.

''You know,'' Doug said as he helped put dishes into

the dishwasher, "as soon as I get in touch with the roof guy again, I'll go down to Shilshole to work on the painting, if you don't mind."

"Of course," Beth said quickly. When Kayla woke up, it might be better if Doug were out of the house. Adam was so happy, she didn't want another Kayla-Doug quarrel to start.

Adam had been trotting back and forth between the bedsitter and the kitchen, reporting. "Mommy's still asleep." As Doug left, to distract Adam and perhaps let Kayla sleep undisturbed, Beth took Adam upstairs with her for the bed-making tasks.

It was almost eleven when they came back down, and they found Kayla seated hunched over the kitchen table. She looked sick.

"Oh, Beth, I'm sorry. I'm really sorry. I don't know what you must think. Hi, baby," she added to Adam as he ran to her. Tiredly, she leaned over to pick him up and hold him.

"Have you had anything to eat?" Beth asked, although she really didn't want to know.

"Forget eating for a while, okay?" Kayla said. "Is Dad

around?"

"No. It's such a great day, he went out to paint. I do think you should have something. Coffee, maybe?"

"Maybe later, okay?"

"Mommy, you come back," Adam said, trying to get Kayla's attention.

"Look, baby, Mommy doesn't feel too good. You go play or something." She pushed him off her lap, and he backed away, looking up at her, frowning slightly.

Beth sat down across from her, reaching out to Adam. He went over to her, and she picked him up to hold him.

"Did it just get too...difficult?" Beth asked awkwardly.

She felt confused, out of her depth. How in the world should she handle this?

Kayla sighed. "That's as good a reason as any, I guess. It was a mistake to come here. Dad's going to be furious, and I must admit he's entitled to be." Her voice had taken on a note of harshness.

"What are you going to do?" Beth asked. "I mean what else is there to do?"

"Good question. What else is there? I'm kind of at the end of my rope. What I should probably do is pack up my kid and get out before Dad comes back. Save a big row with him."

Panic rushed through Beth. *No, don't take Adam away!* She must talk to Doug, make sure there wouldn't be a quarrel.

Kayla looked up. "Beth, bring me up to date. How did I get back here? I was with my friend Wanda, this girl I met in rehab. We hit it off from the first. I really like her. She's smart. Independent. Nobody takes advantage of Wanda. I learned a lot from her. Did she and what's-his-name, her boyfriend, drop me off here? The last I remember was he picked us up about a block from the rehab place. Then we sort of celebrated awhile. He had visited her, and they had set it up for her to leave. She asked me if I'd had enough of the stupid place, and I had, so she let me tag along."

"Wanda called here last night," Beth explained. "Actually, it was early this morning. She talked to your father and…" Beth paused. How much should she say? "It was arranged that he would come and pick you up from where they lived. I think he said the boyfriend—John Hull, I believe his name is—was staying with his parents."

"I don't remember that," Kayla said vaguely. "I have these kind of blackouts."

"Anyway," Beth said briskly, "Doug went over to get

you, and brought you home." Adam stirred in her lap and she released her hold on him, so he slid down and ran out of the kitchen. Somehow she must keep Kayla from taking Adam and running away again. She *must*. But that meant Kayla must stay. She felt she was in some dark tunnel with no way out.

"So that's how it happened," Kayla murmured. "Was Dad very mad?"

"Disappointed," Beth said carefully. "But when things don't work out, it is a disappointment, of course. Then we just need to think of something else."

Adam came running back into the kitchen holding his gold-star card from Sunday school.

"See, Mommy?" He held it up with one hand and held up four fingers with his other. "Four. Four stars."

"That's fine, honey. Beth, what's he talking about?"

"I've been teaching him to count, and we started taking him to Sunday school. He gets a gold star every time he attends."

Kayla looked at the card he was showing her so proudly. "Well, that's just great. You're a good boy," she said, and Adam beamed up at her. His world was right again. For the moment.

Beth almost gritted her teeth. *Love your child,* her mind railed silently. *Love your little boy. He's starving for your love.* She got up quickly from the table and went to the refrigerator, fearful that Kayla might see something in her expression. She opened the door and took out a carafe of orange juice.

"Wouldn't you just like to drink some orange juice?" she asked.

"Actually, I think milk might be better, if you have any," Kayla said. Beth put back the juice and took out a quart of the whole milk she had been buying for Adam. She poured out a glass and set it before Kayla. Kayla picked it up, her hand shaking slightly, and took a sip. She shivered slightly and put the glass down. "I know I should eat something," she said dully. Then, almost grimly, she took another sip of milk.

"Cookie?" Adam asked hopefully of Beth.

She couldn't help smiling. "Okay, but just one," she told him. "I don't want you to spoil your lunch. See? Look at the clock. When both hands get up here it's time for lunch."

She had to get out. She must call Doug. Pushing down the feeling of panic, she left the kitchen after putting Adam at the table opposite Kayla.

Upstairs, with the bedroom door shut, she dialed Doug's cell phone. He answered almost immediately.

"Hi, love, what's up?" He sounded anxious.

"I needed to talk to you. We've agreed that we've got to look after Adam, and I'm worried. Kayla's up and we were talking, and she's about to give up completely. She said something about taking Adam and leaving."

"Oh, no! We can't let that happen!"

Suddenly, Beth recalled something that Pastor Cooper had said to her. "Listen, I've just thought of something. Once at Coffee Hour at church, Pastor Cooper said something about the 'rights' of grandparents. I think we should follow that up, don't you?"

"Absolutely. Much as I hate to admit it, my darling daughter is a basket case when it comes to motherhood. We've got to protect Adam somehow. Maybe we can go that route if we have to."

Beth breathed a sigh of relief. At least they were in agreement on this. "I left a message on the church answering machine for him to call me, but he hasn't yet."

"Good idea. I think I'll come home, too. It's about my feeding time and, beautiful day or not, I can't seem to keep my mind on what I'm doing. I'm using up a lot of turp rubbing out things I just painted in."

"Come on home, then. I'll start lunch." She tried not to sound as hopeless as she felt.

At Beth's urging Kayla stayed in the kitchen and ate lunch with them, but didn't seem to have much appetite. Doug said nothing about her having left rehab again, which made Beth breathe easier. She wasn't sure whether he did it to protect Adam from getting upset or because he wanted to wait until they had talked with Pastor Cooper. When they finished, Adam slid down from his place and wandered off. It was almost his nap time, and sometimes he was reluctant to nap when he wanted to do something else. As soon as he was gone, Kayla spoke to her father.

"Dad, I'm sorry I blew it again. I was talking to Beth a while ago. You've both been great, but maybe I'd better just call it quits—nothing's working out the way I'd planned. I hate to burden you both for no reason. It's coming on to summer. I know some people in New England who have a big lodge-type place. They cater to people who spend winters in Florida and summers on Cape Cod. I think I can get a job there. I did before. They gave me a little cottage where I could keep Adam. He's about big enough to leave on his own when I'm working. He could play around on the beach and…stuff." Her voice trailed off.

"He's too little!" Beth exclaimed before she could stop herself. The idea of three-year-old Adam "playing around on the beach" by himself appalled her. Adam, without any library books he so loved. Adam, not having his card with his gold stars. Adam, picking up bits of discarded picnic food to eat. Adam, getting knocked down by a sudden wave. *No. Please!* Beth got up quickly and started to clear the dishes off the table. For the first time since Kayla had come she wanted to *hit* her, smack her across the face. *No! You will not take Adam away and ruin his life!*

Doug spoke, using a calm and reasonable tone. "I don't see that working, Kayla. Not yet. He's just too young to leave on his own. Are you drinking now? Have you had anything to drink today?"

Beth hadn't expected him to add that. She turned from the dishwasher in surprise, to see embarrassed color rise to Kayla's pretty face.

"You got it, Dad. Wanda's boyfriend, that John something, when he came to pick us up, gave us each a bottle of vodka to stash in our purses. He said it was a 'getting-out' present."

Doug reached out to take Kayla's hand. "What makes you think you could make it work out this time, Kayla?" His voice was gentle, and Kayla's eyes filled with tears.

"Well, I guess I don't *know*. I guess I'm just, well, hoping."

"Can we wait awhile on that?" he suggested.

Beth made herself keep quiet, but her mind was screaming, *No, Doug. Don't let her con you.*

Kayla's tears spilled over. "But we've tried, Dad. You and Beth..." She bowed her head and started to sob, then picked up her napkin and blotted at her face. "Look, I'm a mess. Can we talk about it later? I'll go put Adam down for his nap. I could use a nap myself. Okay?"

"Okay," Doug said. "It's still only spring. Let's give it a few more weeks, shall we?"

"Look," Beth said, going back to the table. "If you want to try to work in New England this summer, what's wrong with going ahead and trying it and leaving Adam here? Maybe later, when he's older..." Her voice faltered. She wasn't sure where she was going, but went on. "In a year or so he'll need to start in preschool. I mean..." *Let us keep him here awhile longer. Protect his little world until he might be better able to protect it himself. Buy Adam some time.*

` "Sure," Doug said, taking his cue. "We don't need to decide everybody's fate this minute."

Kayla looked from one to the other, puzzled. Then an odd look—almost sly—came and went quickly in the wet blue eyes. Beth's heart sank. Befuddled, confused, mixed-up, Kayla had suddenly got the message that her father and his wife cared about Adam—and how could she, Kayla, use this? Kayla's own words echoed in Beth's mind. *"We drunks usually try a con first…"*

Kayla gulped and her rare smile came like sunshine. She was actually beautiful when she smiled. "You two are the greatest. Just the greatest," she gushed. "Okay, then, I'll go round up my kid and we'll head for slumberland. I love you both." Still blotting at her face, she got up from the table and fairly ran from the room.

Doug breathed a sigh of relief. "That was close. I guess my tough love effort backfired, if it makes her want to give up and leave."

Knees suddenly weak, Beth sat down at the table. "Doug, we cannot let that happen. I couldn't stand not knowing where Adam was, or what he was doing. And suppose she gets the job again—could she hold it? She's mentioned that she had been fired from some jobs."

"No," Doug said grimly. "Kayla can't hold a job. Did Pastor Cooper call back, by any chance?"

"Yes, he did. He said he'd stop by—didn't know exactly when, but probably this afternoon. He had one meeting to go to, which he thought might not last too long."

"Maybe we could talk Kayla into counseling…or something. Maybe her failures, her needs, is why he feels attracted to her. I think our pastor is one of the world's helpers. He wants to mend all the broken people. And Kayla certainly qualifies."

"Maybe so." But Beth was doubtful. "If we could keep Adam for just a few years, until…" she continued uncertainly. How in the world could they salvage Adam—without Kayla? There seemed no way except— Startled at her own thought, she tried to keep her face expressionless. Unless she had been wrong about Pastor Cooper and Kayla. Suppose, just suppose— Sharply, she brought herself back to what Doug was saying.

"Yeah, maybe until Adam's up to, well, latchkey age. An age where he can sort of…"

Where he can sort of what? Beth thought. *Until maybe he's ten and needs some help with his homework but there's nobody there to help? Or maybe when he's thirteen and he starts skipping school and thinking of dropping out and nobody notices? Or maybe when other kids start offering him drugs, and he learns that, on drugs, life is less painful? Buy Adam some time, but how much time is enough for a child at risk? Twenty, thirty years from now Adam, the man, will be the direct result of Adam, the child, surviving his childhood. Will he, or will he not, learn the joy of achieving by starting with his little gold stars? Will he, or will he not, stay in school and reach his potential because he had help with his homework when he needed it? Will he, or will he not, learn right from wrong because there was someone there to teach him? Somewhere in the depths of Beth's mind there sounded the dim echo of Cyrus's voice when he was in the hospital. "When you do it for the least of these, you do it for Me."*

Across the table Doug gave a little shiver.

"What is it?" Beth asked.

"I hate to admit it, but all of a sudden I'm scared to death."

"Me, too," Beth said.

The roofers came about an hour later with another load of blue tarp to cover more of the roof. Doug went out to talk to them while Beth prepared the snack she knew they would expect. When they had gone, she and Doug discussed the roof, able for a time to push away the Kayla and Adam problem.

Seated at the kitchen table, Doug handed her a sheet of paper folded over. "'If you have tears, prepare to shed them now.' That's a quote from Shakespeare. Remember I used to make some speeches to curriculum committees selling school books."

"What is it?" Beth said, taking the sheet of paper.

"It's the roofing guys' estimate for a new roof."

"A new *roof*." she gasped. "You mean a *whole* new roof?"

"A whole new roof. As he was struggling with the tarp on this lovely sunny, windy day, he said—well, I'll clean it up a bit, since I'm speaking to a lady. He said we can't make do much longer with patches on patches on patches. It took him more than half an hour to figure out his estimate, and he was using a calculator at the time."

Beth unfolded the sheet and gave a low moan. "This can't be right, Doug."

"I'm afraid it is. That's exactly what I said when I first saw it, and then he explained."

"How could he explain this? It's a fortune."

"He did explain it. If you go out in front and look at this house—it's a showplace. It's a beautiful, big, elegant old home. It has large rooms. And it all had to have a roof over it. Not to mention that it's not a nice, flat, cheap roof, but has all those ups and downs—I forget what he called them. Just those dormer windows in front alone—well, each has a tiny roof over it. Do you follow me?"

"I'm afraid I do," she said weakly. She was remembering how much money she had just spent on Kayla's new wardrobe and before that on the several—actually, many—things Adam had needed. How much was there left in her reserve? She'd better call the bank. That hollow feeling in the pit of her stomach seemed about to become a permanent thing. She must not burden her sons-in-law with this.

"And you're not going to do it alone," Doug said, "so if that's what you're worried about, forget it. I'm not broke yet, you know. We're not exactly rolling in dough, but we both have fairly good pensions, and I'm getting better and better money for my paintings."

"Yes," she said vaguely. For some reason that she didn't quite understand, she wanted to—somehow—pay cash for this job, not get a renovation loan. Now, why in the world wouldn't she want to simply get a loan? It would be easy enough. The B and B was a modest but successful business.

Then she realized why. The future was not as certain as it had been before Kayla had brought Adam into their lives. If it came to a choice between taking good care of Adam and giving up her business—it was no contest. *Adam must have the time he needs.* No matter what sacrifices they had to make.

Doug was looking at her keenly.

"I can make a good guess as to what you're thinking."

"We have to pay it all, or as much as we can, and not have a loan hanging over our heads, in case—"

"Are you sure about this?"

He reached over and took the estimate.

"Yes," she said, her mouth feeling dry, "Call them."

Frantic ideas darted about in her mind. Suppose Kayla got a job she liked and went away—far away—leaving Adam. Or suppose Doug was right and Kayla became a good wife to Pastor Cooper. Or suppose—somehow—Kayla was gone, and she and Doug with Adam sold out the B and B and moved into Kate's little gray house, which was still vacant. Could she really give up her B and B? There had to be a way out of this. Some way. *Dear God, if You've given me this job to do, tell me how.*

* * *

It wasn't until almost five o'clock that Pastor Cooper finally arrived. Kayla went into a small panic. She was at the kitchen sink, grating some carrots for a dinner salad, when the door chimes sounded. She liked Beth's carrot, raisin and nut salad.

"Both new guests are here," Beth said, "so that's got to be Pastor Cooper." She put aside the nut chopper.

"Look," Kayla said, "you entertain Preacher-man in front, will you? I'll go out back and get you the table flowers. Come on, Adam. Let's duck out."

Beth agreed. "All right, if that's what you want. But open the basement door and call down to your father. Tell him Pastor Cooper is here."

She had the pastor seated in the living room when Doug came up from his workshop. He looked rugged and outdoorsy in his work clothes of jeans and turtleneck sweater. No matter what Doug wore, he always managed to look imposing, Beth thought fondly.

Pastor Cooper was in a business suit and carrying a leather portfolio, and after greetings, he came right to the point. "Bessie gave me your message, Beth. What is it? How can I help?"

They told him, prompting each other, about Kayla's latest failure. She couldn't help but notice the quick look of sadness in his eyes.

"And what made me call you," Beth explained, "is that we've kind of hit a dead end. Kayla's just given up. And she's feeling guilty, as if she were imposing on us."

"Which she is, actually," Doug interposed. "But she is my daughter, and there's Adam to think of."

"And she wants to leave and—and take Adam with her," Beth said.

"And we can't let that happen," Doug added. "We can't."

"No. Of course you can't," Pastor Cooper said. "You

both realize, don't you, now that she's drinking again, her personality will not be the same? If she's sliding back into the out-of-control state there could be a lot of difficulties ahead. Addicted people tend to be users in more senses than one. They will do anything to protect their addiction.''

Beth silently agreed, remembering the sly look in Kayla's lovely eyes when she realized their vulnerability about Adam.

Doug looked solemn. "There has been trouble in the past,'' he said slowly.

"I was afraid of this,'' Pastor Cooper said, leaning forward. "And I've done a bit of phoning, asking questions. In this state, as legal grandparents, I'm sorry, but you don't have much clout.''

"What do you mean?'' Doug asked. "She's my daughter. Surely I have a right to protect her welfare. And my grandson's.''

"She is an adult, Doug. You really have no control over Kayla's actions, her behavior or her decisions. And as for Adam, he's *her* son. The courts almost always rule in favor of the mother of the child. There have been Supreme Court rulings on this. But you're not alone, if that's any small comfort. I've collected all of this for you.'' He unzipped the portfolio he had on his lap. "Read it at your leisure. You'll be shocked, but I hope also encouraged somewhat. There are unsung thousands of older couples or single grandparents in this same situation. People—older people, retired people—are raising their children's children, taking on second families to raise. It's happening all over the country.''

"Good grief,'' Beth murmured, taking the stack of leaflets, papers and one book that he held out. "It's that bad?''

"That bad, and worse, but there are some helps along the way. Support groups, seminars, resources when things get too rough.''

"We were wondering," Doug said tentatively, "if maybe we could talk Kayla into some sort of counseling or—" He stopped because a dull flush had risen in the pastor's young face.

"I've had to decide I can help only...in a very limited way," Pastor Cooper said slowly, obviously dragging the words out. "In addition to being a clergyman, I'm also a licensed counselor. I should be able to help but I don't think I'm the best one to work with Kayla. I've..." He paused, as if searching for the right words. "I've thought about it and, although I've only met Kayla twice, I think I can see where this is going, and I'm more sorry than I can say. This has never happened to me before." He paused again. "But the plain truth is, I'm...attracted to Kayla. She's a lovely woman. I'm bound by certain rules, ethics, if you will. It could become an awkward situation. Please understand."

"But Pastor Cooper," Beth said in dismay, "what are we going to do?" The question burst out.

"I'm sorry. I have no idea," he said bleakly.

Chapter Eleven

After Pastor Cooper had gone, Beth and Doug talked about it. They spoke in low tones in case Kayla came back in.

"Poor guy," Doug said. "I had kind of hoped that he could help with counseling…or something. And I must admit, I admire a man who understands himself."

"And is honest enough to say so."

"Yes," Doug said. "And he's got his career to protect. He doesn't dare…" He continued. "You know, it was losing Frank that really hit Kayla so hard. I think maybe if Frank had tried harder, had been willing to wait a little longer for her to straighten out… On the other hand, she had a problem when they married. We'd had trouble. But I think Frank was the real—maybe the only—love of her life. I never saw a woman so much in love as when I went to Kayla and Frank's wedding. I thought she'd made it for sure, but old habits die hard, I guess. She thought the sun rose and set out of Frank's belly button. When Kayla lost Frank, I guess there was nothing left for her."

After a dull silence, Beth started leafing through the pamphlet and other items that Pastor Cooper had collected for them. "I think we'd better accept the fact that we're going to have to take care of Adam," she said finally. *How?* her mind wailed. *How can we do that?*

"I think you're right. I can't stand the thought of…not doing it. What's that stuff?"

Beth handed him a leaflet. "We aren't alone anymore," she said. "But read that. Pastor Cooper was right. Kayla is Adam's mother. Actually, it's *Kayla* who has control of Adam. We don't. That's the account of a court battle of one set of grandparents for visitation rights only."

"Visitation rights? Did they win?" Doug frowned over the leaflet.

"No. Read that last line. All they wanted to do was see that the child wasn't suffering abuse from the stepfather. The court ruled against them."

He muttered, "And it says here there was a history of abuse. And the court kept giving the child back to the mother." He paused. "I can't really see Kayla abusing…"

"No, but I can see her neglecting, overlooking, forgetting, you know, things Adam needs. I don't—" She said firmly, "Doug, I don't really want her to take him to Cape Cod and let him roam around on some beach." Was she saying too much?

"No, I don't, either," he agreed.

At that moment Adam peeked around the door. He was holding a single daffodil. "Mommy says Peachy man gone?"

"Yes, he's gone," Beth said, smiling. "Tell Mommy." Adam disappeared and they heard him running toward the back door again.

"I guess I'd better get back to preparing dinner," Beth said, sighing.

"Here," Doug said. "Give me that stuff. I'll go stash it in our room. We can look it over later."

Kayla had not only cut fresh flowers, she had been on the service porch arranging them and had done a good job of it.

They had finished dinner and Beth was putting the dishes into the dishwasher when the phone rang. She answered it in the kitchen.

"Hi," a husky voice said. "Is Kayla there? This is Wanda."

Beth turned to Doug. "Will you tell Kayla that Wanda's calling?" And while he went to find her, she listened until Kayla picked up the extension in another room. As she hung up she couldn't help but hear Wanda say, "Are you busy tonight, kiddo? If you're not, I can fix us up with..." before she replaced the receiver.

Silently she went back to her task. Was this another crisis coming? Wanda and Kayla were not a good combination, but how in the world did you advise a grown woman about her friends? She tried to push aside the thought, but it wouldn't go away.

At the end of the day, when she and Doug were together in their room, they went over the information Pastor Cooper had collected for them. Kayla had indeed gone out, so they had the child monitor on in case Adam woke and needed them. Pastor Cooper's information was grim.

"I get the feeling this one is going to be useful," Doug said, leafing through the book Pastor Cooper had left. It was a survival manual for grandparents raising a second family. It pulled no punches. He read parts of it to Beth, and both sank into discouragement.

"I can understand the laws protecting parents' rights," Doug said, tiredly putting the book aside. "But they are all based on the idea that the parent in question is able and willing to care for the child and keep the child safe. When the parent isn't able… Do you think we should talk to an attorney, find out what our rights actually are?''

"Oh, Doug. Surely it won't come to that," Beth said. "Kayla means well. It's just—" And then she, too, was at a loss for words. Where was Kayla now? What was she doing? Would Doug need to go and find her somewhere and bring her back? *Should we encourage Kayla to go to Cape Cod and leave Adam?* Instantly she rejected this idea. How would she have felt if someone had tried separating her from either of her two daughters? No, that wasn't the way to go. There had to be some other solution. *Please, God, there must be some other solution.*

The next morning, just as the breakfast rush was over, Jill called. Feeling a sudden sense of foreboding, Beth assumed her brightest voice.

"Mom," Jill was saying, "we need to talk. Both Kate and I think so."

"Absolutely," Beth agreed, pretending to misunderstand. "We haven't had a good gabfest for a long time. We'll just have to make time."

"No, Mom. It's about this Kayla situation," Jill said firmly. Jill had been a very successful, hardheaded businesswoman, and when she wanted to get to the point, she got to the point.

"I don't understand what you mean, dear," Beth said, still evading.

"Kayla's back, isn't she? You can't stay on this merry-go-round, Mom. We're going to have to find a way out of it. Kate and I have decided that we've got to step in. And you know Kate is stuck at home, so we'll have to go over to her house. What are you doing this afternoon?"

"This afternoon?" Beth asked, stalling for time. "You know I'm so busy I can't really just take off an afternoon just like that with no notice." She would need to talk to Doug first.

"Quit hedging, Mom. What afternoon *can* we get to-gether? We've got to have a family conference. We've got to work out something."

Beth felt a lump in her throat. They were both worried. They were only trying to help. She gave in.

"How about tomorrow?" she asked.

"Tomorrow it is," Jill said briskly. "Say, about one o'clock, right after lunch? All the kids are in school and you can bring Adam. He'll love that play stuff in Kate's backyard. Her kids don't use it much anymore."

"All right," Beth said. "Tomorrow at one at Kate's. If I can't make it, I'll call—"

"I'll pick you up," Jill said, with a note of grimness in her voice. "Ten minutes before one. Bye."

It was an especially busy morning. The unpredictable Seattle weather had suddenly turned bright, and Beth had sent Doug off to work on his painting. They would need all the money they could get, for the new roof. Kayla had slept in, not coming out for breakfast. Beth had handled that breakfast alone, as Doug had had to see to Adam, and she felt tired and vaguely discontented.

And Adam was becoming impatient and fidgeted about, alternating between trying to "read" a book and reminding her that it was storytime. She put him off again for the bed making, and was sorry to see the old frown come back. A tantrum would erupt if she didn't hurry, but she didn't want to hurry. It was her fault, after all. She had let him become accustomed to the story reading, and today she didn't have time.

She wondered what was on his three-year-old mind. He was so used to being shunted into the background. Was he thinking that she was just like all the other grown-ups? She had forgotten how *constant* the needs of very small children were.

She hurried desperately through the bed making and the

tidy-ups, but it was past lunchtime when she finally had a moment to say, "All right, Adam. Which story do you want today?" He had his special favorites and sometimes he recited passages from memory as she read them. He was improving in so many ways with the care and attention she and Doug were giving him. She mustn't let this good progress stop.

It was past one when she went downstairs to find Kayla seated glumly at the kitchen table.

"Sorry I couldn't pull myself out of bed this morning to help out," Kayla said. "But I'm a little hungover. We did too much celebrating, I guess."

"Have you eaten anything?" Beth asked, and Kayla made a face and shook her head.

"Later, maybe."

"Celebrating what?" Beth asked before she could stop herself.

"Wanda and John's engagement. Mr. and Mrs. Hull are going to pay for the wedding. Wanda wants a proper wedding. It's not going to be a big deal, just something simple, but a real wedding. Wanda insisted."

"Isn't the wedding the bride's parents' responsibility?"

Kayla laughed. "Well, Wanda isn't that much into Miss Manners. Wanda's okay. She's really sharp. She knows what she wants. Mr. and Mrs. Hull didn't really think John should marry her at first. Didn't think she was good enough, I guess. Anyhow, Wanda just laid down the law. Told them off. John's really besotted. When she and John threatened to just walk out, the old folks came around. It's as Wanda says, they have a right to their happiness. I'm learning a lot from Wanda. She's nobody's fool."

Beth didn't let herself answer, but busied herself preparing lunch. Wanda was the wrong person to influence Kayla. That was clear. Maybe she should talk to Doug about it. *Absolutely,* she must talk to Doug about it.

* * *

Somehow she got through the rest of the day. There were extra phone calls, too, as the tourist season was coming on. She breathed a sigh of relief when she heard Doug's car drive in. He had finished the second Shilshole Bay painting. Now it only had to dry awhile in the basement until he could frame it.

That night, when they were alone, she had a difficult time beginning. How could she tell him that her girls were worried? Would they try to interfere? Well, they already had. She was brushing her hair in front of the mirror.

"You're very quiet tonight," he said, tying the cord of his robe. "What's on your mind, love?"

"Jill and Kate," she said, plunging in. "I'm going to have to tell you something you may not like."

He grinned. "It won't be the first time in my life I've listened to something I don't like. What is it?"

"I'm sorry about this, but the Bennetts have always been a close family and…well, we tend to interfere with one another's decisions, I'm afraid. Always with the best of intentions, of course. You may remember how long I waited before I told the girls I was going to remarry only a year after their father died."

Doug laughed and said with feeling. "How could I forget? It was like asking for the hand of the maiden in the tower. Remember, I sort of presented my credentials to Kate. Jill was more open to the idea, I recall, but Kate fought the whole thing for a while. So, what's up now?"

"I don't know how, but they know Kayla's back and they're worried. I'm sorry."

"Well, they can join the club." He was suddenly serious again. "What's actually on their agenda?"

She told him about Jill's call.

"And what are you going to do?"

"Go over there. What else can I do? But I think we—you and I—need to decide what I'm to tell them."

"I agree," he said slowly, not looking at her. Then turning away from her completely, he added, "Beth, are you out of your depth with this?"

"What do you mean?"

He took a moment to answer, then spoke carefully. "You and Ralph raised two well-adjusted, sensible, successful young women, able to take charge of their lives." He paused. "And I didn't. Now you seem to be stuck with the consequences. Actually, they're *my* consequences."

She got up and went to him. "Oh, don't talk like this, Doug. When people are married, they share."

"The good, the bad and the ugly?" He was still turned away.

"It isn't ugly. Kayla's made some mistakes. But Adam's a joy."

"He is, isn't he?" He sounded wistful.

She slid her hands over his broad, bowed shoulders. "So, how should I handle my girls tomorrow?"

He reached up and clasped one of her hands. "My gut feeling is there's nothing like the truth—up to a point. Why don't you tell them that, yes, Kayla's a problem, but—and this you'd better be tactful about—this is something we—you and I—prefer to take care of ourselves. Can you do that? We decided not to tell Greg about the roof. We're handling that ourselves. What bugs me with the next generation down is that they always rush to the rescue, when we don't need rescuing."

"Good, that's the way I'll handle it," Beth said, hoping she could.

However, the next day it wasn't that easy, especially with Jill. Beth had taken care with her makeup and clothes, but Jill wasn't fooled.

As soon as Beth got into the car, Jill said bluntly, "Mom, you look beat."

"Well, thank you," Beth said lightly. "And you didn't even notice my new sweater." When shopping with Kayla, she hadn't been able to resist this pale mauve embroidered sweater for herself. Now, with the roof expense, she rather regretted the purchase.

"Hadn't got to that yet," Jill said airily. "It's lovely, Mom. You always did have great clothing sense. That's perfect for summer."

They found Kate stretched out in a hammock in the back garden of the lovely home Ian had provided for his family. Jill pulled up two lawn chairs, and they sat down. Adam headed happily for the swing.

"Don't ask me how I feel," Kate said, "because I might tell you and you don't want to hear it. The last couple of months of pregnancy are the pits. I feel like a balloon."

"Well, you do look like a balloon, come to think of it," Jill said. "Shall we get to the point before your kids come trooping home from school demanding something to eat?"

Beth plunged in. "Stop right there, girls. Yes, Doug's daughter is back. She couldn't make it at the rehab center again, but we're dealing with it all right. She's really a rather nice person." *Bite your tongue, Beth. She's not nice at all.* "If one of you girls had a problem, Doug would do everything in his power to help you. I'm sure you realize that."

"That's a given, Mom," Kate said. "Doug's fine. But you've already raised your family. You've paid your dues."

"Not really," Beth said quietly. Both daughters glanced at her sharply, on the point of arguing, but she spoke first.

"I'm married to Doug. I'm his *wife*. My 'dues,' as you call them, include helping my husband if he needs my help. And at this time he does. And so does that little boy. No.

Don't say anything. Just pause a second and think about *that*. I talked to Cyrus when he was in the hospital. He reminded me of one important fact.''

"But, Mom—" This was Jill, impatient and on the verge of annoyance.

"He said, 'When you do it for the least of these, you do it for Me.' Just think about that," Beth said, hoping she sounded decisive.

"We are. We have," Kate said. "And that's important, certainly. But what in the world is that basket-case daughter of Doug's going to do now? Has she exhausted all her options? Is she just going to hang around sponging on you and Doug, allowing you to raise her son? Answer that!" Kate was speaking unusually sharply.

"I can't answer that," Beth said simply. "Ask me next week, maybe. We're taking it a day at a time, trying to work things out, but nothing is accomplished overnight."

"It's been *weeks!*" Jill fumed.

"And maybe it will be weeks more. We don't know yet. I do appreciate your concern. I really do. But I also feel that this is something Doug and I can handle. You shouldn't worry about it." She knew that she was drawing a line in the sand, that—probably for the first time in her life—she was separating herself from her children in a very real sense. It made her want to cry.

Both daughters felt it, too. Kate's expression was one of exasperation, and Jill began to drum her fingers on the arm of her chair in anger. She had rejected their help before they could even voice it.

"In other words, 'Butt out,'" Jill said flatly.

"It isn't that," Beth said, almost pleading. "But it's that Doug and I…" How could she say it? How could she tell them both that when she had found Doug, she had found the only real man-and-woman love of her life, that Ralph, the father they had both loved dearly, had never been that?

Kind, patient, gentle, plodding Ralph. He had deserved more from her than faithfulness and "duty." That was her private cross to bear.

"What is it, then?" Kate asked, moving slightly in her hammock, trying to find a more comfortable position for her small, distended body.

"Give me some time with this," Beth finally said, feeling helpless. "Kayla's only been back a little while, and Adam—" She stopped. Better not to bring up the subject of Adam again, but it was too late.

"I can probably help you there," Kate said. "I mean, after this baby comes. I'll be tied down anyhow taking care of my new infant. Two wouldn't be any more trouble, and my other three are quite self sufficient now."

Jill interposed. "Kate, you're out of your mind. You've forgotten how much work a new baby is."

"Well, we could share it," Kate protested.

"How? I live on the other side of the city," Jill snapped. "With Seattle traffic it took nearly forty minutes to get here today."

"It isn't necessary," Beth said decisively. "I don't need any help. Really, I can manage quite well." Kate would have her hands full with this new baby. It had been several years since Katie had dealt with night feedings, sudden infant illnesses and all the other crises that were part of infant care.

Jill got up suddenly, really angry now. "Well, this is going nowhere. I'll go push Adam's swing. If Mom can't face reality, it's pointless to even consider bailing her out."

"Wait," Beth pleaded, feeling her throat tighten. "Don't take that attitude—"

But Jill had reached the swing and gave Adam a push. He howled with delight. Beth sank back in her lawn chair.

"What did you expect?" Kate said sourly. "Mom, you're being made a fool of. When people love people, they hate to see people made fools of. That's a cockeyed sentence, but I think you get my meaning.''

''Yes, I do,'' Beth said, ''and don't think I don't appreciate you girls trying to help, but—''

''But you and Doug want to be saps,'' Kate finished bluntly.

Beth didn't answer. She was making an effort not to cry. This was the first really serious disagreement she had ever had with either of her daughters, and it hurt. More than that, she knew she was hurting them, too. *Is Kayla worth this? No way!* The unwelcome thought was suddenly in her mind. *But Doug is. Doug is worth everything,* her mind countered.

She clung to this idea as they prepared to leave. The situation was made worse when Adam, objecting to leaving his joyous swinging, threw a real tantrum.

''Sometimes when kids act like that, I want to throttle them,'' Jill said grimly, as Beth tried to quiet the angry little boy.

She didn't entirely succeed, and on the way home, Adam was surly and petulant. Jill was coolly polite. The usual ten-minute drive between Kate's house and hers seemed to take forever. How could she explain to Jill that Adam had probably never had anything in his short life that he hadn't had to fight for, and that this was a three-year-old child's way of doing it? She felt increasingly hopeless.

Finally at home, she was met by Kayla. ''What happened?'' Kayla asked, seeing Adam's angry, red little face.

''Kate has swings in her backyard, and Adam didn't want to leave— Are you going someplace?'' She glanced at her watch. It wasn't even two o'clock yet. The visit to Kate's hadn't lasted very long. She wished beyond anything else that Kayla would just take care of Adam for a while.

''Yeah. Some folks are giving a bridal shower for Wanda. Somebody's picking me up in a few minutes.''

"That sounds like fun," Beth said woodenly, hoping to hide how upset she felt. Kayla looked lovely. She was wearing one of the outfits they had bought together, a pale off-white skirt with pinkish highlights. "Aren't you going to take a wrap? Don't forget this is Seattle. If you stay after dusk, you'll need something. Didn't we get a little jacket that you could wear with that?"

"Yeah, we did, but I spilled something on it. I think this will be okay. Unless—" She stopped.

"Unless what?" Beth asked, watching Adam go over and embrace Kayla's legs, muttering into her skirt. He was still pouting. Kayla had fixed her hair in a new way. It was very attractive.

"You wouldn't consider lending me your sweater, would you? Listen, baby, if you mess up Mommy's dress, she'll clobber you," she added, pushing Adam away. He glared up at her and, disgusted, ran into the bed-sitter, always his haven.

"Which sweater?" Beth asked.

"The one you're wearing," Kayla said, looking impish.

"You'd take the clothes off my back," Beth said, trying to make a joke of it. "All right. Take it. But be careful. I paid too much for this and I knew it at the time."

"Oh, Beth, you are the greatest," Kayla said happily, taking the expensive sweater.

Again that night Beth and Doug turned on the baby monitor for Adam, as Kayla hadn't come home from the shower. They had no idea where she was. The party must have ended hours ago.

"I know she's drinking again," Doug said. "And I'm sorry your girls are upset about this situation."

Beth told him as tactful a version of this afternoon's visit as she could and still remain truthful. She had vowed never again to do anything to make him feel shut out.

"I never can tell if she's been drinking or not," Beth said, turning down their bed.

"You've never lived with an alcoholic before." Then he added, "Beth, I'm more sorry about this than you know."

"Oh, don't worry about it," Beth said, hoping she didn't sound as discouraged as she felt. "Kayla certainly looked lovely when she left. She was wearing that white-and-pink skirt we got when we were shopping, and I lent her my mauve sweater, the one with the embroidery in the front and the back. She's a beautiful girl."

An odd silence stretched between them.

"Doug? Did you hear me?"

"Yes, I'm afraid I did. I'm going to ask this, but I don't think I'm going to like the answer." He sounded grim and was looking at her steadily. "Tell me, Beth, why did she need to borrow your sweater?"

"Why? Well, because she spilled something on the jacket that goes with that skirt she was wearing. Why would you ask such a question?"

"Do you think you can remember the specific clothing items you and she bought when you went shopping? I'm no good at women's clothing."

"Doug, what are we talking about? Of course I can remember what we bought. Where are we going with this conversation?"

He sighed deeply. "It's the same old merry-go-round. What we need to do is go and look into Kayla's half of the bed-sitter closet."

"Why?"

"Because I doubt her new friends are buying her drinks. She's having to pay her share, and probably more. My educated guess of the moment is that she's selling things. You said a jacket? I'll be very surprised if she still has it. Whatever it cost you, it probably went for one-tenth its value for a bottle of vodka. Now, if you're not up to snooping in someone else's closet, I am. What'd the jacket look like? Or will you put your scruples aside and come with me?''

"Oh, Doug," Beth moaned. "She wouldn't have done that. Surely."

"Sweetheart," he said gently, "we are dealing with an alcoholic. Much as I love her, she is not a responsible person. She is an addict. She is sick." He paused a moment. "Will you come with me?"

"Yes," Beth said faintly, hating the thought of it. When was this going to end?

She felt deeply shaken. They tried to be quiet so Adam wouldn't awaken, and they went through Kayla's half of the bed-sitter closet. The jacket was gone. So were two other items. They shut the closet door quietly and left Adam still sleeping soundly. *Where was Kayla now? Who was she with?*

Then suddenly, from out of nowhere, a question flew into Beth's mind. *Where is my jade ring?* The one she had taken off and left on the kitchen window ledge yesterday. The one she hadn't been able to find later? Oh, surely not! She mustn't tell Doug until she had looked further. There was the possibility that she herself had put it someplace else, and would yet find it, but she felt a certainty that the jade ring was gone.

Dolefully, not saying anything more, they went back upstairs. Doug was very depressed. She could feel it. What in the world were they going to do?

Beth sat down on the side of the bed. "This is what Pastor Cooper meant when he told us to expect a change in Kayla's personality."

"Yes, drinking does that. Any mind-altering substance does. Basically, Kayla's a good person. But I've been this route before. When she's drinking, she's…different. And I'm not really sure what I can do about it."

"Well," Beth said briskly, "there's nothing we can do

about it tonight. Morning and breakfast come around pretty fast, so I suggest we get some sleep.'' She wanted, desperately, to tell him about her missing jade ring, but held her peace. But she wasn't at all sure that Kayla was ''basically a good person.''

Doug smiled and touched her cheek briefly. ''So right, as always.''

But sleep was slow in coming to both of them. Later she was awakened by the noise from the baby monitor. A glance at the clock told her it was ten minutes past four. There were thumping and muttering sounds that couldn't possibly be Adam.

Quickly she slid out of bed and, struggling into her robe, headed down the stairway. She could see the ceiling light was on in the bed-sitter. When she went in, she saw Adam sitting groggily in the center of the make-down couch, and Kayla putting the embroidered sweater on a coat hanger, fumbling awkwardly.

''Here,'' Beth said. ''Let me do that, and I'm going to turn off the light.'' Hurriedly, she took the hanger and sweater and clicked off the light, leaving only the dim glow from the streetlight outside.

''Oh, thank you,'' Kayla muttered thickly. ''That's a lovely sweater. I gotta lotta compliments on that. Everybody loved it. S'beautiful. I…I tried not to—'' She stopped, seeming to have forgotten what she had begun to say. She stood swaying in the middle of the room.

Beth went to Adam, gently laid him back down and pulled his blanket up over him, murmuring softly. Still more asleep than awake, he settled in snugly and drifted off again.

''Let me help you,'' Beth said to Kayla, and began to help her undress. When this was done, Kayla seemed to gravitate to the window seat. ''Love that ole window seat,'' she was crooning. So Beth got another blanket to cover her there.

When she was sure Kayla was settled for what was left of the night, with one more glance at Adam, she left the bed-sitter.

Doug was seated on the bottom step. "All okay?" he asked, sighing.

"All okay," Beth said. "And she brought back the sweater."

"I'm glad of that. Better hang on to it." Again there was the grim undertone. "Might as well go on up," he added tiredly. "I'm not quite ready to tackle breakfast preparations just yet."

"Neither am I," she murmured, sliding her arm through his as he rose, and together they went back upstairs.

Sleep was out of the question for both, but by tacit agreement, they didn't talk about it anymore. Both lay quietly waiting for the dawn and the alarm clock's first ping.

Oh, dear God, what now? She was sorry for Doug. She was sorry for Adam. She was sorry her herself. And, yes, she was sorry for Kayla, too.

Then, half sleeping, she realized she had begun to pray. Wordless, silent prayers of the mind that she didn't understand, and didn't need to. But it made her feel better, as praying always did. God would get them through this.

The roofing men came when they were in the midst of the breakfast activity, so Doug had to leave her, but Adam was already dressed and into his day. Kayla was still sleeping.

By the time the checkouts and goodbyes had been completed, it was time for the roofers' coffee break, so Beth hurriedly heated their customary cinnamon rolls. When they had finished and resumed work, she commented to Doug, "I don't think they get this fancy of a coffee break at their other jobs.'' She was half laughing when she said it, as the men were a good-humored crew, ready to joke and clown about.

''You can bet on it,'' Doug answered with a grin. ''They've got a good deal with you, and they know it. But maybe it'll pay off in a better job, who knows?'' He was heading down the basement stairs to start framing his painting.

What was next? The upstairs and the beds. Beth quickly put the roofers' dishes into the dishwasher and turned it on. Adam was leafing through several books—unfortunately in the middle of the kitchen floor—making up his mind which story he wanted her to read. He hadn't begun to get impatient yet. He looked so dear.

Oh, yes, the beds.

''Come on, Adam. We're going upstairs now,'' Beth said, and Adam obediently began gathering up his books.

The door chimes sounded. It couldn't be guests this early, Beth thought as she went into the front hall and opened the door.

A middle-aged couple stood before her. Both wore conservative business suits. She got the distinct impression they were not B and B guests. There was something very purposeful about them.

''Mrs. Endicott? Are you Mrs. Endicott?'' the man asked in a no-nonsense tone that startled her.

Beth had to think a moment. Endicott? Oh, that was Kayla.

''No. I'm Mrs. Colby. Mrs. Endicott is my, uh, my daughter-in-law.'' Something in the man's manner made her cautious.

''Is Mrs. Endicott here?'' Again the strictly-business voice.

"Yes, but she's... She isn't up yet. May I ask what you need to see her about?" She felt the beginning of alarm.

"I'm sorry, ma'am, but we have a warrant for Mrs. Endicott's arrest. May we come in, please?" They were both taking out plastic ID cards.

Chapter Twelve

Beth's mouth was suddenly dry, and she felt an almost violent surge of protectiveness for Kayla. For Doug. "I don't understand," she managed to say, then added, "May I get my husband?" Doug should know about this. Doug would straighten it out.

"Of course, ma'am. May we come in?" he repeated.

"Yes, yes, of course," Beth said, opening the door. "There must be some mistake. I know it's a mistake."

The two officers entered and stood in the hallway. "I'll...I'll get my husband," Beth said, and hurried back toward the kitchen. When she got to the basement door off the kitchen, she was shaking. She opened the door and called.

"Doug! Come up here!" The tone of her voice alerted him, for she heard him drop the frame and mount the cellar steps two at a time.

"What? What?"

"The *police* are here," she said disbelievingly. "Two of them. For Kayla. They said something about a warrant. There's some mistake. It's got to be a mistake."

"What's she got herself into now?" There was more annoyance than fright in Doug's tone. "Where are they?"

"I left them in the front hall," Beth said, but he had already left the kitchen. When he reached the front hallway, he spoke cordially. Trust Doug to stay in control.

"Good afternoon. I'm Douglas Colby. I understand you are inquiring for my daughter?"

"Yes, sir," the man said. "I'm Detective Fulton and this is Sergeant McCrae. Seattle Police. We need to see Mrs. Kayla Endicott. Is she here?"

Doug was about to answer, when Adam appeared at the top of the stairway. "Gamma Beff?" He had gone on ahead with his armload of books.

"Oh, dear, I forgot Adam," Beth said distractedly. "Go wait for me in the bedroom, Adam," she called up to him.

"Mrs. Endicott?" prompted the detective.

"You'd better wake her," Doug said to Beth, a sigh in his voice. "We'll see what this is all about."

Beth knocked softly at the bed-sitter door, then opened it and went in. Kayla was still on the window seat, sleeping deeply. Beth shut the door after her. She shook Kayla's shoulder gently, and then more firmly as Kayla tried to struggle out of sleep.

"Wha-at? Beth? What's up?" She sat up, clutching her blanket around her shoulders.

"Wake up, Kayla," Beth said with low insistence. "Wake up. There are police here. They…they want to talk to you."

It seemed to take Kayla forever to focus on what Beth was saying. "Police? For me? What for? I haven't done anything." But she was awake now.

"Here, Kayla, put on your robe. At least speak to them. See what they want. It must be some mistake."

"Yeah, right. Lemme get some water on my face." Kayla stumbled to the basin behind the screen in the corner, and Beth heard the water splashing. She felt a sense of unreality. This wasn't really happening. It couldn't be. To the best of her knowledge, no one in her family had ever been arrested. No one had ever done anything to be arrested *for*. None of this made sense. *Please, God let this be over before any more guests arrive!*

"I don't get it," Kayla was mumbling when she came back. She was tying the robe about her slender waist. "Where are these jerks?"

"Kayla, they're policemen," Beth cautioned, opening the bed-sitter door.

The detective was quite close. He spoke at once. "Kayla Endicott?"

"Yes," Kayla answered, and started to add something, but the detective spoke first.

"This is a warrant for your arrest for delinquent child support mandated by court order number..." His voice droned on.

"You're kidding," Kayla gasped. "He wouldn't do that! Frank wouldn't do that!" She was obviously stunned, but reached out and took the paper the detective held toward her.

"Read the warrant, ma'am," he said. "Now I'll have to ask you to come with us."

Doug intervened. "Come with you where?"

"I'm sorry, sir. We have to take Mrs. Endicott in for booking." Now he spoke almost kindly, as if he sensed their confusion and realized how unaccustomed they were to police visits.

"You mean to jail?" Beth asked, and instantly felt stupid. *They were going to take Kayla to jail! Unbelievable!*

"I'm sorry, ma'am," the detective said, turning to her. "Mrs. Endicott is now under arrest. The procedure is that she has to come with us. My advice—" he turned to Doug again "—is that you call your attorney."

"I...I'm not sure we have one," Doug said uncertainly, a dull flush of embarrassment mounting in his face.

"Mr. Kemp," Beth said. "I know an attorney. Albert Kemp. He helped me when I turned my home into this bed-and-breakfast."

"He might be your starting point," Detective Fulton said agreeably. "Now, Mrs. Endicott, if you will get dressed, Sergeant McCrae will accompany you." He indicated the bed-sitter door, and the female officer moved toward it. Kayla had stood before them, white-faced and stunned. Now she seemed to come alive.

"I don't believe this," she moaned, starting to cry.

"If you'll get dressed, Mrs. Endicott?" the female officer prompted. Kayla turned back to the bed-sitter.

"Can...can't I help?" Beth offered, but the detective shook her head.

"Sergeant McCrae will assist Mrs. Endicott," he said formally.

"Mommy?"

They all turned and saw Adam standing at the bottom of the stairway. He had left his books somewhere, crept down and was looking at the scene in the hall in wide-eyed alarm. At three, he couldn't possibly understand their situation but he could sense their anxiety.

"Oh, no," Doug muttered, going toward him, but Adam was too quick for him. He ran toward Sergeant McCrae, a tiny bundle of anger.

"Go 'way," he shouted. "Go 'way!"

Doug swooped down and picked him up just before, little fists flying, he could attack the female officer.

"I'm sorry," Doug apologized. "I'm really sorry. My grandson has an uncertain temper at times. Come on, buddy." He held Adam's squirming little body, trying to quiet him. Adam gave in and stopped shouting, but his face held its angry frown.

Beth became aware that a constant sound in the background had suddenly stopped. All morning there had been the steady tapping of the roofers' hammers as they put on the new material. Now it seemed almost too silent in the hallway.

"Why are they stopping?" she asked inanely. This whole thing was like some sort of dream where nothing made sense.

"Because it's started to rain," Doug said, indicating the glass panel in the big front door, with drops of water on it.

Detective Fulton spoke. "May I ask if this is Mrs. Endicott's little boy?"

"Yes," Doug said. "Why?"

"With Mrs. Endicott out of the house, is there someone here who will care for the boy?"

"Yes, of course. He's my grandson," Doug said.

"Well, I guess that's all right, sir, but I have to report it to Child Protective Services. They'll send someone to check. It's just routine, you understand."

"Yes, of course," Douglas said politely, his face grim. It was clear he was controlling his own temper with an effort.

When Kayla emerged with the policewoman, she was dressed and no longer crying, but she looked stricken.

"Daddy," she started, but couldn't continue. She moved as if in a trance.

"They say you have to go in with them. I'll get in touch with an attorney, and we'll work it out," Doug said to Kayla. Beth felt he was trying to be reassuring, but she sensed his feeling of frustrated helplessness.

Detective Fulton offered a word of encouragement. "The system calls for an arraignment, sir. They usually set bail at that hearing, so if you folks get to a lawyer, he can help you."

"Thank you," Doug said, just as Adam exploded into

protest again at Kayla's leaving. They all seemed to be concentrating on the furious, frantic little boy struggling in Doug's strong arms.

"I'll be back, baby," Kayla tried to reassure him. "Mommy's coming back." She reached over and patted him. It seemed to help because as soon as the door was shut behind Kayla and the two officers, Adam started to calm down.

Doug turned to Beth. "What was the name of that attorney? I've forgotten it that quickly. I guess I'm really over the hill."

"Nonsense," she said briskly. "It's Albert Kemp. I'll call his office right now. He's a member of our church, and if he doesn't handle this type of case, he'll know someone who does."

Beth was able to reach him almost at once. And Albert Kemp did know someone.

"Yes, in fact, my sister's boy is in criminal law," he said. "Daryl Taylor. Here's the number."

Beth winced at the term "criminal law" in connection with Doug's daughter, but she had her pencil ready, took down the name and phone number and thanked him. She turned to Doug, who had his handkerchief out and was blotting the remaining tears from Adam's flushed face.

"His nephew handles this kind of case," she told him. "His name is Daryl Taylor, and I've got his number. Do you want to call him? Albert said to use his name as a referral. Let me take Adam." She reached out her arms and Adam came to her.

"Book?" Adam said forlornly, his blue eyes still wet.

"Soon, darling. We'll get to your story soon." Doug dialed the new number. Her heart ached as she watched him, loving everything about him. *Please, God, protect Doug. Help him with this. Help me to help him.*

Daryl Taylor wasn't in, but Doug explained carefully to

his secretary what the problem was, and asked that he return the call as soon as he could.

"This is going to cost us," Doug commented, a worried frown on his rugged face. "And what with the roof, well, I don't know."

"We can always resort to a loan for the roof," Beth said, "if it comes to that. Kayla's needs must be met. We can't let her stay in jail a moment longer than necessary."

"I agree, but I hate to put you through something like this."

"Forget about me. I'm doing fine," Beth said. It made her uneasy again when he wanted to take all the responsibility.

"I don't understand this," Doug said. "It's not like Frank to be this vindictive. He's not that small-minded. I wonder if he's still working at the same place." He glanced at his watch. "L.A. is on Pacific Time like we are, so he'd still be at his office."

"Where does he work?" Beth asked, shifting Adam's position because he had started to fidget in her arms.

"Some big insurance company in Los Angeles. Let me think a minute. He's a claims adjuster there, or he may be the department supervisor now—that was his goal during his marriage to Kayla. He's a pretty solid guy." He snapped his fingers. "Got it." He picked up the phone, dialed directory assistance and asked for Los Angeles, picking up the pencil Beth had put down. In a moment, he was writing down the number.

He turned back to Beth. "This is the speaker button, isn't it?"

"Yes."

He pressed it so she could hear the conversation, too. Just a few seconds after Doug had given his name and asked for Frank Hughes, they were connected. The strange man's voice came into their hallway, firm, pleasant and controlled.

"Doug! Of all the people to hear from! I hope I'm glad you called. Is everything all right with Kayla?"

"No, it isn't," Doug said bluntly. "I'm going to give this to you straight, Frank. Kayla's just been arrested for nonpayment of the child support payments."

"Oh, no." It was almost a moan.

"Did you arrange this?"

"Absolutely not, Doug! But I'm afraid it got out of my hands. Just a minute, let me find a button to push here. I want this conversation to be just between us." There was a pause and then Frank Hughes resumed speaking.

"Think back to when Kayla and I broke up. She was in a pretty bad way. I had to get her away from Becky. Becky was being badly affected by Kayla's drinking and some of the friends Kayla was seeing at that time. Please understand, the divorce—the complete break—was a necessity." Frank Hughes's voice held an almost desperate sincerity.

"I guess I can understand that," Doug agreed reluctantly.

"Knowing Kayla's job history, I followed the lawyer's advice about the child support thing. It was mainly because I knew Kayla would never pay it, and if she didn't pay it, she wouldn't keep coming around to mess up Becky's life and mine. But at that point it went out of my control. It became a court order, part of the system. As I understand it, it's the District Attorney's job to enforce those orders. I take it they have."

"Yes." Doug's voice was tight. "Two police officers have just taken Kayla away. She was in shock. When she comes out of shock, assuming she does, she'll find herself in jail. Maybe that sounds heartless, but we're dealing with these facts at the moment."

Frank Hughes moaned. "I am so sorry. What can I do? I don't know how to stop this, even if I could."

"You probably can't," Doug said. "A court order is a court order. At least you've eased my mind. We were pretty good friends once. I didn't think you would deliberately arrange this."

"Well, thanks for that, anyhow. I would hope that we can still be pretty good friends. Wait a minute. Who's going to pay for this? I know Kayla can't."

"I guess my wife and I are," Doug said. "Who else?"

"No! Absolutely no! I did not intend that," Frank protested.

"Doesn't matter what you intended, Frank. You know that old phrase about the wheels of justice—if it's part of the system now, well, that's that."

"Wait a minute. Okay, say you have to pay it to help out Kayla. What's wrong with my just sending the money back to you when these wheels of justice send it my way?" Frank offered.

Beth shook her head and whispered, "No, Doug. No, we can't do that." Adam, not understanding the conversation, imitated her, shaking his head, too, which brought a slight smile to Doug's face.

"My wife is shaking her head, Frank. If you sent the money back after the court or whatever collects it, that would probably be either illegal or at least unethical. Incidentally, how are you both doing?"

"Us? We're doing fine. You know Megan and I married?"

"Yes, I'd heard that. I wish you both well."

"Thanks. And we've increased our family. Megan wanted one of our own, and we hit the jackpot with twin boys."

"Well, double congratulations," Doug said, really smiling now. "I wish you both all the best, and that comes from the heart."

"Thanks, Doug, more than I can say—all things considered." Frank sounded choked up.

"Which brings to mind another question. If Megan is caring for Becky and two new babies, she isn't still working, is she?"

"Not for a while, no," Frank said, but added hastily, "But we're doing okay. Really."

"Frank," Doug said, "you can use this money, can't you? As sole provider and all?"

"I said we're doing okay," Frank persisted.

"I was a sole family provider once myself, buddy," Doug said. "And since Kayla isn't able to help raise her own daughter, some financial support is justified, so don't argue. Plus, my wife is now nodding her head, so we have her approval. We will pay the child support, and don't send it back. Let me do this much for Becky, okay? At least until things are better for you and Megan."

Frank finally agreed, but added, "I'm going to investigate at this end. Maybe there's a way I can get it cancelled now—to avoid something like this in the future. You're going to have to live with that, Doug, because I'm going to do it."

"Okay, but for now we pay up this delinquent amount," Doug agreed, and, after sending his love to Becky and the others, they rang off.

"Thanks for backing me up on that," Doug said to Beth, and she felt a flood of love for him. Somehow, they would do it. They must. But what else would Kayla manage to wreck?

"Book!" Adam reminded, suddenly looking fierce, and both Beth and Doug had to laugh.

"Yes!" Beth said, just as positively. "Book! Doug, I'm

going to read this poor child his story. If time gets short, will you help with the beds?''

"Yes, of course I will. Better than that, I'll make them. I can listen for Daryl Taylor's call upstairs as well as down here.''

The attorney didn't call back until late afternoon, as the evening's guests were checking in. He had been in court. Beth was busy greeting people, giving them their little Seattle maps, and Doug was carrying suitcases upstairs. He cast her a desperate glance and took the call on their bedroom extension for privacy. She had to wait until the flurry of arrivals was over to find out what Daryl Taylor had said. He had called back again about twenty minutes after his first call.

When the new arrivals had gone for the evening, Beth and Doug both collapsed into big living room chairs.

"Well, it's the usual, good news and bad news,'' Doug said, sounding defeated. "Daryl Taylor is sharp. He got right onto it, I'll say that. That's the good part. He called someone somewhere and found out Kayla's arraignment isn't until tomorrow morning. That's the bad news. Sometime between ten and noon—that's the closest they can tell him.''

"You mean Kayla has to stay in jail overnight?'' Beth asked, shocked.

"Yep.'' He was trying to sound matter-of-fact, but she sensed his hurt.

"Oh, Doug, I'm so sorry.'' She reached out to him and took his hand. How difficult this would be for Kayla! *Please, God, let Kayla at least learn something from this.*

"Then,'' he continued, "I'm going down in the morning to go to court with him. He's got a bail bondsman on tap, so it's going to cost us. I'm assuming they take plastic. I forgot to ask. If they don't, I'll go early and hit one of the bank machines for some cash. I guess you'll have to cope with most of breakfast and the guests leaving by yourself.''

''That's all right. Don't worry about me.'' But even as she said it, she dreaded coping with it, plus Adam, who would be hovering in the background with his daily selection of books. It was frightening to realize that she and Doug were his only anchors, his only security. Poor little boy. She pushed the idea aside. She'd better start thinking about getting some dinner, but the idea appalled her. She was just too tired.

''What do you say we call out for a pizza?'' Doug asked, and she knew, with a surge of love for him, that he had divined her thought.

''Great idea,'' she said, holding back tears. ''Adam liked it the last time.'' She didn't need to add that poor Adam had learned to like whatever was given to him. Was he still hiding bits of food? She hadn't had time to really search for a while.

Oh, Kayla, what have you done? But it was no good blaming Kayla. Kayla seemed to be one of life's maimed, one of life's misfits, destined to flounder away her time in bleak confusion. *Oh, God, please help Kayla.*

She stood up suddenly, saying, ''I'll call the pizza place,'' and hurried to the hall phone. She mustn't let herself slide into depression. She had done that after Ralph's death, when she had felt so guilty. With a kind of desperate intensity, she picked up the phone and started frantically pressing the buttons.

When the pizza and salad came, she made a pretense of enjoying it, but she knew she was forcing herself, minute by minute, to get through the evening. All she wanted to do was escape into blessed sleep. But it all had to be done. There was the dishwasher to load and later unload. The breakfast table to set. The melon balls and fruit juice jugs to be prepared. The muffins to set out in the warmers.

Adam must be bathed and put to bed with his bedtime story. *Everything…everything…everything…*

And over and under, through it all, was the knowledge that Doug was feeling increasingly guilty as he worked beside her, trying to do more and more. What had happened to their wonderful September love? It seemed to have disappeared like daylight into darkness at the end of the day. She forced herself to hide her worry, her tiredness, her increasing feeling of hopelessness. *What are we doing to do?*

Upstairs, when the endless day was over, they both fell into bed without enough energy left over to even talk.

And morning seemed to come almost immediately. Where had the night of rest gone? They spoke little as they showered and dressed to face the day that neither wanted to face.

Doug had to leave during breakfast, and she determinedly kept her perfect hostess smile as he did, though her heart ached for the humiliation he would face bailing his daughter out of jail.

She tried to concentrate on the positives surrounding her. The guests were happy, well fed, enjoying themselves. Adam—this wonderful little person—was gaining weight, and depending on things he found valuable for the first time in his short life. He had his gold stars. He had his library card. He had shelter, food, clothing…and love. She tried to hold on to these things. They would—somehow—pay the delinquent child support. They would pay for the roof…

Trust and believe.

She was thinking this as the door chimes rang out, and she excused herself graciously from the last guest to open the door to a thirtyish woman with a briefcase plus a clipboard and a rather harried smile.

"Hi. I'm Gretchen Holloway, from CPS—Child Protective Services. I'm looking for Mr. or Mrs. Colby?"

"I'm Mrs. Colby," Beth said smoothly, her heart plummeting. "Will you just step into the living room? I'll be with you in a moment."

"Sure. I can see you're busy," the woman said pleasantly. "Take your time. I've got some stuff to fill out." And she obligingly went over to the corner and sat down out of view of the hallway as the last guest left for the day.

Beth silently thanked God that Adam was already in his bed-sitter, sorting through his books on the window seat. *Adam, please don't make a scene. Not in front of the social worker.*

Beth tried not to hurry the last guest out for her day of exploring the sights of Seattle. Then she went into the bed-sitter. How could she explain to this uncertain, unpredictable child? She sat down on the window seat beside him.

"Adam?" she said gently. "Put that down for a minute and listen."

"Wut?" He put aside a book and looked up at her, a question in his eyes.

"A nice lady, a very nice lady, has come to see us. And I want—now listen very carefully—I want you to *like* her. I want you to be *very* nice to her. Do you understand?"

"Yep. Okay." His wide blue eyes now held complete trust.

"You're not going to cry or yell at her? You're going to be very, very nice to her, right?"

He was nodding seriously. "Okay. Right." Then a slight frown came. "She a good lady?"

"She's a *very* good lady. She just wants to ask us some questions. So everything is…okay. You understand that?"

"Sure. Okay." But the little face had become very serious.

"Adam," she added as an afterthought, "it will make me *very happy* if you are nice to this lady."

"Okay," he said, very decisively now, and Beth breathed a little sigh of relief.

This, after all, was the same little person who had given her the broken half of his dusty cookie when she had said she was hungry. She reached over and hugged him.

"You wait here, Adam," she said, getting up. She glanced at her watch. It was ten forty-five. *What is Doug doing now? Where are they? How is Kayla coping?* She kissed her fingers to Adam and left the bed-sitter.

She found Gretchen Holloway bent over her clipboard, writing busily, in one of the deep chairs in the living room.

"I'm sorry to be so long," Beth said.

"No problem," the social worker said, putting down her clipboard. "I'm always behind on the never-ending paperwork. And I can see I caught you at a bad time."

"No worse than any other time," Beth said, then wondered if that was the right thing to say. She sat down opposite the other woman. "My husband isn't here just now," she added.

"No, I suppose not. Now, let me see. I have to start filling out one of the never-ending forms, so I guess we can just get going. These are routine questions—have to ask them." She glanced up with her pleasant smile. "I'll need to see the little boy—Adam, his name is?—before I go. According to the police report, his main caretaker, his mother, is absent?"

Yes, Beth thought, *you might say "absent," since she's in jail.*

The social worker was now shuffling through her large briefcase. When she found what she was looking for, she forced the paper up among other papers under the crowded clip on the board. "Who is Adam's caretaker here? And—" she glanced up and around "—what is 'here,' by the way. Is this a boarding house or something? It looks a little grand for that."

"It was my home. It's now a bed-and-breakfast. Today's guests have left," Beth said.

"I see. Well, I'm not quite sure where we are in that situation," she said. "But I can find out." She smiled reassuringly again. "My job is to get the best arrangement available for this child, this Adam—" she had glanced down at the paper again "—Endicott."

He's not a name on a paper, Beth thought desperately. *He's a person. He's mixed up. He doesn't understand. He's—*

"Because Adam is at a vulnerable age," the social worker went on.

Yes, Adam is vulnerable. What we do here today for Adam is vital.

The social worker glanced up, smiling again. "And right now, you're feeling pretty confused and protective, aren't you?"

"Yes," Beth said, knowing her tone revealed it more than her answer.

"Well, take it easy. I'm on Adam's side, too. Just tell me what Adam's situation is."

And Beth found herself pouring out the story, about Kayla's sudden arrival, about Kayla's problem, about Doug and her trying to understand and help, not really knowing how. About Adam hiding food—should she really have said that? and about his gold stars and his library card, and about his loving to sit on the window seat, staring out whenever it rained... "I guess I'm doing this all wrong," she ended.

"Not at all," the other woman said. "You're doing things as right as you can do them. Don't be discouraged. You'd be amazed how many people are coping with just this kind of sad situation. And you've given me a good picture of how things are here, with Adam—" she glanced down at her clipboard "—Endicott."

Despite the woman's obvious kindness and understanding, Beth felt a slight chill. The little person who was Adam Endicott was in the system now. This Gretchen Holloway, or some other person, would be checking up on Adam Endicott to see how he fared, how he progressed. It was as if they were somehow taking Adam away from people who were his own. She tried to push the thought aside.

"I know it's scary," the other woman said. "Do you think I could talk with Adam a bit?" She was making motions to get up, putting aside her clipboard.

"He's in the bed-sitter—the little room we call the bed-sitter because it has a make-down bed in it," Beth explained haltingly.

"And where is that?" Miss Holloway asked.

"I'll show you," Beth said, getting up.

"If you'll just get us settled, see that Adam is at ease, then excuse yourself for a few minutes, I can take it from there," Miss Holloway was saying as they left the living room. "Would you and Adam be comfortable with that, do you think?"

Beth swallowed hard. "I'm not sure what Adam would be comfortable with," she said carefully. *And I am not at all comfortable with that.* "Why don't we see how it plays out?" she evaded.

"Fine. Whatever. Every child is different," Miss Holloway said reassuringly.

Adam was still on his window seat, surrounded by his big storybooks. He glanced up warily as they entered.

"Adam," Beth said, making her voice steady with an effort. He looked so little and uneasy. "This is the lady I talked to you about. She's come to see us. Her name is Miss Holloway."

"Hello, Adam," Miss Holloway said, pausing just inside the door. "Okay if we come in?"

"Sure. S'okay," Adam said, staring at her.

"Thanks." Miss Holloway went inside, "Okay if I sit down?"

"Sure." But as he said it he glanced over at Beth, and she nodded encouragingly, though she saw his small body stiffen.

"I see you have a lot of books. Do you like books?" Miss Holloway asked in an interested manner. When it seemed as if Adam wasn't going to answer that at all, Beth couldn't resist speaking to fill the pause.

"Adam loves his books. He has some of his own, and we get some every week from the library." She knew she shouldn't have interrupted. Miss Holloway shook her head just slightly, and Beth felt annoyed. *If the child surrounds himself with books, he obviously likes books. No wonder Adam won't bother to answer. Adam isn't exactly a chatterbox, but he isn't stupid, either. Adam Endicott has found his first escape from the ugly realities of his life.*

"Would you show me some of your books?" Miss Holloway persisted, undaunted.

Adam gave a gusty sigh and slid down from the window seat, carrying one of his books. At that moment the blasted door chimes rang out.

"Adam, I've got to answer the door," Beth said, feeling desperate.

With Adam's resigned "Okay" to reassure her, she went into the hall and opened the big door. She would make short work of this, whoever it was.

It was Pastor Cooper. His first words were "Did I come at a bad time? I just wanted to stop in before I start on my daily round."

"Yes. No. I mean, oh, you have no idea—" Beth said, with a welling up of gratitude so intense she couldn't complete her thought.

"Beth, you're upset. What do you want me to do? Tell me. Right now, this minute. I'll do it."

Sanity. Blessed sanity. "Just go into the living room and wait for me," she said steadily, as if she might be commenting on the weather. "You see, Doug isn't here. Kayla was arrested and taken to jail, and Adam is talking to the social worker, and we need to convince her that Doug and I are good caretakers for Adam, so you see…" For some reason she couldn't say another word.

"I do see," he said quickly. "I'm not here unless the social worker wants to meet the family preacher. *Then* I'm here. Gimme a call if you need me." And he disappeared into the living room.

Chapter Thirteen

Just as Pastor Cooper left the hall, the phone rang and Beth picked it up distractedly. It was someone wanting to book a room. Beth went into her courteous refusal, attempting to end the conversation when she really wanted to scream "Go 'way!" as Adam might. The caller persisted, and Beth recommended a couple of other places he might call. Then she had a legitimate excuse for ending the call.

"I'm sorry I can't be more helpful, but I have another call waiting."

What is Adam saying to the social worker? Is he saying anything at all? Does the social worker think he should be someplace else? The low murmur of voices came from the bed-sitter.

"Hello?"

"Hi, it's me." Doug's beloved voice came to her. "You sound stressed. What's up?"

"Nothing I can't handle. What's up with Kayla? Where are you?"

"Just outside the courtroom. I came out to make this call. This is going to take a while. Kayla wasn't with the first group they brought in. Daryl Taylor's a nice guy, very helpful. He knows a lot of people in the justice system. He's making some calls. I may not be back for lunch. Are you sure you're okay?''

"Fine. Don't worry. Just do the best you can for Kayla. I love you.''

"I love you, too. See you later—as soon as I can.'' He rang off, but he had sounded worried, harried.

Beth hung up the phone, listening to the sudden silence from the bed-sitter.

Bracing herself, she went in. Miss Holloway and Adam were seated side by side on the window seat. Miss Holloway had just finished reading a line from one of Adam's big, flat books. She closed it with a smile and handed it to Adam.

"I see Adam likes being read to,'' she commented unnecessarily to Beth, with a quick glance at her watch. "I'm going to have to be going. I've got a caseload you wouldn't believe.'' She got up, turning back to Adam. "Thanks for the story, Adam.''

"Okay,'' Adam said, and put the book aside. Then, turning around, he got on his knees, pushed aside the curtain and looked out front. It had become his custom, when he knew someone was leaving, to watch them go as if he might be thinking "Good riddance.'' Beth and Doug had laughed about it.

Beth braced herself as she took the social worker out into the front hallway. "Adam's all right for now, isn't he?'' She couldn't help asking.

"I think so,'' the social worker said. "But I'm not sure about this bed-and-breakfast situation. True, the child is with relatives. That part's fine. A lot of grandparents are taking care of their children's children these days. But with strangers coming and going—that I need to check out with my supervisor. I'll have to let you know about that. I'll be in touch.''

Beth shut the door behind her and went back into the bed-sitter. Adam was safe, at least for today. Back in the bed-sitter, she paused at the doorway to watch him watching. He was always a little tense and wary, it seemed. Well, why shouldn't he be?

''Has the lady gone?'' she asked Adam's stiff back.

''Yep. In her car. Now.'' That was rather detailed for Adam, and Beth went to stand behind him. *Adam, you dear little person.* He was talking better these days; at least he was saying more. Now he turned around and gave her his sunniest smile.

''Lady read a story,'' he offered.

''Why did she do that?'' Beth asked, sitting down beside him.

''I told her she could.''

''Why?''

''Is *my* book,'' Adam said decisively, as if that explained everything. Beth had to stifle a sudden impulse to laugh. He was such a sweet kid.

''Where'd you go?'' he asked, almost accusingly

''I was answering the phone, remember?'' Beth said. ''Did anything else happen? What did the lady say to you?'' *Adam, remember—and please talk—I need to know.*

Adam thought about her question, then he said, ''She didden take it.''

''Take what?''

''My library card. I said she could look at it if she didden take it. And she didden. And then—'' He paused, frowning slightly. ''I tole her.'' This was a *lot* of talk for Adam.

''You told her what?''

''I tole her she could read me a story. If she wanted. And she did.'' There was a note of finality in his tone, as if that was all he was going to say about that.

He had certainly done his best. *Adam, I love you. You handled that beautifully. I couldn't have done better myself.*

"Well, Pastor Cooper is here, Adam. I have to go talk to him. Can you play here awhile?"

"Okay." He slid down from his window seat and went to the toy box.

Beth found Pastor Cooper pacing in the living room.

"What's going on, Beth? It sounded bad," he said, rising from his chair.

"It is bad. Come and sit here," Beth said, going to one of the couches. Then she told him fully what had happened. He seemed to wince slightly at the idea of Kayla in jail.

"I've heard of Daryl Taylor," he commented. "He's a good lawyer."

"Doug seems satisfied with him, but the real problem is Kayla. What can we do now? Have we done everything we can?" Despite her best effort Beth's voice wavered. Pastor Cooper reached out and touched her hands, which were clenched in her lap. She tried to relax.

"And I haven't been much help," he said. "I'm so sorry. I was thinking on the way over. Let me run this past you. Do you think we all might forget I'm the family pastor?"

"I'm not sure what you mean," Beth said, sensing what might be coming. *Oh, no.*

"I've thought…about Kayla a lot. In fact, it's hard to keep her out of my mind. Do you think there is any chance I might…just become a sort of friend of the family? With the idea that it might eventually be more?" He looked so earnest and intent that it touched her heart. "Do you know what Doug thinks about it?" he added.

"He would be in favor of it," Beth said steadily. Nothing but the truth would do here. "But I'm not," she added.

"May I ask why?"

"Of course. Your work. If Kayla were part of your life, how could you focus on your own work?"

"Kayla seems to be at loose ends. She doesn't seem to have any...anchor."

"My point exactly. She doesn't seem to have any real reason for living. I can't understand her—her continual need to..."

"To escape? That's what addicted people are doing, Beth. They find life too difficult, for various reasons, so they find ways to avoid their problems. In doing it, of course, they create even bigger problems. I think of it as a kind of mental treadmill. It must be a terrible way to live. Is she actually back on the downward spiral?"

"I'm afraid so. She's drinking again, and this sudden arrest... I don't know what's going to happen now, or how Kayla will respond to this. Doug and I are going to pay the money she owes."

"That's very generous of you."

"Not really. She is Doug's daughter—" Then she heard Doug's car in the drive. "Oh, that's Doug. Maybe he has Kayla with him. Excuse me." She got up and hurried to the back door.

"Wait!" Pastor Cooper said suddenly. "I don't think I should be here if Kayla's with him. It would embarrass her."

But it was too late. They heard Doug and Kayla coming in, sounding angry and obviously in the middle of an argument. Kayla came rushing in ahead of Doug.

"Well, I'm going to take a long, hot shower first! I feel dirty! I can't stand being dirty!" She stopped in dismay when she saw Pastor Cooper there with Beth. Doug was right behind her.

"Try to calm down, Kayla!" Doug was shouting. Then he, too, stopped. They obviously hadn't expected an audience.

For the first time in her life Beth couldn't think of a

single thing to say to smooth over an uncomfortable situation. Pastor Cooper came to the rescue.

"It's the nuisance of a preacher again," he said easily. "Just pretend I'm not here, but keep in mind that this isn't the first family argument I've been in on, so I'm an old hand, you might say."

Doug suddenly laughed, half in embarrassment, half in relief. He turned to Kayla. "Go take your shower. You're entitled."

"Terrific! Great! Just what I needed!" Kayla said furiously, and dashed through the room heading for the downstairs bath.

"Mommy!" Adam had heard her voice. He came running out of the bed-sitter, but Kayla brushed past him. They heard the bathroom door slam, and Adam in the hallway banging on the door. "Mommy! Mommy!"

"I'll get Adam," Beth said desperately. She was deeply shaken. She had seen the anger, but also the panic in Kayla's wide, frantic eyes. What a horrible situation for someone to be trapped in. It took a while to quiet Adam down and ease his hurt feelings. It was fully fifteen minutes later when she felt she could leave him to return to the living room.

Doug and Pastor Cooper were still there, talking intermittently. Doug looked up as she came in. "I was just telling Pastor Cooper about it. Who would you guess that Kayla used her one phone call in the jail to call? Keep in mind that I'd already told her I'd get a lawyer."

"I have no idea," Beth said, sitting down. Nothing Kayla did would surprise her.

"Her dear friend, this Wanda person."

"But why?" Then, without speaking it, Beth knew why. Kayla was feeling guilty, frightened and surrounded by her father's new family. This new family who didn't seem to have any problems they couldn't handle. People who might seem in Kayla's eyes to be perfectly in control of their lives. Surely it must have been too much, more than she could cope with. What had she said? *"I've messed up two men's lives."* And here with her father's perfect new family was the man to whom she felt attracted but with whom she was afraid to become involved. *Kayla, Kayla, where is this going to end?*

"Of course she would call Wanda," Beth said in quick understanding. "Wanda—flawed, selfish, demanding—is probably the only person Kayla's met since she came here that she doesn't feel inferior to. Feeling inferior can be a pretty devastating thing, Doug."

"I think Beth's put her finger on it," Pastor Cooper said softly.

"I suppose so." Doug's voice was tired. "What do you think?" He was speaking to Pastor Cooper.

"Do you know what she asked of, or said to, Wanda when she made her call?"

"More or less. She must have told her about the arrest, her present dilemma. Apparently Wanda asked her to come over when she was released. If Beth's right—that maybe Kayla sees Wanda as someone who really understands her particular problem—I guess it's only natural that she'd run to her for…comfort? For reassurance?"

The pastor was nodding. "Wanda probably looks like a safe haven. She's not going to criticize or pass judgement on Kayla. She's probably very understanding of Kayla's particular demons, probably has some of her own."

"And in the meantime, while my daughter struggles with her demons, guess who's caught in the middle?"

"Adam, of course," Pastor Cooper answered, and Beth felt a new respect for him. "That's the real tragedy here," he continued, his expressive eyes revealing more than he realized about his own feelings. "Adam has no idea what's happening, or why. He's getting a very skewed idea of the world he has to somehow live in for the rest of his life. He will try to figure out how he can best cope. And how much will his immature decisions, as he goes, damage his life? Kayla—like anyone suffering an addiction—has no idea the price she is making everybody else pay. You both do realize this?''

''Yes, we've started to realize it,'' Doug said, and Beth nodded grimly.

She didn't trust herself to speak for the moment. She ached to reach out to touch Doug, to comfort him, to comfort Pastor Cooper, but at the same time she wanted to smack them both.

Kayla isn't worth all this!

Half an hour later, when Kayla came back into the bed-sitter, they could hear her. There were slammings and thumpings and a couple of shouted protests at Adam. There was the opening and banging shut of the bed-sitter door, and Adam was thrust out into the hallway. They could see him from the living room, a heavy scowl on his face.

''Mommy mad,'' he said, coming straight to Beth.

She took him up onto her lap. He would say nothing more; he was sulking.

When Kayla came back into the living room she looked lovely. ''Well, folks, your bad penny is taking off for the evening. I'm invited out.''

Both men had stood up.

''Do you have any money?'' Doug asked, sounding uneasy.

''Enough,'' Kayla said shortly.

''I'm just leaving,'' Pastor Cooper said. ''Can't I drop you someplace?''

Kayla studied him, then gave a sudden, brittle laugh. ''Why not? You all realize, of course, that I'm going on a binge. Why shouldn't Preacher-man take me there?" She seemed to think this was very funny.

"Why not, indeed?" the pastor said good-humoredly. "It's a kick and a half, isn't it? My car, such as it is, is right out front."

Beth and Doug saw them off, Kayla still laughing as if everything were all some big joke. Somewhere Beth had heard about laughing to keep from crying. It seemed to fit Kayla's mood.

Beth was still holding Adam. Did he feel heavier? Had he possibly gained just a little more weight? She hoped so. Adam's world might be topsy-turvy, but at least he was getting enough to eat here.

As they shut the big front door, the phone started ringing.

"Oh, no." Beth sighed. "Will you hold Adam?" And as Doug took the little boy, she picked up the receiver. She wasn't going to take *any* reservations. Period. Things were too confused. She answered the last ring pleasantly—and then all thought of their own problems flew from her mind.

"Mom. It's Jill. Ian's taken Kate to the hospital. Can you come?" Composed, take-charge, in-control Jill was crying.

"Yes! Of course! Where? Where?" Beth demanded.

"Swedish Hospital. Ian called from his cell phone. They were just getting Kate into the ambulance. She went into early labor. They think she's going to miscarry." Then Jill was crying in earnest.

"Come on," Doug said. "I could hear enough. We're headed for the hospital, right?"

"Yes, will you—"

"Yes. To everything. Don't worry. I'll handle things here. My car's still in the drive."

Doug let her off in front of the huge hospital. She wished fervently that he could come up with her. But someone had to take care of Adam. Someone had to welcome incoming guests later. In a few minutes she was in the maternity ward. Ian, bless him, was there. Both her daughters were so fortunate to have good husbands.

"Beth." Ian came to her quickly. "They've taken her into the delivery room. The baby's coming and it's too early." He looked desperate.

"She'll be fine," Beth said, hoping and praying silently that she was right. "All we can do is wait. She's with the experts. Have you made arrangements for the other children?"

"Yes, one of the church women was going over to help out when Kate's labor started. It's too *early*—" His voice broke. "Mrs....I can't think of her name. Mrs. Olsen called me right after she called the ambulance. I don't know how late she can stay. I should have asked. I couldn't think."

"Give me your phone. I'll call and find out." Beth knew she sounded calmer than she felt. Mrs. Olsen could stay until four, but the children would be home from school then. Their oldest, Raymond, would handle things until his father came home. Beth forced the Kayla issue to the back of her mind.

Then they settled in to wait an interminable amount of hours. When the doctor, still in his rumpled green cottons with the green cloth cap still on his head, came in, both Beth and Ian stood up. Ian reached over to clasp Beth's hand. They had both been sick with worry.

"She's okay," the doctor said, smiling. "And Ian, you have a lovely new daughter. And she's okay, too. That one's a bit scrawny yet, but give her time, she's a little toughy. She'll be ready to see in a few minutes. But Kate's resting for a while. You can't see her until later."

Ian sat down very suddenly in the nearest chair and Beth couldn't hold back the tears. She wasn't in the least embarrassed, because Ian was crying, too. They hung on to each other until a smiling nurse came and took them to the big glass wall so they could look in at the babies.

"That's yours," she said, pointing to one. "That's the new Beth."

The new Beth was indeed rather red and scrawny, but Ian said she was beautiful. In a little while they were allowed to look in on the sleeping Kate.

"You couldn't hear me," Ian said, driving Beth home, "but I never prayed harder or longer in my life." He looked like Beth felt: exhausted. He didn't even come in, but elected to go straight home to tell the other children the great news.

"I'll stop and pick up some fried chicken for dinner," he said. "The kids like that."

"Everything's okay here," Doug reported when Beth got into the house. "The two new guests arrived. And Adam's decided to behave himself for a while. What do you want for dinner? I'm in a cooking mood. And no, Kayla hasn't come back yet. She and her friend Wanda are probably out for the night."

"We'll set the child monitor again," Beth said. She was so relieved that Kate and the new baby were all right that she couldn't be upset even about Kayla, but she felt awfully tired.

"You look wilted," Doug said.

"I am. The stress, I guess." She felt depleted. She hadn't realized how long she had worried about Kate and this pregnancy. It had been there for ages in the back of her mind. Now it was gone and she felt somehow empty. What was it Ralph had said to her long ago, at a time when she had been desperate with worry about one of their daughters? His kindly voice echoed in her mind. *"Motherhood is not for sissies, Beth."* She felt an odd need to cry, her relief was so great. Maybe she was just too tired for that, too.

"I think it's best if we have an early night." Doug's voice came into her dreamlike state. They were at the kitchen table, just finishing their meal. "I'll see to Adam and clear things up here. Why don't you just go up to bed? Kayla will come in when she comes in. I'll set the monitor."

"Good." She didn't protest. "I'll go on up." She kissed Doug, then Adam's upturned face, and started up the long stairway. It had never seemed so long before.

Well, at least darling Katie's problems were solved. She had her new baby girl, and when she woke up, she would be full of plans. Kate was such an active person, involved in so many things with her family and her church. And now Kate could fix up her little gray rental house next door where she and her first husband, Claude, had lived before his death.

Beth paused a moment on the long stairway. The idea darted into her tired mind from out of nowhere. *Such a nice little house. Compact. Snug. Only two bedrooms. No long stairways.* Then it was crowded out by another thought. *What am I going to do about Kayla? About Adam? I'll have to think about it. But not now. Later.*

Wearily, she continued upward.

During the night she was vaguely aware of two interruptions from the monitor, but Doug attended to both. Morning would come too soon.

And it did. The next day, getting this group of guests off with a delicious breakfast in them lightened her spirits considerably. She was humming about midmorning when Kayla came slowly into the kitchen. She heard Adam before she heard Kayla.

"Mommy, see my books?" Once again he was in the middle of the kitchen floor and, as always, he tried to get his mother's attention. Beth felt a rush of affection for him.

For the first time in his short life he was experiencing some security.

"Hi, Beth." Kayla's voice was tired.

"Sit down, Kayla. I'll get you some coffee. Did Doug tell you the news? About Kate and the new baby?" She had already talked with Kate briefly on the phone and was delighted with the world in general. It was going to be a beautiful day, and Doug was off painting a picture of it.

"Yeah. Great. I'm glad things were okay for her." It was evident that Kayla was trying to sound enthusiastic. "I'm sorry about last night," she added in a low tone.

"What about last night?" Beth asked. At the moment nothing would make her unhappy.

"Oh, I thought Dad would have told you. He got so mad. I do that. I go through life disgusting people. I guess that's my mission. And I seem to have a real talent for it." Her voice had become hard.

For the first time Beth turned and looked at Kayla. Kayla was really angry, as angry as she had been yesterday when Doug brought her home. There was almost a snarl in her voice. And why should that be so surprising? Just because she herself was so happy, it didn't follow that everybody else would be happy, too.

Instinctively, Beth tried to smooth it over. "Kayla, please don't feel like that. You've got a problem. We all know that. Don't be so hard on yourself." She wanted Kayla out of this negative mood. Maybe Kayla would take care of Adam. For a change.

"Dad says if I'm to stay on here I've got to shape up and help. Okay. I'll help. I admit I haven't been too much help to you so far ''

Beth felt a sudden flare of anger. What had Doug said to Kayla? It would have been nice if Doug had bothered to mention it. Had he told Kayla she could *live* here? Permanently? *It's my house.* Kayla's eyes filled with tears and she brushed at them angrily. *Self-pity.* Beth thought in contempt.

"Sit down," Beth said, knowing she sounded grim. Well, she felt grim. "I'll get you some coffee. What else would you like? Cereal? Toast?"

"Whatever," Kayla said, sitting down at the kitchen table. "But think of something—some work—I can do today." Kayla's voice was tight. "I told him I'd help. And I'll help!"

Beth felt like swearing, which she never did. Actually, she wished Kayla hadn't come home. She had plans for today, and Kayla was not part of them. But Kayla was drinking again. She couldn't leave her here on her own. What if Kayla got drunk? What if somebody came to the door? What if that CPS woman came back? Or called?

"All right," Beth said. "I'm going over to Kate's house as soon as I finish here. This all happened so fast that Kate wasn't able to finish arranging the new baby's nursery. I told her I'd get it ready. You can help me with that, if you want to."

"Okay. Good. And before that I'll help with the beds here. And when Dad gets home you tell him everything I've done! Okay?"

"Yes, if that's what you want," Beth answered. Maybe she would tell him a good deal more than that.

Adam was so delighted to be returned to the house with the swings that he didn't make a row when he was told that story time wasn't going to happen today because there was too much else to do. They really must get him something to play with here in their own backyard, Beth thought. A swing of his own, maybe even a slide. He'd love that, and he needed to be outside more. She would talk to Doug about that, among other things.

Kate and Ian's three children would be at school, so

Kate's house would be empty. Beth was glad nobody else would see Kayla in this angry mood.

Beth stopped the car in front of Kate's house, wondering how she was going to get through the next couple of hours. Kayla had sat sullenly silent next to her on the drive over. As Beth turned off the engine and set the brake, Kayla spoke for the first time.

"So, that's where Kate lives. It's pretty grand, isn't it?" There was clear resentment in her tone.

Beth felt she was near boiling point herself. They'd be lucky if they got through this without open warfare.

"Kate hasn't always lived here," she said quietly. She was remembering Katie's difficult widowhood years, and her courage living through them with her two children. "Kate has had some rough times. That little house next to this one—the gray frame house—that was Kate and Claude's. She had been a widow for several years before she and Ian married. This house—the big one—was Ian's. They were next-door neighbors."

"Oh, really. I didn't know," Kayla said, glancing back at the small gray house. "It's…kind of shabby, isn't it?" There was just a hint of satisfaction now in Kayla's tone.

"It's empty now," Beth said. After she and Ian married, Kate had rented the little house to a nice elderly couple, Mr. and Mrs. Hyslop. Mr. Hyslop had Alzheimer's and Mrs. Hyslop took care of him. He was a gentle, confused old soul. Finally he passed away, and she went to live with their daughter—this was a few weeks ago. Kate was going to fix it up a bit before she rented it again, but she hadn't got to it yet when she started having difficulties with her pregnancy.

"I guess we'd better get started," Beth said. She was feeling a little calmer. She wanted to be busy, not talking with Kayla when she was in this mood.

"Swing!" Adam reminded them from the back seat.

"Yes, yes. We're going in right now," Beth said, getting out to take Adam from his car seat. She didn't fail to note Kayla made no move to help. "Ian fenced in the back," she added to Kayla, "so Adam will be safe there while we're inside." Not that Kayla would care, of course.

"Oh, we don't need to worry about Adam," Kayla said. "He won't go anywhere. He knows better." She got out of the car and stood looking up at the house. Then she followed Beth around to the back. Adam was rushing in ahead because he knew where they were going.

Maybe it hadn't been such a good idea to bring Kayla here, Beth thought. It all probably looked very opulent to her, and she obviously resented Kate apparently having so much when she had so little. *And whose fault was that?*

Beth opened the back gate and they went into the rear area. There was the well-kept sweep of lawn, the flower beds here and there. Then there was the excellent collection of children's play equipment, plus the barbecue area on the flagstone terrace in back of the house. Yes, it would all seem very grand to Kayla.

"We'll go in the back way," Beth said, "after we get Adam settled."

Adam rushed for the first swing and got into it, trying to pump up some motion. Kayla stood silently, looking around, making no move to help him get started. Beth went over and gave him a push and was pleased to hear him laugh. It was so good to hear Adam laughing. She wished Doug could hear.

"Okay, let's get going," Beth said, hoping she sounded more cheerful than she felt, but her heart sank. She'd have to take Kayla through Kate's beautiful kitchen with all the polished wood, stainless steel and copper. It was really a *House Beautiful* kitchen. Then, of course, the lovely dining room with its elegant china cupboard filled with expensive china. If only she hadn't had to bring Kayla along. She must try not to be so judgmental of Kayla, but it was hard not to, when comparing her with Jill and Kate. On the other hand, they had had a completely different life. She should try to be more understanding, but, with Kayla's personality, it would be hard going.

"Wow," Kayla said when they entered the kitchen.

"Everything's so neat. I guess someone came over from the Ladies' Guild to clean away the breakfast things. The kids certainly didn't, in their rush to get to school."

Kayla gave a sudden harsh laugh. "Speaking of your church people, guess what? Preacher-man was working up to asking me for a date yesterday. You know, when he so kindly offered to drive me over to Wanda's."

Beth's heart sank. So poor Pastor Cooper was trying to follow through on his feeble friend-of-the-family idea. "Well, you could do a lot worse," she said somewhat tartly. She still didn't think it would be a good match for Pastor Cooper, and she felt defensive. "Are you going out with him?" She couldn't help but ask it, hoping that Kayla hadn't agreed.

"Not on your life," Kayla snapped. "I don't need that kind of trouble—although I have to admit I was tempted. He's quite a hunk. But I've got more sense than to get involved with a man of the cloth. Can you imagine such a thing?"

Actually, no, Beth thought. *Not in a million years,* but she didn't say it, reminding herself again that this was Doug's daughter.

"He's a nice person," Beth said finally.

"Of course he's a nice person. And I wish him well," Kayla said drily. "I wish him a long happy life with somebody sometime. But not with me."

They were progressing down the hall and had come to the living room. "Oh," Beth said to change the subject, "let me show you a picture your father painted. Kate has it over the fireplace. In here.'' She led the way into Kate's living room. Kayla went to the fireplace and stood looking at the picture.

''It's your back garden. He's good. I have to admit it.''

''It is good, isn't it?'' Beth came to stand beside her. If they could just get through the tasks here and get back home, maybe Kayla would go and sulk in the bed-sitter.

''Okay, where's all this work I'm supposed to do?'' Kayla turned suddenly from the picture.

''Upstairs,'' Beth said in a businesslike tone. ''Right out here.'' She led the way through the hallway and up the stairs. She hoped all the bedroom doors were closed. Kayla had seen enough fine furniture for the moment. But apparently Kayla's mind was no longer on Kate's possessions.

''I had a great talk with Wanda last night. She's a terrific person. Real hardheaded, good sense.'' There was an undertone of satisfaction in Kayla's voice now.

''Good. It's nice that you're making some friends,'' Beth agreed. Anything to keep Kayla placated until she cooled off. ''Right in here. This is going to be the nursery.'' Beth opened the door and they went in.

The baby furniture had been delivered. There was the crib, the bassinet, stacks of baby blankets and comforters, still in their plastic wrappings. All sorts of colorful baby paraphernalia were stacked here and there from the several baby showers.

''What a mess. First, of course, we'll need to wash this stuff the baby's going to use. Kayla, do you think you can work that washer and dryer downstairs? I can show you,'' Beth offered. ''Would you like to do that or something else?''

''Please, Beth, I can work any washer or dryer on the planet, since any washing I do has to be in Laundromats. I don't have a lot of fancy equipment. Let me do the washing, and you work in here.''

"Good," Beth said in relief. "Let's get started."

Kayla worked doggedly for the next two and a half hours, until the new Beth's nursery was perfect for her arrival home.

"Well, are we finally finished?" Beth asked as she got the last clean stack of baby clothes into a drawer and shut it.

"Almost done," Kayla answered. She was standing just inside the door, looking slowly around the new nursery. "Looks good," she commented. "We did a real job of work here. Be sure you tell Dad."

"Yes, we did," Beth answered.

"You know, in case you ever wonder," Kayla said, "I do appreciate all you've tried to do for me, Beth. You've been real great with Adam. He's not an easy kid to get along with." There seemed to be no anger in her tone now.

"Why, thank you," Beth said uncertainly. She was going to say something else, but she heard in the distance the slamming of a door. "Can that be Adam?"

"Yeah, probably. Last time I was down in the service porch he was griping about being hungry. That kid's a bottomless pit."

The peaceful moment was gone. "Of course. Why don't we stop someplace and get something on the way home?" Beth suggested.

"A burger maybe. Adam likes burgers," Kayla agreed.

Although her anger seemed to be gone, on the way home Kayla was almost as silent as she had been before. She only made one comment. "Looks like Adam gave up. He's asleep in the car seat, now that he's full of burger."

"Well, his lunch was late and it's well past his nap time," Beth answered. She was already thinking of the rest of her day. Was Doug home yet? Two new guests wre coming in for the night. She'd need to think of something for dinner; then there were the breakfast preparations to deal with. Maybe she shouldn't have worked so hard in the nursery. She could have left some for another day—the new baby wasn't going to be released from the hospital just yet. She wanted to simply lie down and fall asleep, as Adam had.

As she turned into the drive she saw with relief that Doug's car was there, and her heart lifted. Somehow she would get through the day.

"I'll take Adam," Kayla said, pulling him, still asleep, from his car seat. As soon as they were inside she disappeared into the bed-sitter and shut the door.

Beth breathed a sigh of relief.

At eleven o'clock that evening, when all the chores were finally finished, the four-poster in their bedroom had never looked so good. Almost as soon as her head touched the pillow Beth was engulfed in sleep. Then, an instant later, or a long time later, there was a haunting sound that came and went. Somewhere in the distance, Adam was calling. It faded in and out, wavering.

"Mommy? Mommy? Mommy?"

Beth moaned and tried to push the sound aside but it continued forlornly.

"Mommy? Mommy?"

"Doug?" Only half awake, she reached over to touch him.

"I heard it. It's the monitor. He's awake. I'll go down." He was getting up. She heard him struggling into his robe, then reached up and snapped on the light.

"I'll come with you," she said, forcing herself toward full wakefulness.

She followed him down the stairs, holding on to the banister because she still felt half asleep. They reached the bed-sitter door almost at the same time. It was open, and one of the lights inside was on. Only Adam was there, sitting up in the wide sofa bed. He was weaving a bit groggily. He was holding a piece of folded paper out to them.

"Take iss," he said sleepily. Then, "Mommy gone." There was a pause during which he swayed slightly. "Mommy come back?" Then he toppled over into sleep again.

Doug went over and plucked the paper from Adam's lax fingers. He flipped it open and read. Then he handed it to Beth.

"She's gone. For good." He stooped over and scooped up the sleeping child, holding the limp body close to his broad chest. Beth looked down at the note. It was in Kayla's large, scrawly writing.

Dad and Beth,
I give up. Sorry things didn't work out. Wanda's fed up, too. We're taking off. Don't worry about me. In case you would. I've got a line on a job for the summer. Take care of Adam. He's better off with you two than with me.

Kayla

Beth looked up at Doug. His face was gray with shock as he cradled the sleeping child.

Beth felt stupid. Kayla had left her child, *How could a mother leave her child?* Then, *Kayla's gone. She's not coming back.*

Doug spoke first, his voice sounding far away.

"I'm sorry, Beth," he was saying. "I'm so sorry I got you into this."

Chapter Fourteen

"But where could she go?" Beth asked. "She doesn't have any money. She couldn't afford plane fare, or even bus fare."

"Check the closet," Doug said.

Beth crossed the room to open the closet door. It was almost empty. All of Kayla's new clothes were gone, and some of Adam's more expensive things.

"Oh, Doug," Beth said. "She took some of Adam's things but she didn't take Adam. Why—" She stopped, already knowing the answer before Doug could say it.

"To sell, Beth. She took everything she could sell, to get a few dollars traveling money. Is anything else missing?"

But even as he asked it, Beth was glancing around the room. The potpourri jar was no longer on the coffee table.

"The little green jar," she said weakly.

"The one that belonged to your grandmother. And she'll probably sell it for a couple of dollars. Some hock shop gets a real buy there," he added bitterly. "I feel sick about this."

"It's not your fault." Beth made herself say it, but she felt a rising anger. At Kayla. Even at Doug. It was *his* daughter who had come barging in to wreck the smooth, happy tenor of their lives. *But to leave her child!* "Does Kayla say where she's going?" she asked evenly, not looking at Doug. She didn't want him to see the outrage in her eyes.

"No. But I doubt if it's that job back east she mentioned. Probably something closer to here. Beth, beloved, do you realize what I've gotten you into?"

Yes, I realize what you've gotten me into, Beth thought, but she didn't say it. She didn't trust herself to speak yet.

"You realize what this means," Doug continued. "She left her *child.* Adam needs care. Years and years of care. And he's my responsibility. You've already raised one family."

"Don't remind me," she snapped. "Look, I'm sorry. I didn't mean to say that. We can't settle anything tonight. It's late." She glanced to where the small clock radio had been. It was gone, too. "It must be midnight," she added. "We…we can talk about it later. After the guests have left. We…can work it out." But even as she said it, her mind was screaming silently. *How? How can we work it out? Can we run a business and take care of a troubled little three-year-old child?* "Put Adam back to bed," she added, suddenly very tired.

"All right," Doug agreed after a moment. "No point in trying to do anything now. There's no knowing who her friend Wanda put her in touch with. She could be headed anywhere. Kayla always did pick losers as friends." He put Adam down on the sofa bed, covering him up gently. Adam muttered something and snuggled under his warm covers.

She left her child, Beth thought again in disbelief. *How can a mother leave her child?* She shivered and tugged her robe more tightly around her. ''Let's go back to bed,'' she said dully.

Tomorrow. They would think about it tomorrow. She couldn't think about everything now. She was too exhausted. Doug looked exhausted, too. What in the world were they going to do? That CPS woman had been doubtful about leaving Adam in a B and B.

But morning brought no answers. Doug worked steadily beside her as they got through the breakfast and checkouts for the two guests who were leaving. His silence was almost morose, as if he were withdrawing into himself to some dark and private place she could not enter.

Adam wandered around disconsolately, getting in the way with his storybooks. He seemed to be coming down with a cold, too, which worried her. Having a small child who demanded to have his nose wiped every five minutes during the checkout of guests seemed irritating beyond belief. *Where is my patience?* Beth wondered. *I've always been so good with children.*

One departing guest even remarked about it. ''How odd,'' she said. ''I thought the B and B directory said this place didn't take children.''

''We don't,'' Beth explained quickly. ''This is…my husband's grandson. He's just, uh, visiting.'' Even as she said it, she felt the guilt of lying. *He's living here. Kayla has left him here.*

After both checkouts were gone and the other guests were out exploring the city of Seattle, she looked around for Doug. At last they could talk. Then she saw him in the doorway in his down-filled jacket that always made him look bigger than life. He was jingling car keys in his hand.

''Are you leaving?'' she asked. *We must talk, work things out.*

''Not for long, Beth. I'm just going over to check things

out at the Hulls. I won't be long. You mind looking after his highness?''

"No, of course not," Beth said evenly. Of course she would look after Adam. She did most of that anyhow. She was in a foul mood. Maybe she could lift herself out of it before he came back. Wasn't he the love of her life? She must try to remember that.

Upstairs there were beds to strip and remake, and laundry to collect. But before she started she called the church and left a message for Pastor Cooper. He must be told that Kayla had gone. It was only fair. She hoped Doug would return before the pastor arrived.

She had finished the beds and had read Adam one story when the door chimes sounded from downstairs. Over Adam's loud objections she hurried down to answer. She hoped it was the pastor. It was.

"Come in," she said, her heart aching for him. She wished Doug would come back. "Let's go in here." She led the way into the living room.

"What's up?" he asked, taking the chair she indicated. "Your message sounded urgent."

"Well, it was. We've got a crisis here, I'm sorry to say." She paused because Adam came wandering into the room, looked around vaguely and wandered out again. He was probably missing Kayla. She felt a sudden rush of anger against Kayla.

"What's wrong, Beth? Tell me." Pastor Cooper's eyes held deep concern.

"It's Kayla," she said. "She's left. I mean, she's actually gone. Moved out."

"But Adam—"

Beth shrugged hopelessly. "She's left Adam with us. She told us to take care of him. Here." Beth took Kayla's note out of her pocket and handed it to him.

He bowed his head over it, and she wondered briefly if

he felt like crying. She certainly did. Kayla's life was such a wasteland. He got up and walked to the window, turning his back while he read the note. She couldn't see his face. It was several moments before he turned to face her.

"Well, that's that," he said, his voice sounding bleak. "I guess I've made a real fool of myself. I should have known better— I'm not a child. I've worked with addicted people before—long enough to know they...aren't responsible. They can't be expected to be."

Beth looked at him with compassion. What high hopes had he had for pretty, flaky Kayla? How much did he really care for her? How big a price was he going to pay for feeling attracted to such a lost soul? Well, they would all pay a price for Kayla—in questions, in concerns, in worries that came in the middle of the night.

Where is Kayla now? What is she doing? Is she all right, Lord? Kayla is out there somewhere, drifting. Help her, please. Please. Beth felt a moment of shocked surprise. She was actually praying for Kayla!

"I'm sorry," Beth said. "I'm so sorry."

He gave her a small smile. "I'm sorry, too," he said, coming to her to hand back the note before he sat down. "What are you and Doug going to do?"

"I...I'm not sure. I'm...frightened." She stopped. She hadn't intended to say that. Then she rushed on. "I don't understand Doug. He's so...quiet about it. I know he's upset, but..."

"But what?"

"I don't know. I can't put my finger on it. Of course we're going to take care of Adam. What else can we do? I just can't see *not* taking care of him. Who else is there, now that Kayla's gone? And it won't be easy. There are complications already. The worker from the Children's Protective Services was here. She's doubtful that they would even let Adam stay here—in the middle of a thriving

B and B. Then, what if Doug and I do start raising Adam and, maybe ten years from now, Kayla decides to make another try at motherhood and wants Adam back? How would Adam be affected by that? He's had enough instability already in his short life.''

''Well, my advice is to do it legally. You and Doug protect yourselves as much as you can,'' Pastor Cooper said. ''You and Doug should apply for legal guardianship immediately. Kayla…with her problems, could well change her mind again and come back. You're right about that, and the courts would back her up.''

''Doug mentioned that possibility,'' Beth said miserably.

''Is Doug going to do that? Did he say?''

''I don't know. I can't seem to reach him. He's gone all quiet.''

''See if you can press the point,'' the pastor said. ''The fact that Kayla left Adam of her own volition, and she herself *told* you to take care of him, might give you some leverage in court. And if you think it would help if I talked to Doug, I'll be glad to. If you can't talk him around, let me know, and I'll back you up. You do need to get this settled as firmly as you can, for Adam's sake.''

''I know,'' Beth said, feeling a wave of gratitude. This man was, as Cyrus had said, ''sound.'' Despite whatever disappointment he might be feeling because Kayla had flitted in and out of his life, he was putting all that aside to help if he could. She reached out and touched him briefly. For an instant, they clasped hands. *My friend,* Beth thought.

He had to leave before Doug returned, and Beth waited for Doug. She used the time to read another story to Adam, which at least made him happy. Doug still hadn't returned by the time she put Adam down for his nap after lunch.

The beautiful house lay silent around her as she left the bed-sitter and shut the door quietly. She stood a moment in the hallway, looking around almost as if she were seeing it for the first time. More than thirty years of her life had been spent in this place. Slowly, savoring it, she stared up at the high ceilings, the richly polished wood of the banister. She reached out and stroked it. Then she started up the stairs to walk through the upstairs bedrooms and upper hallway. This house had been her friend for a long, long time. It had given her an ongoing interest in life as she had gone dutifully through the years of her marriage to kind, patient Ralph. It had been the gracious home into which their daughters could freely invite their friends as they grew from childhood to womanhood.

Then she turned and came slowly downstairs again, straightening a picture here, adjusting a drapery there. She paced slowly through the large downstairs room. *Home,* she thought. *Home.* She had loved this grand old house and it seemed, in some odd way, that it had loved her back. It had helped fill the emptiness of her first marriage—life before Doug.

She sat down in the living room, absently reaching over for her knitting, which she kept intending to work on but almost never did. It would be nice to have time to knit again. And suddenly, from nowhere, a line from Pastor Cooper's Sunday sermon popped into her mind. *"Please know that when God shuts one door, He opens another. You can count on that."* Now, here, at this moment in her life with Doug, was God shutting one door? And if so, what door would He open?

She stared vacantly across the lovely room, her hands on the mass of bright knitting yarn in her lap. What was it that Cyrus had said that day in the hospital? Something about God giving her a special assignment. And she must give it her best shot. From somewhere in the bottom of her mind, Cyrus's words echoed up. *"Remember, Beth, your best shot."* She knew she was smiling, without really knowing why.

* * *

She was still sitting there holding her knitting, gazing off into space, when Doug finally came back.

"Well, I was right," he said tiredly. "Kayla and Wanda took off together, and God help them. I also got the clear impression that the Hulls Senior are secretly more than relieved. However, their son John is devastated."

"I'm sorry for them. For Kayla. For Wanda. For all of them," Beth said soberly.

"Well, right now I'm sorry for us. For poor Adam." Doug sat down heavily beside her. His big hands hung by his sides. His whole body seemed to sag.

"Have you had any lunch?" she asked, putting the knitting back into the bag.

"Lunch," he said vaguely. "Uh, no, I guess not. I wanted to think, and I drove out to the end of that Burke-Gilman Trail and wandered along there for a while."

"Not all forty-nine miles of it, I hope," Beth said, smiling. Somehow she couldn't stop smiling.

He smiled back. "No. Just until I kept getting in the way of the serious walkers—which I'm not—then I turned back. But I'm really not hungry right now."

"Tell me what you were thinking about." She reached over and took one of his hands in hers, wanting to help him, to make things right again. And with God's help, she knew she could.

"What was I thinking about? Dear lady, I was thinking about what I've been thinking about for days. What I can't get out of my mind. Alleged mind."

"And what would that be?" She felt in a kind of euphoria. *All things are possible with God.*

"Us. You. Me. And, of course, *us* now includes Adam. What I'm trying to say in my awkward way is that I have no choice but to take on his care. No choice, Beth. Please understand that. I was never a real parent to Kayla. And

I've got a second chance now. I can be a parent to Adam—and he needs it. He needs...he needs...everything. You've done your stint at parenting. And you did it nobly. You've got the B and B that you created yourself, and that you love.''

"Yes," she said dreamily. "I've really loved this. I did create it. And I do take satisfaction in that. I made a something where nothing was before. I guess I got a chance to do my 'thing.'"

"My point exactly, love. I can't take that away from you. And, speaking with blunt honesty, keeping Adam here in a busy B and B just isn't working out.''

"I agree, Doug. And I doubt that the CPS will permit it. They'll think Adam will be better off in foster care, so—''

"Never!" Doug said. "Never. That little guy isn't going to be bounced around from one foster home to another. I can't let that happen, Beth. Please understand that.''

"I do understand it. I wouldn't permit it either," Beth said. "Adam deserves a fair chance in life.''

"Right," Doug said. "It's been going around and around in my head. I've realized almost from the beginning that we can't keep him here and still run the business. I went down all the blind alleys. Should I hire a nanny to look after him until he's ready for school? Then maybe I could send him to a good boarding school. Then I—''

"But, Doug, that leaves out the most important ingredient in child raising—love. There has to be love first.''

"Yeah, well, I guess I finally realized that. He has to be cared for by someone who loves him. So that means—''

"I love him, too," Beth said softly.

Doug looked at her keenly. "Granted. And you've been great. You've given him most of the care he's gotten here. I didn't miss that, Beth. But with the business and all, how can—?" He stopped because she pressed his hand. He looked at her with a question in his troubled gaze.

"Let me talk for a minute," Beth said.

A half smile tugged at his mouth. "Okay. You talk."

She lifted his hand to her lips and kissed it gently. "You missed what I said a moment ago. I said, 'I *got* a chance to do my thing.' Past tense, Doug. I *did* it. And I loved it. But I've decided it's time to move on. And everything is falling into place for us. All the necessary pieces."

He looked at her. "What pieces are those?"

She sat up a little straighter, releasing his hand. "You— if I know you as well as I think I do—were just about to go all noble and offer to take on Adam's care by yourself. Make the big sacrifice, and take Adam away. Well, dear heart, it doesn't need to be a sacrifice to anybody. It can be nothing but good. For all of us. First of all, we have as close as possible to a perfect marriage."

"Amen to that."

"Secondly, there is nothing more I can do with this business. And, frankly, I'm getting more and more tired of these frantic breakfast preparations in the dead of night when I should be in bed. Third, Katie needs her mother closer to her when she's coping with a new baby and three other kids. Fourth, Katie hasn't rented the little gray house. And fifth, I've had two firm offers to sell this place in the past couple of years. And I kept the names and phone numbers of the people who want to buy a thriving B and B."

"You're kidding," Doug started to laugh.

"No, I'm not kidding. I've never been more serious in my life. I said it's time to move on. And that's the direction I want to go. I *want* to be a parent again. You'll never believe this, but I *want* to see that Adam gets his fair start in life and do all the work that entails. I *want* to deal firmly with the temper tantrums when he gets his annual shots to keep him healthy. I want to help him with his homework. I want to deal with the PTA when the time comes. I *can* do it. Adam is *smart*, Doug. He just hadn't had his chance yet. He's going to need a lot of care to realize his potential. If my guess is right about that little brain of his, he's going to end up a graduate student in some prestigious university somewhere, specializing in something that costs us a lot of money. We're going to need *money*. And the B and B is a ready-made gold mine if we sell it.''

''But you can't sell this place. You love it. You've enjoyed it so much.''

''Yes. *Enjoyed*. Past tense. But it has served its purpose. It's time to move on. Now I want something else. You and Adam, Doug. You two are a package deal.'' She was half laughing now. ''We've got our work cut out for us. There's so much to do in the next few months. It's a whole new start for us. But we can make it work, Doug. I'll call Katie about the little house. We can do whatever fixing up is necessary. I'll list the B and B for sale and get in touch with those two couples who wanted to buy it last year. We can invest the money in some secure mutual funds for Adam's future. We both have our pensions—more than enough for our needs. Don't you see?''

''But, Beth…are you *sure* about this?''

''I've never been more sure about anything in my life before. It's all coming together for us, and for Adam.''

''Sell this place? You *love* this place! You know you do.''

''But I love you and Adam more.'' *Cyrus, I'll give it my best shot.* ''Don't you see?''

''Yes,'' he said softly. ''I see.''

It was a magical moment.

Suddenly Beth saw Adam in the doorway again. He came purposefully toward them. His little face wore its most serious expression. He slapped his storybook down on Beth's knee.

''Book,'' he said firmly, and Doug's laugh rang out.

Oh, life was good. Very good indeed.

*   *   *   *   *

Dear Reader,

I hope you enjoyed reading *September Love,* a story I've wanted to write for a long time. Today in America there are more than three million children living with their grandparents. For whatever the causes—drugs, drinking, the general collapse of our moral structure— a whole generation of young people have simply abandoned their children to their parents to raise.

Then the grandparents, instead of living a leisurely retirement, must start all over—booster shots, PTA meetings, managing college tuition—during a time of life when they are less able to do it. These are the silent, unsung heroes of our turbulent time. I wanted to tell you a story about them. This is it. So the next time you see a harried grandparent coping with an energetic three-year-old, take a moment for a smile and a cheerful word. They deserve it.

Blessings,

Virginia Myers

Love Inspired

AN HONEST LIFE

BY

DANA CORBIT

Charity Sims had been raised to be the perfect
preacher's wife—but the one man who intrigued
her was the one man her mother didn't approve of:
contractor Rick McKinley. Charity was determined
to make the loner a churchgoer. And Rick was the
one person Charity could count on when her life
was shattered by a devastating truth....

Don't miss

AN HONEST LIFE
On sale December 2003

Available at your favorite retail outlet.

Take 2 inspirational love stories FREE!

PLUS get a FREE surprise gift!

Mail to Steeple Hill Reader Service

In U.S.
3010 Walden Ave.
P.O. Box 1867
Buffalo, NY 14240-1867

In Canada
P.O. Box 609
Fort Erie, Ontario
L2A 5X3

YES! Please send me 2 free Love Inspired® novels and my free surprise gift. After receiving them, if I don't wish to receive anymore, I can return the shipping statement marked cancel. If I don't cancel, I will receive 4 brand-new novels every month, before they're available in stores! Bill me at the low price of $3.99 each in the U.S. and $4.49 each in Canada, plus 25¢ shipping and handling and applicable sales tax, if any*. That's the complete price and a saving of over 10% off the cover prices—quite a bargain! I understand that accepting the books and gift places me under no obligation ever to buy any books. I can always return a shipment and cancel at any time. Even if I never buy another book from Steeple Hill, the 2 free books and the surprise gift are mine to keep forever.

113 IDN DU9F
313 IDN DU9G

Name	(PLEASE PRINT)	
Address	Apt. No.	
City	State/Prov.	Zip/Postal Code

* Terms and prices are subject to change without notice. Sales tax applicable in New York. Canadian residents will be charged applicable provincial taxes and GST. All orders subject to approval. Offer limited to one per household and not valid to current Love Inspired® subscribers.

LI03

©2003 Steeple Hill Books